KU-497-598

THE WILDERNESS

C. J. HARPER

**SIMON &
SCHUSTER**

London · New York · Sydney · Toronto · New Delhi

A CBS COMPANY

First published in Great Britain in 2014 by Simon and Schuster UK Ltd
A CBS COMPANY

Copyright © 2014 Candida Harper

This book is copyright under the Berne Convention.
No reproduction without permission.
All rights reserved.

The right of Candida Harper to be identified as the author of this work
has been asserted by her in accordance with sections 77 and
78 of the Copyright, Designs and Patents Act, 1988.

1 3 5 7 9 10 8 6 4 2

Simon and Schuster UK Ltd,
1st Floor, 222 Gray's Inn Road,
London WC1X 8HB

Simon & Schuster Australia, Sydney
Simon & Schuster India, New Delhi

A CIP catalogue record for this book
is available from the British Library.

PB ISBN: 978-0-85707-700-4
eBook ISBN: 978-0-85707-701-1

This book is a work of fiction. Names, characters, places
and incidents are either the product of the author's imagination or are
used fictitiously. Any resemblance to actual people living or
dead, events or locales is entirely coincidental.

*Special thanks to everyone who submitted a photo
for the cover image of this book.
Every effort has been made to contact copyright holders
of images and to obtain their permission.*

Printed and bound by CPI Group (UK) Ltd, Croydon, CR0 4YY

www.simonandschuster.co.uk
www.simonandschuster.com.au

THE

The Library at Warwick School
Please return or renew on or before the last date below

9/14

16 MAY 2018		

Campus Library Services Limited
71671

WARWICK SCHOOL

Also by C.J. Harper

The Disappeared

Rainbird, this one is for you

I wake up. Tyres crunch the gravel outside the warehouse. The next thing I know, there's an almighty crash and a shard of glass cuts through the air and shatters against the wall, a few centimetres above my head.

They've found us.

'Get up!' Kay says, pulling at my arm. 'Come on!'

I throw off our makeshift blanket and stumble to my feet. There's a second crash and I watch as one of the windows turns into a wall of splinters, then smashes to the ground. Kay yanks me into a back room.

'It's The Leader's guards,' she says, flinging open the door of a store cupboard, pushing me in, and closing the door behind us.

We've had it. We're trapped. I hear shouts and the slap of boots against the concrete floor. I can hardly see; there's just the dawn light illuminating the edges of the cupboard door. Any moment now it will be flung open.

Kay is scrabbling around by my feet.

1

'What are you doing?' I hiss.

'Look.'

I squint into the darkness; Kay has pulled up one of the floor tiles and beneath it is a hole.

'Get in,' she says.

I don't wait for further explanation. I clamber down into the gap. Kay follows right behind me. She moves so fast that she kicks me in the back. As soon as she's in, she pulls the tile back over the hole and we're plunged into thicker darkness. I can still hear the guards crashing about.

'Move,' Kay whispers.

She's right up behind me. I stick out a hand and feel my way forwards. Above us, there's a bang as someone slams open the store cupboard door. I freeze. Footsteps pace right over our heads. More banging, then a clatter as something falls to the floor. He's throwing around the contents of the room looking for us. The noise stops. I hold my breath. I imagine the uneven tile catching his eye. I cringe, waiting for it to be plucked away, revealing us cowering. I close my eyes. The footsteps move over us again and back towards the door. Further away, thumps and shouts continue.

'Go,' Kay says.

Go? How much further can I go? But reaching out I find that there's plenty more space to move forwards again.

And that's when I realise that we're not in a hole.

We're in a tunnel.

We crawl forwards in silence. The tunnel turns a corner and the banging and yelling from the warehouse die away.

2

'How the hell did you know there was a tunnel here?' I ask Kay.

'Ty told me.'

'What? When?'

I've been with Kay almost every minute since we escaped from the Academy two days ago.

'He was here tonight, when you were asleep.'

I stop crawling. 'Why didn't you wake me?' Ty and Janna told us they would come and see us during the day, but they never showed. 'You know how worried I was when they didn't turn up.'

'You were very asleep. Ty said you were big tired and you needed to be resting.'

For efwurd's sake. 'I do apologise if I was snoozing; all that leading a rebellion must have tired me out.'

'Don't start big-wording me. Be thinking about not getting got.'

I swallow my sarcasm and start crawling again. We spent months planning how to escape from the Academy and the day before yesterday it finally happened. I used to believe that Academies were training schools for kids who had failed their Potential Test, but then I wound up in one and I discovered they're also a dumping ground for anyone the Leadership think is trouble.

I told Janna, a journalist, what really goes on in an Academy and she helped me to gatecrash a press conference where I explained to the nation how their Leader allows children to be beaten and abused in his precious

Academies. At least, I thought I was telling the world, but then I found out the broadcast wasn't live. Even so, the Leadership weren't happy that I'd told a hall full of journalists that Academy kids are half starved and punished with electric shocks. A pack of guards appeared and started trying to take people away for 'debriefing'. There was a massive fight and the Academy students, the Specials, joined in. When a fire broke out we took our chance to escape.

Except, not everyone escaped.

I shut that thought down. I can't think about that now. I've got to focus because fewer than forty-eight hours after we escaped, the guards are after us again. I don't want to go back to the Academy. Please don't let them find us down here.

'Listen,' I say, 'just t—' I bite my tongue as I bump my head against something hard and smooth. We've been crawling through the foundations of the warehouse, but now I think we're clear of the building. 'Is this the end?' I ask.

'Ty said we can get into a pie.'

'A pie?'

'You know, that thing, like the water is in. In the bathroom.'

They don't teach Academy Specials to read and they're not big on expanding their vocabulary either. Kay has picked up a lot of new words since I met her, but sometimes her speech is still a bit crazy. 'You mean a pipe.' I shudder. I feel in front of me again. The hard smoothness is curved. 'Do you mean this pipe?'

Kay squeezes past me.

'This one is not a water one. This one is for wires.'

'You want me to crawl through a cable duct? How are we even supposed to get in there?'

She's patting the pipe. 'Ty says we have to move it.'

'Ty should have spoken to me, too.'

'Don't talk now. Help me. Slide it down.'

I touch the pipe; it's covered in a layer of dirt. I can feel it shifting. Kay is twisting it. Whoever built this tunnel must have cut right through either end of a section of pipe, so that it's free to rotate. I use the flats of my hands to push it downwards. There's the sound of earth trickling and when I lift my hands to reposition them further up I find the edge of a hole. It's easier to pull the pipe down now that there is something to grip. It's pretty clever really that you can hide this entrance by turning this section of pipe so that the hole is facing away into the dirt.

'See?' Kay says.

I can't see anything in the darkness, but I can feel. I poke my top half into the pipe and stick my arms out. Reinforced plastic, or something similar, curves around me. Under my knees are cables in protective sleeves. There are a lot of them, but there's still enough room in the tube to crawl. Just.

Kay has stuck an arm in behind me. 'This is what Ty said. Let's go.'

5

My throat constricts. 'Do we really need to get in the pipe? We're already hidden,' I say.

'Blake—'

'Do you even know where this tube leads?'

'Ty said—'

'Forget Ty, how do *we* know it's safe?'

'It's safe.' She pauses. 'It is.'

I wriggle backwards out of the narrow pipe into the wider space. 'But Janna told us to wait for her here at the warehouse while she found someone for us to stay with.' Even as I say it, I know that I sound like a whining little boy.

'Janna didn't come back. We waited and she didn't come. Ty comed back.'

'And he didn't even bother to wake me up!'

'Blake, I will tell you all the things he said, but now we have to go. Ty told me this pipe because he wants to help us.' She speaks quickly; she wants to get away and she wants to do it now. But I don't want to go.

'Jana wants to help us, too,' I insist.

'Janna is a journalist. She doesn't know about being an Academy Special. She doesn't care about the bad things The Leader was making happen in the Academy.'

'She was going to find someone to tell my story. She knows people, newspaper editors and TV people.'

'Yes, and if they believe you, or if they say you're a crazy boy who helped all the bad Specials in the Academy escape, she doesn't care because she still gets her money.'

'But Janna said—'

Kay makes a strangled noise of frustration. 'Janna's not here. *The guards* are here.'

'Maybe we can wait here for the guards to leave.'

'If we go back I think they'll be waiting.'

'How do you even know they're The Leader's guards? Maybe it was—'

'I saw their van.'

'You saw the van?' King hell. What else was Kay up to while I slept?

'The vans waked me up. I looked out to see if it was Janna, but it was the guards. I ran to get you and all the smashing started.'

'What are they doing here? What do a vanload of armed guards want in an old warehouse anyway?'

'Maybe they're wanting The Leader's son.'

It's alarming to hear her say that out loud. Even though it's days since my mother told me the truth, it still seems impossible that the ruler of the country is the father I always believed was dead. The thought of my mother makes me suck in my breath. She died trying to get me out of the Academy. It's all my father's fault.

I bite my lip. 'How would they even know that I'm here?' I ask.

Kay doesn't answer, but I know what she's thinking.

'Janna wouldn't have bothered to help us escape and then turned us in,' I say.

She still doesn't answer.

I think back over the events of the day before yesterday. Back to the moment when I exposed The Leader for the monster that he is. It's true that Janna did take a lot of persuading to help me to get The Leader to incriminate himself at the press conference by admitting to the way that Academy Specials are treated. And when it all ended in chaos, Janna ran off without a backwards glance for anyone. She only ended up helping Kay and me to escape through chance.

'We should go in the pipe now, Blake.'

I stare into the impenetrable blackness and a tentacle of fear unfurls in my stomach. The truth is that I don't entirely trust Janna either, but I'm clutching at straws because I'm terrified of getting into this narrow pipe. I am desperate for a reason to get back above ground where I can breathe properly. 'We don't know that the guards are definitely after us,' I say. 'I think we should go back and see if—'

A muffled voice is coming from the other end of the tunnel.

They've found the entrance under the tile.

2

'*Get in,*' Kay whispers.

More voices join the first one. Kay grabs my arm and pulls me into the pipe. The cables creak beneath my knees. I turn back and see a faint light coming around the corner of the tunnel.

'Move the pipe!' Kay says.

It's much harder to turn the section of pipe from the inside. We can't be sat on that part or it won't move. Kay shifts to the left and I squeeze up to the right then we have to lean over and try to twist the pipe.

The voices are getting louder.

I grip the top edge of the hole and push the pipe back round towards the solid earth. It moves.

Just as a bright light comes round the corner the pipe lurches under my touch so that the hole is now twisted right round and is facing into the dirt. From the outside you would see nothing but smooth plastic.

'What the hell is this?' The voice sounds strange through the plastic. I'm frozen on my knees.

'It's a torch,' says another, deeper, voice.

A torch? That wasn't us.

'It's covered in dust. Must've been there a while.'

Did they see us go into the cupboard? If they did, they're not going to stop until they find us.

I can only hope that they don't shine their light too close. If they notice the lines on the pipe where it's been cut, they might get suspicious.

'Ain't nobody down here,' the deep voice goes on. 'Reckon this is where they hid the good stuff from customs. It hasn't been used for years. Stinks and all.'

There's a heavy sigh. 'We're going to be here all efwurding day. Tremaine said we can't leave till we've got bodies.'

The sound of their shuffling fades to nothing as they move back towards the hole in the cupboard.

The quiet wraps itself around me. The sides of the pipe seem to be contracting. 'Kay,' I whisper, 'if we come out, they're going to kill us.'

'We won't go out there,' she says. 'We can go in this tunnel.'

My skin tightens. I've never liked enclosed spaces and, having just been trapped in the lift at the Academy, I don't know if I can bear to stay in this pipe. 'It's just so . . . small in here,' I say.

'We have to do it.'

10

I take a gulp of air and draw myself into a point of resolution.

'Tell me everything that Ty said to you first.' If I'm going to do this I need to know what's going on.

'You move and I'll tell it to you.'

I can hear her crawling away and I don't have much choice but to follow.

Kay takes a breath. 'I really true did say we have to wake you up, but Ty said he has to tell me a thing. He says five minutes and then we wake Blake up.'

'So why didn't you?'

She ignores the interruption. 'He asked me things about you. I'm thinking Ty wants to know if you really are a Leader-hater.'

'Of course I—'

'He wants to know you're safe because he can get us to be with other Leader-haters.'

'Really? Ty knows people who are anti-Leadership?'

'Yes, he told me this is the Leader-haters' tunnel.'

I try to digest the idea of an anti-Leadership group. Who make tunnels. 'Then what did he say?'

'You know the thing where you talk to the person that is in another place?'

'A communicator?'

'On his communicator there was a person talking to him. Shouting. I could hear it. And it's like a bad thing happened, but Ty wouldn't tell it to me. He said he has to go and he's going to talk to the Leader-haters and we have

11

to stay in the warehouse and wait for him to tell us it's time to go in the tunnel.'

'If he said to wait, why are we down here?'

'Because I didn't want us to be shot.'

I snort. This whole situation is ridiculous. 'Then Ty went and then I was cold and I lied down with you and I must have gone to sleep. When the guards came, it waked me up.'

'You should have woken me straight away.'

'What thing would you have done if I waked you? You didn't want to leave; you wanted to wait for Janna. If I had told you about this pipe I don't think you would be wanting to get in it. You only got in it now because there were guards with guns.'

Which is true. Men with guns is the only good reason I can think of to bury myself underground like this. The weight of the tons of earth that must be packed around this pipe seems to be pressing down on my head. What if the pipe breaks? What if we suffocate in an avalanche of dirt? I want to get out. I want to claw my way out. The intensity of the darkness makes me shut my eyes to block it out. My breath is coming too fast.

'Blake?' Kay asks.

I struggle to focus on getting a sentence out.

'We don't even know where this tunnel leads,' I say, eventually.

'It goes to the people who will help us.'

I'm not so sure about that. I don't know if I really want

12

to meet these 'Leader-haters'. Back in my old life at the Learning Community, before I entered the Academy, whenever anyone whispered about people who were anti-Leadership they called them terrorists. They said that they blew up hospitals and killed children. I know that so much of what I was taught has turned out to be lies, but I'm still a little afraid of Kay's Leader-haters.

'How do we know we can trust Ty?' I ask. 'We don't know anything about him except he works with Janna. What if these people hurt us? What if this tunnel doesn't even lead anywhere?'

A terrible image of us, just crawling around in an underground maze until we die, blazes up in my mind. Efwurding hell. Panic surges inside me again. I want to be out. I need space. And air. My lungs are pressing against my ribs. I fight to get my breathing under control.

'Listen, Blake,' Kay says gently, 'you're a big brainer, so use your brain to think about this. People made that place down under the warehouse, yes? And they cut that bit of pipe so you can get in the pipe, yes? They were making a way, an escape way. It must be a way out.'

This, at least, makes some sense. The only way to get to the end is to keep going. I mustn't think about where I am. I just have to crawl.

'Do you think they've got guards chasing all the Specials who escaped from the Academy?' I ask Kay.

'Maybe. But I'm thinking it's you they want the biggest. It's you that got all the Specials to fight. It's you that was saying The Leader is bad, to all the journalists.'

I wonder how many of the journalists escaped. I'm pretty sure that the ones the guards managed to catch are dead now. And they're not the only ones who lost their lives.

I won't think about Ali now. I can't.

But the guards didn't catch Janna. There's no denying that her sense of self-preservation is strong. 'Do you really think Janna reported us?' I ask Kay.

'Yes,' Kay says flatly. 'Why do you big like her? Is it because she's all pretty?'

'I don't "big" like her. Why do you hate her so much?'

Kay only sniffs in response.

To be fair, I have noticed that Janna is rather condescending to Kay, and even though Kay's upbringing at the Academy means that she's got a very limited vocabulary, she has no problem recognising a patronising tone of voice. When we arrived at the warehouse in the pitch-black, Kay deliberately tripped Janna over and the two of them actually came to blows. Ty and I had to drag them apart.

'Listen, Kay, we may still need Janna's help,' I say. 'I don't think we should be pointing out her faults. And you definitely shouldn't be punching her in the mouth.'

'I can do my own deciding about who I'm going to punch.'

For a few minutes we shuffle onwards in silence. I tell

myself everything is fine. The further we go, the closer we are getting to the end. I listen hard. No sound comes from behind us. In fact, I can't hear anything at all. I slow down and push between the cables to slide my hands over the bottom of the pipe. I want to know if it slopes down, but it's impossible to tell. The gradient could be very gradual. What if we've been going deeper and deeper all this time?

'Don't go slow, Blake,' Kay says. Her voice comes from several metres ahead of me.

Where are we going? What the hell has happened to me? Just a few months ago I was totally sure of my place in the world. I was a big success at school and I knew that there was a great career in the Leadership waiting for me. I thought I was set, but then my world collapsed and I found myself with no home, no family and no future. And now I'm stuck in a tunnel heading I don't know where. For a moment I feel so utterly lost that the absence of any place where I belong throbs inside me. I miss the way that things were. And yet I can't even wish them back because what I've discovered means that old life can't exist any more.

I now know that kids who aren't deemed worthy are hidden away and mistreated, and that people who don't fit in with the Leadership plans are made to disappear. And I know that my father is responsible. If I want to bring down the system that deleted me and abused kids like Kay, then I have to kill him.

I will not fall apart down here. I will get out.

I crawl onwards with renewed energy. I may not have any

15

place to go or anyone to look after me, but I do have a plan, a mission. I've got to kill that man. And that is what matters.

That and Kay. I was so afraid that I'd lost her back at the Academy that I realised just how much she means to me. I want to tell her exactly how I feel, but I can't, not now, not here.

We crawl on and on.

'More people coming to fight us again,' Kay says in a mocking tone. 'It's all times fighting with you. Blake, you don't like fighting. Why do you keep getting to having people want to fight you?'

In spite of everything, my lips twitch. 'You think it's hilarious, don't you?'

'What's that?'

'Funny.'

'Yes, it is hilly-arious. Because you're not good at fighting, are you?'

'I'm better than I was.' I flex my back, it's starting to ache. 'You know, it's strange, at the Learning Community they used to teach us about battle tactics and strategy and stuff—'

'What does that mean?'

'We had lessons called Future Leaders and they taught us about . . . the ideas of war and fighting. The mechanics of weapons and the science of explosives. We had a lot of shooting practice, too. But they never taught us how to actually physically fight with our fists – which would have been more useful.'

'Useful?'

'Something I could use. I could have used some fight lessons.'

'Yes, you could. You could use some fight lessons now.'

It's better when we talk. It helps me keep my mind from spinning into panic again. I let Kay go on about how terrible I was in the fight competitions at the Academy, where the Specials were ranked by how many fights they'd won. She might laugh, but my physical fitness improved dramatically in the time I spent at the Academy. I touch my arm. I think I may have even developed some muscle.

Even in the dark I can tell my filthy hands are leaving a smear on my sleeve. When we started crawling, the earth that had got into the pipe was dry and dusty, but now the cables feel wet with mud.

'*Ah!*' Kay screams.

'What? What is it?' I reach forward for her, imagining in an instant all kinds of horrible things: that she's stumbled on a dead body, or she's cut herself on broken glass.

'A thing! It was a thing!'

'What was it? Are you hurt?'

I've got hold of her shoulder. The darkness is so frustrating. I keep thinking that I need to open my eyes, but of course they already are open and I can't see a damn thing.

'It didn't hurt. It was a surprise. A bad surprise. What do you call those things? Not people, the other things with lots of legs?'

'Caterpillars?'

17

'With four legs and ...' Her clothes rustle as she gestures, but it's no use to me in the dark.

'Animals? Did you feel an animal?' I suppose an animal is better than a guard. As long as it's not a rabid dog. It must have been something small because I didn't feel anything. 'It was probably just a rat.'

Kay sniffs. 'I know rats. I'm an Academy Special. I've seen big lots of rats. This was biggerer, I mean, bigger.'

If one thing has made it into the pipe there could be all sorts of things sharing this space with us. I imagine what I would see if I could light up the way in front of us. My mind fills with things that crawl and scuttle and bite. It's probably best that we can't see.

I feel my insides tightening again. 'Let's just keep moving, shall we?' I say.

So we press on. My knees are burning and my shoulders ache. It feels like we've been shuffling along for hours. The cables are increasingly slippery and I try not to think about what exactly might be coating them. I don't even want to turn around and go back any more, it would be too far. Once again I'm horribly conscious of the earth wrapping itself around us. Enclosing us. I wish that the pipe would crack and the ground would split open above me. I close my eyes again and concentrate on the rhythm of moving forwards.

'Can you hear a thing?' Kay asks.

I tense up, afraid to hear the sound of someone following us. I concentrate. Under the creaking of the cable sleeves as we press on them there is something else. A plinking.

I let out a sigh of relief. 'It's just a drip.'

'What's a drip?'

'A little bit of water.'

'Stop.'

I do as she says, thinking it might help to rest for a moment, but there isn't room to sit so I have to hunch over. As soon as I cease crawling, my knees flame with pain.

'It's water here,' Kay says. 'Give me your hand.'

I reach out and she guides my hand into a shallow puddle.

'Probably nothing to worry about. It's just water that's trickled in. The pipe must have cracked somewhere. You know, a little bit broken.' Which means the cables are wet with water, and not any of the horrible fluids I'd been imagining.

'I think it's not little broken. I think it's big broken. All the dirt got in and that rat thing.'

I really don't need anything else to worry about. My list is already pretty long. 'The pipe must be damaged in places. Does it matter?'

Kay takes a breath to say something and then stops.

'What is it?' I ask.

'I have to tell you a thing. Don't get scared.'

Oh hell. She's going to tell me that there's no way out. 'Go on.' My voice wobbles.

'When I looked out of the window and saw the guards coming . . .'

19

'What? What is it?'
'I didn't just see guards.'
'What else did you see?'
'Blake, it was raining.'

It was raining. We're buried in a leaking pipe and it's raining. Which means water is soaking through the ground to fill the pipe up and drown us.

'Wait a minute, wait a minute,' I say. 'The pipe probably won't let in large amounts of water. We just need to keep calm.'

But, as Kay pointed out, there must be some pretty sizable holes in the pipe. And there are already puddles forming. We need to find the exit as soon as possible.

'Just keep moving,' I say. 'Everything will be all right, if we just keep moving.'

But a few minutes later it's clear that everything is not all right. The occasional puddles have joined to make a stream around our knees.

'When you say raining . . .?' I ask.

'Big raining. Hard. Lots.'

But, it doesn't make sense. Somehow there is a serious

amount of water filling up this pipe. 'It can't just be what's seeping through the earth.'

'You're saying it can't, but it is. It's coming.'

I'm balancing on a narrow edge. I could very easily tip into hysteria. 'We've got to move faster.' My voice sounds like it's coming from someone else.

Crawling quickly is hard. I'm shivering and my trousers are soaking. The cables make the surface of the pipe uneven. My knees are killing me. My back aches so much that every movement sends a wave of pain like burning needles up my spine.

We stop talking and there's only the pathetic sound of us sloshing along in the dark.

'Blake?' Kay says in a tiny voice.

'What is it?'

'I don't know how to do that thing to stop you going down in the water.'

My heart contracts. Poor Kay. I can't even begin to tell her that it's not swimming that we need to worry about. The water is over my wrists now. 'It's okay,' I say. 'I can swim. I'll help you. We're going to get out of here.'

But the further we go the more convinced I am we're trapped. I pray that the water has levelled off, but after a while I know that it's still creeping up my forearms. I close my eyes and listen to the constant dripping of water. I'm so cold yet my knees are on fire. We go on and on and on. Imprisoned in the earth. A scream tries to claw its way up my throat. I force myself to swallow.

Eventually, Kay says, 'Can you see that?'

I open my eyes. The water is over my elbows now. Fuzzy spots are floating in front of me. I can't see anything. 'What?'

'It's more lighter.'

It's a while before I think she might be right. But then I can definitely make out the dark outline of Kay in front of me.

'It is! It's lighter. We're getting to the end,' Kay says.

If there's a light, then that means a way out. Back into the open, out of this suffocating plastic tomb. My arm muscles are twitching with exhaustion, but we hurry towards the light. Soon I can see Kay more clearly. The water still looks black and has reached her hips.

'Can you see anything?' I ask.

'I don't know. Wait . . .'

The light seems to be coming from above. Kay stops. 'It goes up,' she says.

I lean to the side to look past her. The pipe makes an abrupt corner turning upwards. Horror jolts through me. If the pipe continues straight up, how on earth will we climb it?

'Where does the pipe go?' Kay asks.

I can't speak. I squeeze past her and push upwards into the bend. My legs shake as I stand. Straight away, I can see the circle of light above me that is our exit. It's within reaching distance.

It's also covered in bars.

I take hold of the bars, but they won't budge.

'Can we get out?' Kay asks. She's sticking her head above the water, somewhere around my knees.

I can't bear to tell her that we're doomed. 'I'm not sure . . . there are bars covering the way out.'

'Can you get them off?'

Even though I've already tried it, I grip two of the bars and pull. They don't even bend. Then I push. Nothing.

'I can't do it.'

I need to think. There must be a way out. There must. Ty told Kay that this pipe was used as an escape tunnel. It wouldn't be any use to anyone if there wasn't an exit at this end.

'There might be a different hole somewhere,' I say. 'It could be covered up, like at the other end. Feel under the water.'

Kay starts splashing about near my feet. I run my hand around the upright section of the pipe. The cables disappear into a number of holes, but none of them is large enough to be any help. I can't see any other edges or openings.

'I can't find anything,' Kay says.

'Maybe there's a catch on the outside.' I push my hand between two bars and slide it upwards. It jams at the wrist. 'It's a bit tight.'

I feel around the edge of the hole. The bars are attached to a rim. It's like a lid. It must be designed to lift off. It must. I push my other hand through a gap between the bars on the other side of the hole and I strain my wrists to grip the rim with my fingertips, then I pull. The lid doesn't move. I feel around again. There's something sticking out at the side. The lid is bolted on.

I look down at Kay's hopeful face staring up at me. 'There's a bolt,' I say.

Kay looks blank.

'A bolt.' I remember how valuable things like bolts were at the Academy. They called them shrap and wore them as jewellery. 'Like the shrap on . . . on Ilex's belt.' God, I hope Ilex is somewhere safe now.

She nods. The water is up to her chin.

'I can't get my hand out far enough between the bars to try to unscrew it.'

'Let me try. My arms are more little than yours.' She tries to get to her feet but this upright section is narrower than the rest of the pipe and there just isn't enough room.

'You'll have to back up into the pipe and pass me there,' I say. 'Take a deep breath.'

Kay gulps and slips under the water. I crouch down and slide backwards into the now almost full pipe. I open my eyes underwater, but I can only see Kay as a dark blob as she scrambles past me. Once she's standing, I pull the top half of my body around the bend. I'm in a sitting position. I'm up to my shoulders in water.

'I can't reach,' she says.

'Climb on my shoulders.'

But she can't. The pipe is so narrow here that she can't get her knees high enough to climb up.

'I'll go back under the water. You get on my shoulders while I'm down there, then I'll push you up as I come out of the water.' I take a deep breath and duck back into the freezing water. I'm so tired and the water rushes up around me in a way that makes me think it's going to suck me back down the pipe. When I feel Kay's feet on my shoulders it takes all my energy to force my head above water. I break the surface and gasp for breath. Even as I'm spluttering, I look up. Above Kay's legs and body, the bars are still in place.

'I tried,' Kay says. 'It's all watery and my hand is watery.'

'You need more purchase. Pull your sleeve over your hand.' I feel like a rock is wedged in my windpipe.

I listen to her struggling and the moment seems to stretch. Water rushes and drips and splashes around me. We're never going to get the lid off. We're stuck. There isn't enough room for us both to fit in the upright part of

26

the pipe. And the water level keeps climbing. All the fear that I've been holding down threatens to bubble up and take me over. We're going to die here in the cold and the filth.

'I've done it!' Kay shouts.

I look up and the bars have been lifted away. We're saved! I can get out. Out into space and light.

I grasp a cable in each hand like a rope to pull myself to my feet with Kay still on my shoulders. Once she's climbed out, she leans back in and sticks out a hand to me.

'You'll never get me out like that,' I say. 'Move out the way and let me try to pull myself up.'

She retracts her hand. I grip the edge of the hole. I try to heave myself upwards by bracing a foot against the side of the pipe for traction. My arms are shaking. I manage to pull myself up a little, but then my foot skids and I splash back into the water. I try again. There's not enough room to walk my way up the side of the pipe. Fresh panic knifes through my lungs. I can't believe it. I can't believe I've come all this way. I've crawled through the tunnel of death only to get stuck here. At the exit. Because my stupid efwurding arms are too weak to pull me up.

'Blake, get out *now*.' Kay sounds stern, but her face peering down at me is puckered with worry.

I've come too far to die in a pipe. I've lost my mother and poor little Ali. I promised the Specials that I would take down The Leader, so that no one would ever suffer in an Academy like they did again. I have got to get out.

27

I take a deep breath and squeeze all of my energy into my arms and pull and pull ... and when they start to shake and burn I pull some more ... and finally I reach the tipping point and I've got my head out of the pipe and I know I'm going to do it. Kay grips me under the arms and helps yank me out. I flail like a caught fish. When I'm out as far as my waist, I have to lie gasping for a while before I get my legs out.

After being in the tunnel, the light is so bright it burns. I keep my eyes half scrunched to look around me.

We're in a very small concrete building. Wires snake all around us: running in and out of holes and sockets. One wall is covered with meters. A symbol like a crooked figure four is scrawled several times on the back of the broken door with spray paint. Rain is pouring in through the disintegrating roof and the protective sleeves on a number of the wires has been torn or even chewed away. I don't think this place has been used for a long time.

For a moment all I can do is take great shuddering breaths and press my head to the concrete floor in silent thanks that we're out of that terrible pipe. I never want to be closed in again. I look over to Kay. She's hugging her knees.

This feels like the first moment of stillness since we escaped.

Everything we need to talk about collides in my mind and all the horrors clog in my throat. Out of my mouth comes just one word: 'Ali,' I say.

28

Kay understands. She crawls across the floor and we wrap our arms around each other.

The thought of brave Ali fading away on the steps outside the Academy burns through me. I should never have included her in my plans to expose The Leader. I shouldn't have let her get in that lift – and when it broke down and she squeezed through that tiny gap in the doors, I should have told her to run like hell. Instead, she brought us back the override key and, on the way, The Leader's aide shot her. He was trying to get her to tell him where I was. It's my fault. I feel the weight of responsibility for another death lodge above my heart, pressing painfully down. I know it will be there always.

Ali didn't even get to see her brother, Ilex, before she died.

'What do you think happened to Ilex?' I ask Kay.

'I think some good people found him and he is in their house and they're giving him big lots of food.'

'Really?'

'Really yes,' she says firmly. She's trying to make me feel better.

The sound of rain on the roof is lighter now.

Everything is a terrible mess. I am so exhausted that I could just sit here and wait for it all to go away, but Kay climbs to her feet and pushes open the door of the building. I hear her sharp intake of breath.

'What is it?' I ask, getting up to join her at the door.

I see a vast expanse of bare earth broken up only by the

rubble of demolished buildings. The back of my neck prickles.

'We're in a nowhere place,' Kay says.

'It's worse than that,' I say. 'I think we're in the Wilderness.'

All the childhood stories about Wilderness bogeymen come back to me. Even worse than that, I remember the cannibal boys that I encountered in the Wilderness behind the Academy.

Kay's face is pale. The Wilderness is where they send the worst-behaved Specials. She's got her own horror stories to remember. I hate seeing her worried.

'We must have crawled right under the fence,' I say.

Kay isn't listening. 'I didn't know the pipe came to the Wilderness,' she says. 'Ty didn't tell me.' She stares out at the barren landscape. 'If you're not good, the Enforcers make you go here,' she says. 'They say to you about the Wilderness to scare you. They tell you things.' She sweeps her gaze across the horizon. 'This is the place they send *all* the bad ones, isn't it? Not just the Academy Specials. It's all-danger here.'

She doesn't have to tell me. The hairs on the back of my neck are already standing up. I try to focus my mind. 'Are you sure that Ty said this is where the anti-Leadership people are?'

'Yes, big sure. Do you think we should go back?'

I'm not sure there is a way back. The pipe is useless now that it's flooded. Even when the water drains away, there is no way I am getting back in there. And I've tried the fence that surrounds the Wilderness before; it's electrified. Besides, sometimes guards patrol along its length and I'm pretty sure if they saw anyone coming in from the Wilderness they would shoot first and ask questions later.

We're stuck here.

'What exactly did Ty say about where we could find the people who would help us?'

'He didn't say big lots. He said there is the pipe. The pipe is an escape for the Leader-haters – he called them . . . the Resistance.'

'Really?' Resistance sounds a lot less scary than terrorists.

'Yes. He said he can talk to his friend and ask if the Resistance want us to come, then we can go in the pipe because the pipe is a way to get to their . . . hecwaters?'

'Headquarters. But where exactly?' I look around at the desolate stretch of muddy fields and ruins in front of us. 'There's nothing here.'

'No, it's not here,' Kay agrees. 'But I'm thinking it's near. I asked Ty what place it's in and he said Anuldsity.' She says it with a flourish. As if this clears matters up. 'Do you know where that place is?' she asks, as if I'm some kind of Wilderness expert.

'I've got no idea. Did he say anything else?'

'No.' She frowns in concentration. 'Yes! He said Anuldsity is in the south-east! Does that mean Wilderness?'

'South-east is a direction.'

'What?'

'It's a way to go.' I rub my hand over my face. I wanted to make things better so badly, but it's all gone horribly wrong. I don't even know where we're going to get our next meal from. 'What should we do?' I ask Kay. 'Should we try to find the Resistance?' I don't tell her that I'm still a little afraid of them.

Kay eyes the thinning clouds. 'I think maybe it's better to get on a way to go than to stay here not getting any place.' She touches my hand. 'Ty said they would help us and I think it's true.'

'Why? We don't really know anything about Ty. He was just a friend of Janna's.'

'When he talks about The Leader he has the look like you. I can see that he wants to stop him.'

And that's how we decide to search for the Resistance. I put my trust in Kay's ability to read someone's feelings in their face.

The rain has completely stopped so we step outside the hut and take a look around.

We're in the middle of what must have once been

countryside. Roads snake through hills, but instead of fresh green, the fields are bare grey mud. To the right a large building has been reduced to a pile of bricks.

'Which way is south-east?' Kay asks.

I look up at the sky; a pale sun has broken through the clouds. 'I can work it out,' I say. 'I just need something . . .' I turn back into the hut and poke about until I find a strip of metal that holds a bundle of wires flat against the wall. I wrench it from its pins.

'What are you doing?' Kay asks.

I go back outside and stick the long thin piece of metal in the ground. The sun casts a weak shadow. Using my finger I mark the end of the shadow in the dirt.

'Now we have to wait a while,' I say. 'The sun moves from east to west, so when the shadow moves we'll be able to work out which way is south-east.'

While we're waiting I teach Kay about the points of the compass, but neither of us are completely focused. It feels stupid to be standing still. I expect a pack of vicious Wilderness people to attack at any second. I'm constantly scanning the land around us.

I probably don't wait long enough, but when the shadow has moved some way round, I make a second mark, then draw a line between the two dents in the earth.

'Okay,' I say. 'The first mark is east and the second is west, so if we stand with east on our right, we're facing north, which means . . .' I turn one hundred and thirty-five degrees to my right. 'This is south-east.'

34

'That's good,' Kay says.

'It's not horribly accurate,' I admit. 'But we can always do it more precisely later when we've found a better stick.'

We set off in the direction I pointed. Fortunately, one of the few marks on the landscape, something low and black, is just to the left of my calculated trajectory. As long as we keep that on our left, we should be fine.

I hope.

The muddy ground sucks at our boots as we walk. There isn't much to see. What little vegetation there is doesn't add much colour; the grass is yellow, the trees are grey and withered. After a while we end up on a road that's leading in the right direction.

I hope we don't have to go far, but deep down I've already assumed that a group of rebels wouldn't choose to live near the boundary fence. I prepare myself for a long walk.

For a moment the wind drops and everything is completely still and quiet. I don't know whether I'm more afraid of us being totally alone, or of what might happen when we do find someone. Either way I keep looking over my shoulder.

'Tell me how there is this Wilderness,' Kay says. 'Tell to me about the war thing again.'

'We went to war to try to defend another country that the Greater Power had invaded.'

'What's invaded?'

'They brought loads of soldiers – fighters – into a country and started telling them what to do. Of course the Greater Power didn't like us interfering when we tried to help, so they attacked us too. Using new weapons. Lots of bombs.'

'What's bombs?'

'They drop them out of the sky and they explode.' I mime an explosion by scrunching my fingers and flicking them out. 'They break things, even big things, they make buildings fall down.'

'Like at the Academy when there was the fire and then there was that *boom!* and it made everyone fall down?'

'I don't think that was caused by a bomb, but similar to that. Where we are now was the worst hit because the capital used to be around here somewhere.'

'How did the war stop?' she asks.

'The Leadership stopped it.' I frown. 'Or so they claim.' Come to think of it, what do I really know about the Long War at all? 'That's what I was taught in school anyway.'

Kay nods. We both know that neither her school nor mine was a place for reliable information.

The black shape in the distance gradually resolves itself into the remains of a group of houses. They must have been hit by a bomb. Only one front wall stands alone, with its windows smashed and its wooden veranda in splinters. It looks like a mouth full of broken teeth.

The rest is not much more than a pile of bricks and timber. When we reach it I pull a plank from the wreckage and Kay and I manage to hack at it with flat stones until the wood splinters into a reasonable point, then I stick it in the ground, so that we can make another shadow compass and check we're heading in the right direction. While we're waiting for the shadow to move, Kay starts shifting bricks and hunks of plaster.

'What are you doing?' I ask. 'Some of that stuff is sharp.'

Kay rolls her eyes. 'It's not sharp things I'm worrying about.' She looks behind her. 'I want to find a weapon.'

I would like a weapon too. If only I had a gun, then all that weapons training in the Future Leaders sessions at the Learning Community might actually be some use to me. But there's nothing useful in the heap of rubble. Kay has to settle for half a brick, which she keeps in her hand at all times.

Looking at the shadow compass I adjust our course a little and head towards a group of buildings in the distance. We cross several fields of mud sprouting nothing but a few sickly weeds and surrounded by hedges that are not much more than desiccated clumps of twisted twigs. Then we find another undulating road to follow. It must have been pretty once, looking down the hill at the fields. But now everything is grey and withered. I don't understand why the weeds aren't thriving. Surely, left untended, this place should be a riot of greenery? There's something very wrong here.

When we reach the buildings we find the remains of a village. The wind whips brick dust in my eyes. I squint to take in the devastation. Where we stand is barely even recognisable as a street. You can't pick out individual structures. It's just piles and piles of bricks with lengths of wood sticking out. I have to remind myself that these bricks once made someone's home and these shards of wood came from the furniture they used every day.

Behind these mounds is half a house, its side ripped open and its insides spilling out. Twisted between the bricks there's a jumble of sun-bleached clothes tangled like intestines. Beyond that is more rubble, but on the far side of the village is a group of houses still standing, although they slump against each other like wounded soldiers. What happened to the people who lived here?

Kay is picking her way through the mess.

'Can we drink this?' she asks, pointing to a pool of rainwater that has gathered in a dented plastic roof of some kind.

I take a look at the water. It looks all right, but it's bound to be full of bacteria. We haven't got anything to filter it with. My tongue feels coated in grit.

I shrug. 'We may as well. This is probably as good as we're going to find anywhere.'

The puddle is quite deep and we manage a few mouthfuls each. The water tastes bitter, but it feels really good slipping down my throat.

I hunch my shoulders against the wind as we make our unsteady way between the remains of houses. I can't shake the feeling that we're being watched.

At the centre of the village is a crater the size of a football field.

Kay's eyes widen. 'Is that where they bombed the bomb?'

Dropped the bomb, I think – but I don't say it because my jaw has seized up. It's like the middle of the village has just disappeared.

Kay stares into the crater. 'Were there houses there?'

I nod.

'But there's no things left. No bricks and things.'

I don't know what happened to the remains. It's like they were vaporised. What kind of bomb does that? Causing buildings to collapse is one thing, making them disappear is something else.

Kay has already turned away. 'There's some standing-up houses. Let's look for food.'

I tear my eyes away from the crater.

Kay makes her way over, between bricks and roof tiles, into one of the few upright houses. I eye its walls with apprehension, but I climb in after her anyway.

Inside, the ceiling has partially collapsed. The front door has been blown onto the stairs. The furniture and carpets are covered in a thick layer of plaster and broken glass. It's hard to tell what's what.

The next house we try seems less likely to fall down on us at any moment. When we walk into the sitting room a shiver goes through me. Nothing has been touched. The green armchairs are pointed towards the old-fashioned TV. There's a book about gardening splayed face-down on the coffee table. A piano in the corner has a jumble of music stacked on top. It's like we've stumbled into someone's home. Except there's a chill wind blowing through a broken window.

One room that isn't untouched is the kitchen. All of the cupboards are bare. It looks like someone has cleared them out a long time ago. Even the cutlery drawer has been emptied. It's the same in the next two intact houses we find.

In the third house, Kay pulls open a cupboard under the stairs. Behind the coats and wellies and a pair of tennis rackets she finds a shelf holding four pots of homemade jam. The jars have rubber seals and they haven't spoiled in all the years that they must have been sitting there gathering dust.

'This is big good,' Kay smiles, when we crack open a jar to share.

I know it's rash to finish a whole jar, but I'm so hungry and it's great to see Kay enjoying the sweet taste. I find a bag on the row of pegs on the back of the cupboard door and put the empty pot and the remaining three jars in it to take along with us.

Whoever made this jam had no idea that we would be eating it. What happened to them? Did they die in the war? Are they still alive on the other side of the fence? Either way, I'm grateful for the jam in my stomach.

Out in the rubble-filled garden, Kay points at a small wooden hut.

'What's this?' she asks.

'It's a shed.'

Kay is already wrenching open the door. The wood is so weathered that it's crumbling away at the corners like biscuit.

Inside, the tiny space is crammed full of junk. Plastic sacks, spades, rakes, boxes, buckets and a giant fabric umbrella.

'It's rubbish,' Kay says.

'Wait a second.' I pull a folding chair out of the way.

'What is it?' Kay asks.

'It's a bike. In fact,' I say pulling back a rustling tarpaulin, 'there are two – which is good.'

'Why? What do they do?'

'They move.'

We had a number of bikes at the Learning Community. They didn't make much of a fuss about Physical Education there, but once a week we were supposed to get some fresh air. Wilson and I usually opted for cycling around the grounds since it seemed like less effort than anything else on offer. The Specials at the Academy were required to exercise every day, but I never saw anything that might be described as equipment there and going outdoors for a ride would never have happened.

'Show me,' Kay says.

'Okay. Grab that one.'

We manage to yank the bikes out of the clutter and drag them outside. We have to haul them over and between the mounds of bricks until we reach a clear stretch of road leading out of the village. I swing my leg over the saddle and wobble forwards. My legs are still weak from that dreadful crawl through the pipe, but soon I'm gliding along.

'Blake!' Kay laughs and claps her hands as if I've performed a conjuring trick.

'It's easy,' I say riding back to her. 'You'll soon pick it up.'

Half an hour later, Kay still can't find her balance. Each time I let go of the back of her bike she sways and crashes to the ground.

'Stupid thing,' she says and inspects her skinned palms. It would almost be funny to see Kay's disbelief that she is struggling with a physical activity if it were not for her frustration.

'Don't worry, you'll get it,' I say, but she only scowls in return.

Eventually, she does get it and the first time she catches her balance and makes her way wobbling down the road we both shout with delight.

The sun is stronger now and it catches Kay's hair as she rides away. She's gorgeous. For a moment I forget to look over my shoulder. I forget about listening for movement in the ruins behind us and I just think about Kay. I want to hold her. I want to be in a place where she is learning to ride for fun and not because we're desperately seeking a group of people we may never find. If things were different we could be teenagers who don't have to worry about anything except schoolwork and having a good time. We could ride all afternoon and then we could take a break and we'd talk and kiss and touch for hours and hours and nothing would stop us from being perfectly happy.

But that's not the way things are.

And they never will be, unless we make it that way.

We ride for several hours along the winding roads before we stop at a ruined town to look for more water.

'There's some here,' I say to Kay.

She comes over to inspect the puddle in the deep dent in the bonnet of a once white car with a rash of rust.

'That's g—'

Stones crunch behind us.

I spin round. Standing over our bikes is a man. His clothes are in tatters and his hair is tangled and snarled. I'm close enough to see his face twist in anger when he spots us. He lunges into a run towards us.

'Go!' Kay says.

I skirt the car and leap over a rubbish bin. I follow Kay through a hole in a wall on to a patch of yellow grass. We weave between heaps of bricks and rotting pieces of fence, cutting through the gardens of a row of houses. I look behind to see the Wilderness man following.

Kay scrambles over a curling section of wire fence. I

fling myself after her. We're in a narrow alleyway. We run, jumping to avoid the detritus the path is littered with.

The Wilderness man rattles the fence behind us. I hurdle a chunk of stone, then a broken chair. At the end of the alleyway there's the shell of a long low building. The door-frame still stands even though the walls on either side are missing. We run through it and into an open space full of rubble. Kay turns to the right and we weave between fallen masonry and the twisted remains of metal shelving. I shoot a look behind us. The man is still following us. He ploughs through the debris without looking left or right. But he's not in good shape. We're putting some distance between us. We emerge from the long building through a gap in the wall.

'Wait!' I gasp to Kay. 'Got to get back to . . . bikes.'

Kay nods. But it's easier said than done with collapsed houses everywhere.

'This way,' Kay says, and she leads me down the side of the building we've just run through. At the end, our way is blocked by the remains of a wall.

'Get up, get up!' I grip Kay by the knees and give her a boost. She clambers over the wall. I look back. The Wilderness man is coming down the side of the building. I take a running jump at the crumbling wall and find myself gripping the top with desperate fingers. My feet slip and slide as I struggle over. The Wilderness man is almost close enough to touch me.

Kay pulls me down on the other side and we run to the

right and into another skeleton house. I skid on something and slide smack into what remains of a wall. A shower of plaster covers me. There's a terrible creaking.

The Wilderness man thunders into the house with a growl.

I stagger to my feet as a brick smashes to the floor.

I tumble out of the house after Kay, as hundreds more bricks fall down. We turn to watch as what's left of the upper storey come crashing down.

King hell. I gasp for breath.

'I think . . .' Kay says, 'I think he . . .'

We both know the Wilderness man is under there.

I bend over, sucking air into my lungs. 'We have to get back to the bikes before any more of them appear.'

I straighten up.

It's too late.

There are already three of them slipping and sliding their way over a mound of bricks towards us.

Without saying a word we sprint away again. I'm ahead of Kay and all the time that I'm scrabbling over debris and darting around fallen masonry, I'm trying to work us back to the place we left our bikes. I power around a corner and almost run straight into one of those terrifying giant craters, but I realise at the last minute and pull away to the left.

Finally, there are the bikes straight ahead of us. I grab mine and throw a leg over the saddle. I only peddle a few metres before I have to dismount and heave the bike over a pile of rubble. Kay is right behind me. The Wilderness people are further back than I might have expected. They have an odd lurching gait, which is just as well for us because it takes Kay and I several minutes of yanking and lifting the bikes along before we reach a long clear patch of road where we can actually cycle. We have to dismount to clamber over obstacles several more times before we reach the edge of town.

Then we're speeding away on a rough road. I twist back to watch the Wilderness people shrink into nothing.

'Efwurding hell,' Kay says.

I can only agree.

We keep riding. When we reach another flattened town we skirt round it. The only upright structure I see is a tall house that looks as if it has been sliced in half, exposing three fireplaces on top of each other, all connecting to the same chimney. A large photograph of two children still hangs above one of the mantelpieces. It seems voyeuristic to be staring at an intimate family setting like that exposed to the open air. I turn my eyes back to the road.

Every time I think my thigh muscles can take no more I tell myself that it's safer to keep moving. When it starts spitting with rain I finally admit that I can go no further.

'We need to find somewhere to stop for the night,' I pant.

It's pouring by the time we reach a lone farmhouse with its tired roof sagging into the top floor. The back door is ajar and I tiptoe in, listening for sounds of occupation. We creep through the house checking each room. I even open all the cupboards.

'No people here,' Kay says.

I go back outside and pull our bikes into the hallway. I'm about to barricade the door shut when Kay draws the empty jam jar out of the bag and takes it outside to set down in the middle of the garden to catch rainwater.

'Good idea,' I say. I hunt about and find a bucket under the sink and some bowls in a cupboard. I wipe decades of dust away with my damp sleeve and we put them out with the jar.

Sitting in the kitchen keeping watch out of the window, Kay and I allow ourselves a little more jam. The sweetness makes my teeth hurt.

Neither of us is saying what is blatantly obvious. We've seen no evidence of the Resistance. And we may never find them.

'How big is the Wilderness?' Kay asks.

'It's not that bi—'

Oh my God. I don't *think* it's big. I've been taught that it's only a tiny percentage of the country, but . . . but I don't really know. King hell. I just don't know anything anymore. It could be twice that size. It could be huge. Bigger than the other side of the fence. I have to steady myself with a hand on the table. It's as if the ground really is shifting beneath my feet. I can almost feel the earth expanding its boundaries out into the sea. I don't even know the size

48

and shape of my own country. That's how big the Leadership's lies are.

I'm suddenly too tired to tell Kay that I don't know. Instead I say, 'Tell me what Ty said one more time.'

'I told you. Anuldsity.'

'Are you sure that's what he said?'

'Yes. Big sure. He said An-uld-sity.'

It finally hits me. 'I get it. He didn't say Anuldsity, he said *an old city*.'

'That's what I said.'

'It's three words, not one. An . . . old . . . city.'

'You're the one that knows words,' she says with mild reproach. 'What's a city?'

'That's what they used to call districts.'

'That's a big place, with all houses and factories and things, right?'

'Yes.'

'We can find a big thing like that then.'

I hope she's right.

Enough rainwater has collected in the bowls and the bucket for us to have a small drink. Who knows what we're going to do when the rain dries up for good. I replace the containers and Kay says, 'We should sleep.'

'We'll have to take it in turns. The other one can keep watch.'

'I'll go first,' Kay says, and I don't argue.

Upstairs in the front bedroom the light is fading. There are

49

two single beds still neatly made up. I cross the room to the one under the window. At first glance I think the bedspread is white with a stripe of pink flowers at the top and bottom. When I get closer I realise that where the bed is positioned beneath the window the sun has shone in every day and bleached the colour from middle section of the covers. I sit down heavily on the bed. If you look closely, you can see the shadows of flowers on the sun-bleached part. It's incredible to compare it to the top and bottom sections that were shielded from the sun and to see how vibrant the pattern used to be. To my shame I have to swallow hard. For some reason this faded bedspread hurts me more than all the destruction I've seen today. I rest my head on the pillow. I want to unpick why the drained colour makes me sad, but I'm so very tired that I allow myself to be drawn down into a dreamless sleep instead.

When I wake it's dark. Panic grips me, where's Kay?

'Kay?' I say, sitting up.

'Yes,' she says from the stairs.

She's still here, it's all right. I take a shaky breath.

'Are you okay?' she asks, coming into the room.

Listening to her voice, I know how much I want to always be near her. I need to tell her how I feel.

'I'm fine. I . . . When we were in the pipe . . .' I hesitate. 'I . . . I wanted to tell you something.'

'What is it?'

'I was afraid that I would lose you. I was so happy when

50

we escaped the Academy, together. I'm so happy all the time that I'm with you. And I'm scared that something terrible will happen.' I swallow. 'I just want to be with you.'

She's quiet and I think that I've said too much. That she's embarrassed or she thinks I'm an idiot, but then I realise that she's moving across the room, to lie down next to me.

'I want to be with you, too.' And she draws me to her and kisses me. Our bodies press together and the Wilderness and the guards and my aching knees and the pain and the uncertainty all fall away and I am entirely present right here, right now, with Kay. Just Kay.

While Kay sleeps, I patrol the house to keep myself awake. In my sleepy state, my thoughts drift to one of the many dark places in my mind that I've been trying to steer away from: my father.

When my mother revealed that my father is The Leader I could hardly believe it. I'd just discovered that our government is corrupt to the core and then I learn I'm the son of the man in charge of it all. Mostly, I've just felt angry. I hold him responsible for my mum's death and the deaths of my best friend, little Ali and countless other innocent people. I want to make him pay. I want to stop him. But even though I've tried to concentrate solely on eliminating him, another thought keeps coming to me in unguarded moments: what if I'm like him? What if all that evil has somehow been passed on to me? Ever since I found out

51

my true parentage, I've been frightened by the knowledge of his genes inside me, like some kind of internal stain I'll never be free of.

It's ridiculous, but I'm afraid of myself.

I press my fingers into my temples. I don't have to be like him. I make my own choices. I can choose to do the right thing. I won't be like my father, and I—

I'm jolted from my self-indulgent thoughts by something or someone screaming. It's coming from the fields behind the house. I climb onto the side of the bath to lean out of the window, but I can't make anything out clearly in the darkness. In the bedroom next door, Kay doesn't stir and I resist the urge to wake her. After a few minutes the screaming stops, but I stare out of the window for a long time.

I don't know what had happened to those Wilderness people we saw earlier. At school they told us that people in the Wilderness were crazy killers. I don't want to make the mistake of blindly believing what I've been told by the Leadership again, but those people did look pretty vicious and they clearly weren't friendly.

We're not safe here. Should we go back to the other side of the fence or is this hunt for the Resistance worth it?

In the morning I try to gather my resolve. We've come this far. Our options are limited and at least now we know that we're looking for a city.

'Let's go,' I say to Kay, and I try to mean it.

As we're leaving the house, I notice a shoehorn on the tiny table in the hallway. 'My grandmother had one of these,' I say, picking it up.

'Grandmother?' Kay asks.

'She's dead now.'

'Who is?'

'My grandmother,' I repeat.

Kay shakes her head. 'Your what?'

Sometimes the absence of a piece of vocabulary shows so clearly something that Kay missed out on in life that it makes me catch my breath. 'Grandmother is your mother's mother. Or your father's mother.'

'My?'

'Or anyone's. Everyone has a grandmother.'

Kay blinks with surprise.

'Although, of course they might be dead like mine, or you may never have met them.'

'Why would you be meeting them?'

King hell. That's such a sad thing to say. 'Well ... some kids aren't sent away to school like me and you. They live with their parents and quite often they spend time with grandmothers or grandfathers or a whole load of other people who are connected to you by your parents. They're called your family. You should have lived with your family. Me too.'

'But why do people have the time with those grand people?'

'I suppose because they love each other.'

'Why? Just because of the connecting to your mum and dad thing?'

'Sort of.' I think about before I went to the Learning Community when we would visit my grandmother and she always read me the same book about jungle animals. 'When you grow up with someone and spend time together and they take care of you and ... I don't know, it's hard to explain. Sometimes families don't love each other, sometimes they hate each other.' I look at Kay's furrowed brow. This makes no sense to her because she's never had someone care for her in the way that families do. 'This is one of the things that needs to change about this country,' I say. 'Everyone should get the chance to be with their family.'

Kay shrugs. 'Maybe, but I'm not going to love any person just because of that. I'm going to choose who I love.'

We drink all of the water that has gathered in our collection of containers, except what we can fit in the two empty jam jars. I screw the lids on and put them in the bag for later.

Getting back in the saddle is painful. My thigh muscles start to burn before we've gone very far. Kay doesn't complain, so neither do I.

After a while she looks over at me. I wonder if she's thinking about last night and I can't stop myself from smiling.

'Blake? Remember when you told me all about when you were Learning Community and the men hurt you and your friend, and the policeman was all saying, "Don't tell the Academy your name"?'

It was only a few months ago that P.C. Barnes told me to change my name to Blake, but it feels like years. 'I remember. What about it?'

'What was your name? Your name that you had first?'

'My real name is Jackson. John Jackson.' It feels strange on my lips.

'Do you want me to call you Jackson?'

I'm not sure of the answer to that. There was a time when I couldn't wait to stop being Blake. I wanted to escape from the Academy and to get back to my old life. But now . . .

'I can't go back to being Jackson,' I say.

'No?'

'I'm not the same person.'

'Don't you want to be Jackson?'

'No, I don't think I do. When I was Jackson I thought I knew it all. I thought I'd done all this great stuff like passing exams and winning prizes, but really the best things I've ever done have been as Blake. I've learnt what's really important. And I've found you.'

Kay gives me a look that makes me forget to steer my bike for a second.

I take a deep breath. 'I used to think labels were important,' I say, 'but now I think it's more about what you do. Does any of that make sense?'

'Yes. I don't mind it what you're called. I just like *you*,' she says.

Suddenly pedalling doesn't feel like such hard work any more.

We cycle for miles without seeing any signs of life. My skin feels dusty and when I run a hand through my hair I find flakes of something that looks like ash. The longer we ride the grimier I feel.

We pass through the remains of several bombed-out towns that must have been home to a lot of people. Often nothing recognisable is left standing. Where houses and shops do remain upright they are in bad shape; paint peeling, wood rotting, tiles missing. We pass a block of flats with unbroken windows, but there is no shine coming off the smeared glass; it's like looking up at dozens of dead eyes.

In the afternoon we start up a steep hill. It's hard going, even for super-fit Kay. We've barely had anything to eat for the last few days and our water is running low.

Finally we reach the top of the hill.

What we see beneath us takes my breath away.

We've found the city.

And unlike everywhere else we've seen, it appears untouched by the bombs. In fact, at first glance it looks as if an entire district from the other side of the fence has been picked up and dumped in the middle of the Wilderness. Then I see what is missing. Colour, lights, movement. There are no fresh green parks, no lit-up signs and no cars or buses winding along the many roads beneath us.

This is a city of absence.

As we make our way down the hill I can see that many of the buildings have fallen into disrepair; even so, this is the first place that we have seen that is still recognisable as what it once was. I don't see any of the super-sized craters here. This place seems to have got off lightly. The inhabitants were lucky. Although, that's not how I would describe anyone still living in this lost city.

Walking the empty streets makes my skin prickle. The

whole place is awash with whispering ghosts. I can almost see them coming out of their houses, walking down the street, stepping into a shop.

But it's the living inhabitants who scare me most. I'm more frightened here than I have been the whole time we've been in the Wilderness. There are hundreds of hiding places. I imagine eyes at every window and predators around every corner.

'Do you think there are a lot of Wilderness people here?' I ask, looking over my shoulder.

Kay nods. 'If I was in the Wilderness I would live here. This is the place you would look for things.'

I can only hope that no one is looking for us.

At the end of the second street there's a corner shop. A blue-and-white striped canopy over its window has blistered and torn. The wind whips the tatters back and forth.

'Let's look in here for food,' I say to Kay.

She nods.

Inside the shop, the racks of newspapers and magazines from two decades ago are untouched. Unfortunately, the rest of the shop is not. Every item of food has been removed. Looking at the stock labels on the empty shelves, it's clear that even items like tissues and bleach have been taken.

'Someone has been here,' Kay says.

It's the same in every shop we find.

'It's good,' Kay insists. 'It means the Resistance people are here. And they will have food for us.'

We walk right across the district. In the countryside the silence and emptiness wasn't so bad, but here where I expect to see people walking and chatting and eating outside restaurants and waiting for the bus, the stillness sends a chill through me.

And yet, despite the quiet, I know there must be Wilderness people here somewhere. Occasionally, I think I see someone moving out of the corner of my eye, but every time I spin round there's nobody there. Once, I think I hear the engine of a car in the distance, but the noise fades away before I can be certain.

There's been no rain all day and I start to seriously worry about where we can find water. Also, it's clear that someone – probably a lot of someones – has been using up all the resources this place has to offer. It can only be a matter of time before we bump into them. Who will we meet first – the Resistance or a pack of violent Wilderness people?

The sun is descending. I try to decide whether it's safe to shelter in one of the buildings for the night. It would be so easy for someone to creep up and ambush us.

'Let's get up high and look,' Kay says.

We climb the stairs in a block of flats.

Every door we pass has been forced open.

'Someone has been here too,' Kay says.

It gives me the shivers. I feel as if we're just seconds behind someone. I press my face to a window on the third floor; laid out beneath me the city is divided up by criss-

60

crossing roads. The rows of grey houses blend into the dusk. Nothing moves.

'Do you think we should stay in one of these places?' I ask.

Kay casts a fighter's eye over the layout of the flat we're stood in. 'If we do we can hear if someone comes and get ready to fight.'

'Or hide,' I suggest.

Kay rolls her eyes at my entirely reasonable desire to avoid getting hurt and walks into the kitchen. She growls. 'All the food is gone in this one too! People have taken all the good things in every one.'

I bite my lip. Maybe we'd be safer trying to get back to the other side of the fence.

Then, I finally see something that gives me hope. I jolt with surprise.

'What is it?' Kay asks.

I point out the window at a tall building in the distance. Someone has just switched on a light.

We rush back down the stairs, but by the time we reach the street my feet have slowed. What if the light isn't a good sign? 'What if it's Wilderness people?' I ask Kay.

'Do Wilderness people know how to get lights on?'

That's a good question. I don't know a lot about Wilderness people and even less about their understanding of electricity. I'm surprised to find that there's any electricity here at all. Where do they get their power from?

'Maybe we should keep away,' I say.

'Light is where people are and where people are is food and water,' Kay says.

I nod. We've got to find water whether it's dangerous or not.

As we move into an area that reminds me of a business sector, the number of tall buildings increases. It makes it harder to keep a fix on the light and at one point we lose it all together. When we find it again we're close enough to see the outline of the huge building it's shining out of.

In front of the building the road curves in a U-shape. Kay spots something on the ground. 'Look,' she says, bending down and lifting a stainless steel kidney dish. 'Shiny. What is it?'

'It's . . .' I notice the markings on the ground. A hatched-out space marked *Ambulance only*. 'I think this place used to be a hospital,' I say.

'A what?'

'It's a place where they send sick people so that they can be made better.'

In the gloom I watch Kay's face as she struggles to comprehend a world in which ill people are met with kindness. When I think about how Kay has been treated I get so angry. Even with myself. I feel like somehow I should have been there with her through all the bad stuff.

'*Blake*,' Kay says in a low voice. I can tell by her tone that it's not good news. I follow her gaze and there, on the other side of the road, is a man. Even in the moonlight his hunched figure radiates illwill.

'Keep moving,' I say. 'Head for the light.' I feel for Kay's hand, but before we even take a step I realise that we have nowhere to aim for.

The light is gone.

The Wilderness man makes a snarling sound in his throat. Is he a cannibal like those boys who attacked me out the back of the Academy? I spin round, hoping that the light will reappear – but it doesn't.

'It was this way,' Kay says, pointing to the right of the hospital.

I can't believe that we took our eyes off it.

There's a metallic clang as the Wilderness man kicks something across the tarmac. He's heading straight for us.

'Run,' Kay says, and she sprints in the direction she pointed. I follow her. We have to find somewhere to hide. When I turn back, the Wilderness man is lumbering towards us. A small part of my brain wonders why they all seem to have difficulty moving, the rest of me just hopes it will slow him down a bit.

The front of the hospital looms up. The ground-floor windows are all boarded. Kay runs down an alley between the main hospital and a lower building next door. There's a dull thump as the Wilderness man hits something else. I follow Kay down the gap between buildings. She's much faster than me. She'll get away and I'll have to take him on. He makes a noise somewhere between a scream and a roar.

I'm so tired from cycling, I'm panting already. He's going to catch me. My ribs seem to be contracting, crushing my lungs. Must keep running.

I'm wrenched to a halt by a hand on my shoulder. Efwurd, it's another one.

'Kay!' I call out. I jab backwards with my elbow and try to twist out of his grip. Kay comes sprinting back towards me. I struggle violently, but I can't break free.

'In here,' a voice near my ear hisses.

I look over my shoulder in surprise. It's not a man that's got hold of me. It's a teenage boy.

Kay's long strides stutter to a halt by my side. She pulls back her arm to punch the boy, but he's too fast for her and grabs her wrist. 'Quick,' he says.

Footsteps smack down the alleyway. The Wilderness man is coming. He spits out a guttural sound like a curse. I let the boy pull me and Kay through a metal door. He slams it behind us and pulls a bolt across. I'm shaking. The footsteps stop outside the door. The man scratches at it. There's a thump. I suck in my breath.

Then nothing.

'Is he gone?' I whisper.

'Probably,' the boy says.

'Are there other entrances?' We're at the end of a long

corridor. There's a solar lantern stood at the bottom of a flight of stairs and by its feeble light I can see the paint on the walls has peeled off in strips, so it looks like the passageway is covered in tattered fabric. The nearest window is boarded up, but a vine has crept through a crack and is snaking down the corridor.

'It's possible he could get in,' the boy says. 'But he doesn't really want to. He knows I have this.' There's a gun in his hand.

I stare at the boy. He's wearing a shirt and jeans and he's well spoken. He looks like any number of boys I knew at the Learning Community. What the hell is a boy like this doing in the Wilderness with a gun?

'They're not even that dangerous,' a little girl says, appearing from under the stairs.

I jump. Kay doesn't.

'Robin, I told you to go upstairs,' the boy says.

The girl scowls and turns to Kay as if the boy hadn't said anything. 'I'm not scared of the Wilderness people at all,' she says. 'You just have to know how to handle them.'

'Really?' I say. She looks about eight years old. Have I completely overestimated the threat the Wilderness people pose?

The girl nods. 'Yeah, in the last couple of months they've hardly killed anyone.'

Kay and I exchange a look. 'Well, that's a relief,' I say.

The girl sizes us up, taking in our filthy Academy uniforms. 'You're not from one of the cells are you?' she says.

Kay shakes her head.

'Robin,' the boy says in a warning tone.

'*Paulo*,' Robin mimics back at him. Her forehead is scrunched again. She seems to be a very cross child.

Paulo shakes his head. 'I'm going to check the other door and then we're all going upstairs.' He walks away without waiting for Robin's response. The light from his torch spotlights an abandoned stretcher halfway down the corridor. I suppress a shudder.

'Hey,' says Robin in a low voice so that Paulo won't hear. 'You're not Wilderness, are you?'

'Do we look like hairy-faced cannibals?' I ask.

'They're not all like that one.' She gestures with her head towards the door. 'Some of them are nice.' She pouts. 'I made friends with a boy, but our captain said I wasn't allowed to talk to him any more.' She rubs her nose with her fist. 'He's called Jed – my friend, not the captain. I like playing with Jed, but they said we're only allowed out to go on missions and if I'm going to be a useful member of the Resistance then—'

'The Resistance?' I say. 'You're the Resistance?' I can't believe it. 'I mean, is this the Resistance? Here?' My vague fears subside. They can't be bad people if they save desperate people like me and Kay, and look after little girls.

'I don't want to stop playing with Jed,' the girl says, ignoring me. 'Do you know . . .' She lowers her voice and brings down her eyebrows as if she is about to tell a secret. 'I hate our captain.'

'What about—' I start, but Kay cuts me off by elbowing me in the ribs.

'It's hard when you can't see your friend, isn't it?' she says to the girl and gives her a sympathetic smile. 'My friend went away too.'

I think of Ali closing her eyes for the last time and I bite the inside of my cheek.

The girl looks Kay up and down. 'I can be your friend if you want,' she says grudgingly, as if she is bestowing a great favour. 'But don't tell anyone. They told me not to talk to anyone from outside.'

'I won't tell it,' Kay says.

Robin looks up. Paulo's torch is coming back down the corridor. Soon his face is visible again.

'Do you need medicine?' Robin asks me, switching to a businesslike tone.

'No, we need to find the Resistance,' I say.

Paulo considers me. 'You've found them,' he says.

Kay beams at me, but my doubts are gathering again. I never imagined the Resistance would be living in a derelict hospital.

'Are you going to let them stay?' Robin asks.

Paulo looks at us and then back to the girl. It's clear that she's asked an awkward question. I want to explain to him that we're here to help, but Robin doesn't stop talking.

'It's not really up to you is it?' she says to Paulo.

Even I can see that this remark hurts Paulo's pride, but Robin is either oblivious or tactless.

'You have to—'

'I know what I need to do, Robin.' He gestures to the stairs. 'This way,' he says to us. We climb the stairs, our feet crunching on the gritty surface of the steps. Robin hops ahead of us. She reaches the top first and swings recklessly on the rail.

'What's your name?' she asks me. Without waiting for an answer she says, 'I think that you sh—'

'Go to bed,' Paulo says.

'You go!'

Kay's eyes widen. No little Special would get away with talking to a senior like that, but Paulo seems unflappable. 'I don't want to report you, Robin,' he says quietly.

'All right, all right, I was going to anyway,' she says and flounces off down the corridor. 'Hope you like being bossed about if you're staying,' she calls over her shoulder.

I try to relax. If our biggest fear is being bossed about maybe things will be okay.

Paulo is unmoved by Robin's dramatics. 'This way,' he says, turning in the opposite direction to her.

On the damp-stained wall in front of us something painted in white shows up in the gloom. I move closer. I've seen it before. When we got out of the pipe into that shack, this is the wonky figure four that was painted on the back of the door.

'What's that?' Kay asks.

'That's our symbol. It shows we're against the Leadership.'

Now I get it. It's not a number four; it's a capital 'L' with a line struck through it.

'We're against the Leadership too,' Kay says. 'I'm Kay.'

'And I'm Blake. We've come—'

'It's better if you save it till ...' He trails off and we follow him in silence down the murky corridor. I assume that he is taking us to the leader of the Resistance, the captain that Robin mentioned, but before we can get there a door opens ahead of us, letting out the pale glow of another solar lantern.

A young man leans out into our path. 'Paulo,' he says, like an accusation. 'I appreciate that for you the passing of time is merely a dull interlude between your unremarkable childhood and your unremarked upon death, but some of us have many splendid and important things to get done—' He suddenly notices me and Kay. 'Who the hell is this?'

Paulo seems paralysed by the other boy. 'I found them,' he says eventually.

I know how people like this work. We haven't got time to stand about while he makes fun of us. 'If you don't mind,' I break in. 'We were just on our way somewhere.'

He turns on me in a way that almost makes me shrink back. 'If only I'd got that idiot detector fixed,' he says. 'Then I wouldn't have to listen to you telling me that you think you're too important to speak to me. In fact, you'd never have made it into the building. How *did* you make it into the building? I was hoping that those guys with the guns might put people off, unless of course, one of the

70

guys with the guns let you in. Paulo?' He talks really fast. Kay is staring hard, trying to follow the rapid flow of words.

A number of faces have gathered in the dark doorway behind the boy to listen to this exchange.

'A Wilderness man was chasing them,' Paulo says. 'They needed help.'

'Actually,' I say stepping towards the boy and opening my palms so that he knows I mean him no harm, 'I think that we could help you.'

All the eyes are on me. My smile falters. Some of my fear of the Resistance rises again. They don't seem too pleased with my offer of help. In fact the atmosphere is decidedly tense. I look at Kay.

She gives me a questioning look. 'You are the people who hate The Leader, aren't you?' she asks the bully.

Paulo nods his head, but the young man says, 'Who wants to know?'

'We've come from the other side of the fence,' I say. 'We were in an Academy and, well, actually we managed to lead a rebellion and many of us escaped.' I try to sound modest.

'You're saying that you're the one that started the trouble in that Academy?'

'Yes, that was me.' I'm surprised that they seem to have heard about it. Perhaps the story of our success is being passed around the underground.

'The one that burnt down?'

71

'Yes.'

There's a silence and a prickle runs up my spine. Maybe everything I heard about the Resistance is true. These people aren't reacting at all the way I expected them to. I take a step closer to Kay.

'Shoot them,' someone behind the boy says.

And the rest of the faces call out in agreement.

12

A wave of terror crashes through me. Why do they want to shoot us?

'But we're on your side.' My voice cracks.

'The hell you are,' the young man says and he lunges towards me. Before I know what's happening he's got my arms twisted up behind my back. They don't get Kay so easily. It takes three of the crowd to pin her to the filthy floor. Even then she's spitting and cursing.

I'm too astounded to do anything. Why do they want to kill us? Are they really the bloodthirsty savages the Leadership always said they were?

My hands are bound and the boy shoves me roughly into someone else's grasp. I can feel his hefty presence behind me.

'Shoot them,' someone says again.

'No!' I say. 'There's been some sort of misunderstanding, let me talk to whoever is in charge.'

'A misunderstanding?' the young man says. 'Is that

what you call the brutal oppression of a nation, a misunderstanding? Because around here there are what you might call consequences for that sort of thing. You might call them consequences. I call it a bullet to the brain.'

'We haven't oppressed anyone!' I say. 'We've been fighting the oppression. We want to join the Resistance.'

'If you want fighting, let me up and do fair fighting,' Kay says from the ground.

'I don't want to fight you, tiny girl,' the young man says. 'I just want you dead. But first I have a few questions. Take them to the lock-up,' he says to the people holding me and Kay.

And we're dragged away.

Being pulled through the dark, derelict hospital doesn't help my terror. Most of the windows are boarded up, but the solar lanterns give the flaking paint a ghostly glow. We pass a reception desk stacked with files covered in decades of dust. A sign for Radiology hangs crookedly from the ceiling, swaying in the draft.

We're hauled up another flight of stairs and pushed through an old waiting room with padded chairs and an empty fish tank. A low table is covered by ancient magazines with curled edges.

At the end of another corridor we're shoved into a room. The door is locked behind us and we're left in the darkness.

'What the hell happened there?' I ask.

I lift my bound hands and try the door. It's solid and the handle holds firm.

74

'I don't understand,' Kay says. 'Ty said the Resistance would help us kill The Leader. But they want to kill us.'

'It's a mistake. They seem to think we're connected with the Leadership.'

'But we're not.'

'No.'

'But they don't ... what-do-you-say?'

'They don't believe us.'

There's enough moonlight coming through the one unboarded window to make out that the room is empty except for several chairs and a piece of medical equipment that is attached to the wall with a giant jointed metal arm. I walk under it to look out of the window.

'We're too high to escape,' I say. 'It's a sheer drop.'

'They can't keep thinking we're Leadership,' Kay says. 'They'll have to know it soon, won't they?'

'Yes, I'm sure they'll work it out eventually.'

I only hope they do it before they shoot us.

'When they come back, when the door opens, let's punch them,' Kay says.

'It won't be much of an attack with our hands tied,' I say.

'I can do attack with my feet better than lots of people can do with all things.'

Despite the situation, I laugh. 'I know. But I can't. And there are more of them than us. Anyway, surely they'll send someone in charge to talk to us and then we can just explain things.'

'Hmm.'

I ought to make her understand that not all adults are like the enforcers at the Academy, but a wave of tiredness washes over me. 'I wish I was at home, in my bed,' I say.

'Come here,' Kay says.

I push a chair next to hers and sit down. Kay shifts a little closer to me. Our upper arms are touching.

'Blake,' she says.

Something in the tone of her voice catches on to something inside me and I feel it pulling up through me like a zipper. I find myself turning towards her in the same moment that Kay twists to face me. I want to catch her up in my arms, but of course my stupid hands are tied. Her face brushes mine and then our mouths meet.

Eventually, Kay pulls away. 'You're right,' she says. 'We can explain and it will all be okay.'

After a while she falls asleep on my shoulder and I sit very still, trying to believe her.

I doze fitfully for several hours. When I wake and my eyes adjust to the darkness, the first thing I see is the metal arm reaching towards me and I almost shrink away before I remind myself it's not going to move by itself. I'm trying to gather a mouthful of saliva to swallow to ease my dry throat when a horrible thought occurs to me. I need to pee. I try to think about something else, but now that the thought has crept in it's like an alarm that I can't switch off. How is this even possible? My throat aches

76

with dryness. I've barely drunk a thing in the last couple of days and yet . . . I definitely need to go.

Kay stirs. I feel shy.

She sits up bolt upright. 'What's happening?'

'Nothing. It's okay. Nothing's happened. No one has come yet.'

'I need water,' Kay says.

I stand up and press my ear to the door. I can't hear anything.

'Are you okay?' Kay asks. 'Why are you all moving?'

I realise that I'm fidgeting. 'I'm fine.' I could do without having to discuss this with Kay. 'I'm just frustrated. When are they going to give us a chance to sort this out? When are we going to get to talk to an adult?' I don't add that I'm angry with myself that we came here in the first place.

Hell, I really need to pee. I can't believe that there's some idiot threatening to kill us and all I can think about is my bladder. This is not how I want to spend my last moments on earth. I should just go. But where? Efwurding efwurd. If I wet myself in front of Kay then they may as well shoot me.

Kay moves towards me. 'What is it Blake? You can tell me.'

She touches my arm with her bound hands and I remember the kissing last night and I want to kiss her again, but I am bursting. I shift away from her. 'I just . . . need to go.'

'Go?'

77

'You know, to the bathroom.'

'Oh.'

I bang on the door. 'Hello! Can anyone hear me? I want to speak to someone in charge.'

I think I hear someone moving about out there, but there's no reply.

Kay hammers on the door. 'We need water! Blake needs—'

'You don't need to tell them that,' I interrupt. I assume that either everyone is asleep in another part of the hospital or that they're ignoring us, but a few moments later the door opens and a boy in his late teens walks in carrying a solar lantern. We can't be much of a priority if this is who they're sending to talk to us.

'I am Alrye,' he says, closing the door behind him. 'I need to ask you some questions.'

'Can I speak to whoever is in charge?' I ask.

He shakes his head.

'Well, can I use your toilet?'

His forehead puckers. He wasn't expecting that and now he thinks I'm trying to pull a fast one. He shakes his head again. Damn it, I can't hold on much longer.

'I really am quite desperate.'

'No.'

'Well, I can see that cleanliness isn't your first priority here and I guess if you're really going to blow our heads off then someone is going to be clearing up some mess pretty soon anyway ...'

Alrye frowns. He opens the door and gestures for someone to come in. It's another boy about his age, but much larger, with the broadest shoulders I've ever seen. He's obviously one of the heavy squad.

'Take him to the toilets,' Aryle says to him, pointing at me. 'Quickly.'

I don't have to be told to move fast. I'm down the corridor like a shot. Our footsteps echo around the tiles as we walk into the toilets. Shoulders holds up his lantern and I see rust stains from the ancient pipes creeping across the walls. I move towards the urinals, but Shoulders says, 'They don't work. We don't have water for it. Here.' He points to a bucket.

I struggle to get my trousers undone with my tightly bound wrists and then I enjoy what is probably the greatest sense of relief in my life. Until I remember that we're about to be shot.

Now that I'm not about to wet myself I can think clearly. As I fumble about with my buttons I consider kneeing Shoulders in the groin. I don't think there's much point. Even if I managed to floor him, I'm not leaving without Kay.

On our way back to the room I scan the gloomy corridor looking for something, anything, that might be of use to us. Every door we pass has a faded sign about using hand sanitizer before entering. We walk under a section of buckled ceiling with wires dangling down like tangled hair. The whole place is falling apart. As we approach the lock-up room Shoulders swings his lantern from one hand to the other and illuminates a noticeboard on the wall. A newspaper article pinned there catches my eye. Unlike everything else in this hospital, the colours are still bright.

'Wait,' I say with such force that Shoulders actually stops.

'What?'

But I don't answer because I'm staring open-mouthed at the newspaper. There's an aerial photo of a large red brick building with a clock tower that I recognise straight away, even though it's half obscured by smoke and flames.

The headline reads: *HUNDREDS DEAD IN ACADEMY ATTACK BY TERRORISTS.*

'What the hell is this?' I say.

'You should know,' Shoulders says with venom. 'You're the ones that did it. And then you blame it all on us. You make me sick.'

'I didn't do anything,' I say. 'I mean I was in that Academy but—'

'I don't get it. I really don't get it. How can you kill people and just not care?'

'I've never killed anyone!' A plunging sensation in my stomach reminds me that this isn't true any more. There was that cannibal boy in the woods behind the Academy.

'You're Leadership. You've all got blood on your hands.'

'I am not—'

'Shut it.' He knocks on the lock-up room door and Alrye lets us in.

Kay is shaking her head. 'We're Leader-hating too, we're the same,' she's saying to Alrye.

'I'm not so sure that we *are* on the same side any more,' I say. 'I've just seen a newspaper …' King hell, Kay doesn't know what a newspaper is. 'Like the Info but on paper,' I say quickly. 'Not like your Info, not lies. Well, fewer lies. Maybe.' Efwurd, I don't know what is true any more.

'What's your point?' Alrye asks.

'It says you set fire to the Academy.'

'Me?' Alrye says.

'They wrote "Terrorists", but that means the Resistance.'

'That's completely untrue and you know it,' Alrye says.

I don't know it. I don't know anything any more. 'You've got it pinned up for all to see. You're proud of it.'

'We've got it pinned up so everyone can see the lies that are told by your lot.'

'My lot? *I am not from the Leadership.*'

Shoulders sneers in disgust. 'We know you are. We got tipped off you were coming. A boy and a girl pretending to be refugees from the burnt-down Academy and–'

Alrye shoots him a look that shuts him up, but finally I see why they don't trust us; they think we're Leadership spies disguised as Academy kids.

'We really are from the Academy,' I say.

'We're not saying we're people that we're not,' Kay says. 'We came to help you.'

'You're disgusting,' Shoulders says.

Kay is angry. 'Don't you bad-word me.' She squares up

to him. 'Do you want a fight? Stop your bad talking and fight then.'

'Whoa,' I say.

Alrye cuts between them, gently pushing Shoulders away. 'Let's all keep calm. Sit down, you two.'

I pull Kay down on to a chair.

'I'm going to ask you some questions and if you answer them then we won't need any unpleasantness,' Alrye says.

There's a look in his eye that gives me a horrible feeling about the unpleasantness that will follow once we get to the end of the questions anyway.

'Tell me how you found the hospital,' Alrye says.

'We saw a light.'

Alrye tuts and shakes his head. I don't think that light was supposed to be on.

'So the Leadership don't know the location of this hospital?' he asks.

'I don't know. I'm not from the Leadership, so I can't tell you,' I say.

Alrye sighs.

'Let me make them talk,' Shoulders says.

Alrye shakes his head. 'I'd rather do this without you getting hurt,' he says to Kay.

'If you were fair people and I had my hands then I would get you hurt,' she says to him. 'I would get all the lot of you hurt because you're stupid. We *are* from the Academy. Ty sent us. Don't you know Ty?'

Alrye looks at Shoulders. He's obviously considering taking him up on his offer.

'I want to talk to whoever is in charge,' I say.

He opens his mouth to say no.

'If I see the person in charge I will tell them everything. The truth. Everything that they want to know.'

Alrye stares hard at me. I hold his gaze.

'I can't just go waking important people up,' Alrye says, 'but I'll speak to someone.' He walks out and Shoulders follows, leaving his lantern behind him, but not before he has shot me and a Kay a look of disgust. The door closes behind them.

'They're not believing us,' Kay says.

'I know.'

She gets up and walks around the room. In the light of the lantern I can see the floor is speckled with paint flakes and some kind of droppings. The Resistance have let the hospital fall into a state of decay. I wonder if the roof is stable. I stare up at the metal arm. I think it's some kind of imaging equipment.

'We should go,' Kay says after a while.

'I wish we could, but I have no idea how to get out.'

Kay thinks. 'Maybe we have to talk to them more,' she says.

'We've tried talking to them. It's obvious that everything we heard about them is true. They're ignorant, violent thugs.'

She gives me a long look. 'That's what you thought

84

about me, isn't it? You thought I was a stupid Special who was all fighting and nasty.'

'No! I mean . . . well, I guess it took me a while to get to know you. But this is totally different.'

'Just because you've spoken to a person it doesn't mean you know them.'

If someone threatens to shoot me then I think I know enough about them, but I don't say this because the door opens and the bossy young man who shouted at Paulo earlier walks in.

My heart sinks. 'You're joking,' I say. 'I asked for the person in charge. What are you in charge of – the department of sarcasm?'

'That's right, sunshine, and if you weren't about to die I'd want you on my team.'

I give Kay a look. I know everything I need to know about this idiot. He's an arrogant bastard. And we'll be lucky if we can convince him not to hurt us.

'My name is Ven,' he says.

'You're not an adult,' Kay says.

'I see you're the brains of this shambling duo. Well my genius friend, in a spirit of frankness I feel I should let you know that the best you can hope for now is a painless death. And the way to achieve that is to be completely cooperative.'

I think the only word of that Kay understands is 'death'. She clenches her fists, but she can't do what she'd like to with them; her hands are still bound.

'Do you know what?' I say. 'I heard a lot of stories about how stupidly brutal the Resistance was. I was hoping that was one of the Leadership's lies, but it turns out to be true.'

'True, except the stupidly part.'

'How can you call yourself a resistance?' I snap. 'Shouldn't you be helping people?'

'Although our acquaintance is going to be brief, I think it may still be useful for you to know that the only people I'm interested in helping are the Resistance. You know what would be in the interests of the Resistance?'

I shake my head.

'Killing you.'

'I want to speak to your boss,' I say.

'Your options are death now, or you can tell me every-thing you know before you die. I reckon that will buy you an extra three minutes or so. Three and a quarter, if you list your life's achievements.'

I open my mouth, but Ven won't let me get a word in.

'Do the Leadership know the location of this hospital?'

'I don't know.'

'Are the Leadership planning an attack on the Resistance?'

'We don't know,' Kay says. 'We don't know the Leadership.'

He takes a gun from his belt.

King hell. He's not really going to kill us, is he? 'This is ridiculous. We're not the enemy.'

'I've found it's safest to make my own decisions about who's on my side.'

'We haven't done anything wrong!'

'You people have beaten, abused and manipulated everyone from babies to pensioners. And I'm not the merciful type.'

He lifts his gun and presses it to my temple.

Efwurding hell, he's going to kill me.

'Stop!' Kay says.

Ven makes an exaggerated gesture of tiredness and turns to face her without taking the gun from my head.

'I know a thing,' she says.

'We should all take pride in even the smallest of achievements, but hush a bit while I kill your little friend, will you?'

'I know a thing you need to know.'

'Well, it's not how to construct a sentence, is it?'

Kay shakes her head at his unintelligible words and persists with, 'You need to know it.'

'Don't tell me what I NEED!' Ven roars. His anger flares up like a gas flame. The lazy-eyed sarcasm is gone. 'What I *need* is a world where people like you don't collude with a corrupt government that destroys lives. Do you know the answer to that? Hey? I'll tell you the answer to that. We get the efwurding bastards who are responsible and we shoot them one by one.'

He turns his gun on Kay and I know that he is going to shoot her.

His finger flexes.

I spring from my chair; the movement causes Ven to take his eyes off Kay and in a split second she kicks out a foot and knocks the gun out of Ven's hand. We all lunge towards the gun, but Ven reaches it first and turns it on me once again.

'The Leader admitted it!' I shout.

Ven is all composure again. He just looks at me.

'He admitted how the Leadership works,' I say in a rush. 'All the bad stuff they've done, we filmed it.'

The gun is still on me.

'Go on,' Ven says.

'When The Leader came to the Academy he thoroughly incriminated himself,' I say. 'He admitted that corporal punishment is used in Academies and that students are deprived of food and given electric shocks.'

'Did he now?'

I've got his attention. If they really are interested in taking down the government then we could be of use to them and maybe he won't kill us.

'More than that,' I say. 'What would really shock the public is the crazy way The Leader was talking about sacrifices that have to be made. He sounded like a mad man who'd happily sell out any number of children to serve his purpose.'

'Where is it?'

'Where's what?'

'This recording.' Ven says it as if he doubts it exists. 'Have you got it?'

'Well, not exactly. It's in a safe place. I managed to engage the support of a journalist and—'

'So *they've* got it?' I feel his patience snap like an elastic band.

'Yes,' I say. 'But ...'

He extends his gun arm. Oh God.

'No!' Kay says. 'No, she hasn't!'

'Hasn't what?' Ven says, without taking his narrowed eyes off me.

'Janna hasn't got the recording.' Kay's eyes flash with triumph. 'I have.'

14

Ven relaxes his arm. 'Finally you're telling me something worth staying awake for. Where is it?'

Kay reaches into her pocket with her bound hands. 'It's here,' she says.

'Let's take a look then, shall we?'

'You won't be able to view it. You need a computer,' I say.

He turns on me. 'We have a number of computers. You really ought to work on that superior tone, by the way. In my experience it's the people who think they're better than everyone who get their throats slit first.'

I didn't mean to sound rude, but a derelict hospital isn't where I expect to find the latest technology.

'Give it to me,' he says to Kay.

'No,' she says. 'You take us to the computer.'

They stare at each other in deadlock.

'Why must you people waste my time?' Ven asks. 'Fine. But just so you don't get any big ideas, let me tell you that every exit from this hospital has an armed guard on it. If you make a run for it they'll shoot.' He unlocks the door and leads us down the corridor.

'How the efwurd did you manage to get hold of the recording?' I whisper to Kay.

She looks at me sideways. 'I think the thing that you want to say is "thank you".'

I can't work it out. Kay was never even alone with Janna. And it's not as if they're on friendly terms. She must have stolen it from her. 'Thank you,' I say. 'I promise you I really am quite grateful that you managed to get the mad man to lower his gun.' I can't imagine Janna's rage when she finds the AV bug missing. 'I'm just surprised. How did you do it?'

Kay smiles. 'I didn't fight her just to punch her shiny face.'

Oh. I remember their scrap at the warehouse and I'm caught somewhere between shock and awe. I should stop being surprised by how smart and cunning Kay continues to be.

We follow Ven down the stairs and through a maze of corridors. Once, I hear voices coming from behind a closed door, but it's still dark and I assume that most people are asleep. Finally, he ushers us into a small windowless room. There are three desks with computers on. In contrast to what we've seen so far, the desks are clean and the computers are dust free. Ven switches one on and unties my hands.

I reach out to touch Kay on the arm.

Ven tuts. 'Come on then, show me something that will make me stop wanting to kill you.'

I'm starting to suspect that even if Ven believed that we want to get rid of the Leadership too, he would still be sniping at us. 'Why are you even in the Resistance?' I ask.

He catches my meaning straight away. 'I don't have to like you to want you to be free.'

I bite down a response to this and take a look at the computer. I expected pre-war technology that would be incompatible with the AV bug that Janna used to get the footage, but this hardware is brand new. 'Where did you get these from?' I ask.

'You'd be surprised what we can get our hands on,' Ven says. 'There are people on the other side who are prepared to help us.'

I don't show it, but this shocks me. I find it hard to imagine anyone on the other side of the fence having anything to do with this lot, and if they're all like Ven then I'm amazed they accept the help. Maybe they're not all like him. Maybe he's just some jumped-up trainee who's on duty during the graveyard shift. I hope so.

I can feel Ven's eyes on me.

'Just let me pair the computer with the AV bug then I can download the content,' I say.

'How did Janna get pictures of The Leader on that bug thing?' Kay asks.

'At the press conference the only cameras allowed were

the official ones. Janna hid this in her dress. It pretends to be a base station for the Leadership's broadcast cameras and tricks them into streaming their footage to it.'

Kay's forehead creases. She's about to ask me to explain a lot of words.

'Basically it doesn't take the pictures; it just steals them from other devices.'

'Yes, yes,' Ven says. 'Come on.'

I flip through Janna's files. The most recent one doesn't have a title, but next to the thumbnail image is the date of The Leader's visit to the Academy. I open it. Behind me Ven stops still. The screen flickers. Then we see exactly what I hoped we wouldn't.

Nothing.

15

The screen is black. In the centre it says: *ENTER DECRYPTION PASSWORD*.

'Hell,' I say.

'What is it?' Kay asks.

'The recording, it's encrypted.' I look at Ven. 'That means—'

'I know what it means,' he interrupts. 'Do you know what it means for *you*? It means that I've still got no proof that this is what you say it is. Or that you are who you say you are.'

'Wait a minute,' I say, clicking about on the mouse. Ven stands right behind me. He's silent, but his presence feels heavy on my skin. I have to suppress the urge to lean away from him. I mustn't let him see that I am afraid. I tinker for several minutes, but I can tell almost immediately that I won't be able to access the footage. The best I can do is to enlarge the thumbnail image. It shows The

Leader centre stage, glaring out into the audience. I turn to see what Ven makes of it.

'That could be anywhere and he could be saying anything.'

'It could. But it's not. If I'm telling the truth then you're letting some really powerful stuff slip through your fingers.'

He's thinking. 'I need to know more about you two. Tell me how you claim to have ended up here.'

So I tell him. As soon as I start to talk I realise that I can't mention that Leadership men were sent to kill me because I'm The Leader's illegitimate son and he wanted to get rid of me. Instead, I tell him how I was a hotshot at the Leaning Community, but that I got transferred to an Academy when I started snooping around the Leadership's computer records, which is partially true. Kay fills him in on what it was like at the Academy and how we made plans to escape. Then I tell Ven about the press conference and the way The Leader admitted what was happening at the Academies and the crazy way he acted.

'Even though it didn't get aired on TV the Leadership were still really angry. Guards tried to take away the journalists. But the Specials rioted. A fire started and it descended into chaos.'

'Why weren't you caught?'

'The journalist, Janna, she got us out in a van. Her friend Ty—'

I see a flicker in Ven's eyes.

'Do you know Ty?' I ask.

'Never heard of him.' But I'm sure he's lying.

'Ty helped us,' Kay says. 'He said he knew you lot and that you could help us get The Leader.'

Ven's face is emotionless. 'How did you get through the fence?'

Kay relates her conversation with Ty about the tunnel and how we escaped through it when the warehouse was raided by guards.

'I wouldn't use it again if I were you,' I say. 'It leaks.' I can almost feel the cold water swilling around me. 'Badly.'

Ven is silent. 'I could certainly do a lot with that footage,' he says.

'But we can't see it,' Kay says.

'We've got the recording,' he says. 'What we need is the password. And you're going to get it from your journalist friend.'

'You want us to go looking for Janna and persuade her to give us her password?'

He nods.

It's a terrible idea. 'I'm not trying to be uncooperative, but I don't think it's safe for us to go back to the other side. We did have a squadron of guards after us.'

Ven raises an eyebrow.

'I don't even know where we would find Janna,' I add. 'She was supposed to come back to us and she didn't turn up.'

'You'd better start thinking.'

How have I got us into this crazy situation where this boy is ordering me about? Is he even acting with his superiors' knowledge? 'What exactly will you do to me if I say no?' I ask.

'It's not what I'm going to do to you ...' He turns to Kay. 'It's what I'm going to do to her.'

'You are not going to lay a finger on her,' I say, narrowing my eyes.

'Blake,' Kay says, giving me a warning look.

'I think she's sending you secret messages,' Ven says to me in a stage whisper. 'I think she wants you to stop being an idiot.'

'All of you can stop being an idiot,' Kay says.

'That's nice from someone who seems never to have learnt how to talk.'

'You say more about my talking or try to hurt us then I will break your fingers.'

Ven ignores Kay. 'This is how it works,' he says to me. 'If that footage exists then I want to be able to use it. You say we need a password, so you're going to find this woman with the password. But just in case your story isn't true I want to make sure you don't get any smart ideas about running back to the Leadership. You'll leave your pixie girlfriend behind as guarantee.'

I run a hand over my face. I'm not sure it's a smart idea to go running after Janna, but if I refuse Ven's just going to start waving that gun about again. Besides, I'm not against getting access to the footage.

97

'It's not going to be easy,' I say. 'I'm going to need some help. I'll need to look up where Janna's newspaper's office is and I'll need clothes and someone to show me the way back to the fence.'

'You'll have some help,' he says. His eyes flash with amusement. 'I'm coming with you.'

'You should take me, not Blake,' Kay says.

Ven smirks at her. 'I know that you won't be able to empathise,' he says to me, 'but it really does get very tiresome when girls are constantly throwing themselves at you.'

'Take me to find Janna,' Kay says. 'I'm a gooder ... I mean, a *better* fighter. And I'm fast.'

'Clearly. And this journalist – is she your friend too?'

Kay doesn't blink. 'Yes.'

'I think we'll stick to the original plan.'

'But—'

'It's all right, Kay,' I say. 'He's got a point. I don't think Janna would even talk to you.'

'Where does your friend work?'

'She writes for *The Post*.' At least that's where Janna worked when I first met her when she came to interview me and Wilson at the Learning Community. I hope she's still there. I reach for the keyboard so I can look up the address but Ven swats my hand out of the way.

'I'll do it,' he says.

I roll my eyes. 'I'm hardly going to escape via the computer.'

'Why not? Lacking the skill?'

98

'Blake is the best at computers,' Kay says. 'At his school he got all the prizes.'

I've learnt not to boast, but I can't help the warm feeling that comes with Kay doing it for me. Ven ignores both of us.

'How can he find where Janna is on the computer?' Kay asks me.

'It's on the Network. You don't have it at the Academy, but most computers are connected to the Central Information Network. It's like ... a big store of information and you can find out things.'

'You can find out what the Leadership want you to find out,' Ven corrects.

I shift uncomfortably in my seat. Of course, I've always known that the Leadership control the Network, but it's only now that I fully appreciate what that means. For some reason this leaves me feeling annoyed with Ven. 'If you've got the skills,' I say, 'you can find things they don't want you to know. Like I said, I hacked into the classified section of The Register once and—'

'You did mention it.'

I close my mouth.

Ven laughs. 'If you turn out to be genuine, maybe I'll make use of your computer skills later. We need to get moving.' He takes a communicator out of his pocket. 'Alrye, get up here,' he says.

Ven shuts down the computer and, after a minute, Alrye obligingly appears in the doorway.

'Take the girl back to the lock-up room,' Ven says to him.

I touch Kay's hand as she passes me. 'I'll be back. I promise.'

Alrye closes the door behind them and we hear Kay say, 'If you get near me I will smash you.'

I really shouldn't worry about her.

Ven looks me over and wrinkles his nose. 'And you'd better get clean.'

He takes me to a laundry room. Although the paint on the walls is bubbled and blistered like a bad skin condition, the floor has been swept clean and the sweet scent of soap almost overpowers the thick musty smell that hangs about the hospital. Ven quickly picks out a shirt, trousers, underwear and socks and pushes them into my arms. Further down the corridor he deposits me in a bathroom.

'Hurry up,' Ven says, switching on the solar lantern in the corner and closing the door behind him.

The room is cold and damp. None of the taps work, but someone has left me a jug of hot water along with half a bar of soap and a towel. I strip off my reeking Academy uniform and stand in the cracked bath to wash. The surrounding tiles are spotted with mould and there's a thick gash of rust running from the cold tap to the plughole, but at least the bath is empty, unlike the toilet, which seems to be full of fallen plaster.

It feels really good to get clean. When I put on the

freshly laundered clothes Ven left me I inhale deeply and savour the feeling of clean cotton on my skin.

It takes me some time to sort myself out and I wonder whether Ven has gone to talk to his superiors. I'm expecting to be whisked off to speak to someone when I open the bathroom door, but instead I find Ven waiting for me. He hands me another pile of clothes and a backpack. I recognise the red shirt and trousers as a Leadership guard's uniform.

'Put them in the bag,' he says. 'You might need them later.'

I notice that he's got a backpack too, but further questions die on my lips because he hands me a bottle of water and all I can think about is how good it is to gulp it down. Next he produces a chunk of bread from his pocket.

'Eat and walk,' he says.

I match his long strides while I chew the bread. I force myself to eat slowly. I don't want Ven to think I'm an animal.

'Your fairy friend sends her love,' Ven says. 'In fact she licked her lips and made obscene gestures.'

'What?' I feel myself blushing.

Ven laughs. 'You two are disgusting. Actually, she said, "Tell him to not get killed." Which is even funnier really.'

That sounds more like Kay.

'They won't hurt her, will they? Because if any—'

'Keep your voice down. People are still sleeping.'

Ven takes me down the stairs. When we reach the

101

ground floor someone in pyjamas calls down the corridor, 'Where are you going?'

It's the little girl from last night, Robin. Ven ignores her.

'Can I come?' she asks, rushing to catch us up.

I wince when I see her bare feet on the filthy floor.

'No,' Ven says, without bothering to look at her.

'I could help,' Robin whines, but Ven is already striding through a back door guarded by a young woman with a gun. He gives her a look which clearly says she is not to let Robin follow us.

The door closes and the cool air hits me.

'Stay beside me,' Ven says, 'and keep your eyes open. It's not safe out here.'

I look around. The black sky is just starting to turn purple. It's hard to see anything, except Ven beside me. Given how much he seems to think of himself and how much he clearly enjoys bossing other people about, I'm surprised that he is personally supervising me. Maybe his boss told him to do it. Or perhaps he's sneaking me out early before anyone in charge even knows I'm here. Still, it can't hurt to get hold of that password, and if Janna can tell Ven the truth about what happened at the Academy, maybe then I can get some help from his bosses to destroy the Leadership.

Ven is oblivious to my stare. He leads me across a stretch of concrete and into the old ambulance garages.

'Are we going in an ambulance?'

'No.' He points behind the rusting ambulance. 'We're going in this.'

I don't know much about cars, but this is a seriously flashy-looking vehicle. It's black and low to the ground.

'Get in,' Ven says.

At the Learning Community we had a bus and occasionally they'd take us out for trips – museums and galleries mostly. On public holidays like The Leader's birthday we might go to a park or beauty spot. The bus seats were upholstered in some prickly stuff like carpet. The seats in this car are smooth and soft and caramel-coloured.

Ven reverses out of the garage. I don't want to show it, but I'm impressed by his driving. He pulls around the hospital and once we're on the main road he accelerates away. I grip the side of the seat. I've never travelled so fast.

'You're awfully quiet, Leadership,' Ven says eventually.

'If you really think I'm from the Leadership why are you doing this? I could lead you right into a trap.'

'It's nice that you're using your razor-sharp mind to think of me, but I had arrived at that conclusion myself.'

'So you trust me then?'

'No. I'm going to trust the only thing I've seen of you that I can believe.'

'What's that?'

'You've got it bad for that girl.'

'What if I have?'

'I'm sure that you'd do anything to keep her safe, so I'll just let you know that her safety and my safety are now inextricably linked.'

'How?'

'If I'm not back by nightfall, Alrye is under orders to kill her.'

I stare at Ven. He can't really have the authority to have anyone killed, can he? One thing is clear: I've got to get back to Kay as soon as possible. I remember Ven's expression when he was pointing a gun at my head. There's no way I'm going to be able to convince him to take me back and just let us go. I'm going to have to make him understand that we're not a threat. I need to gain his trust, establish a relationship with him. I struggle for a conversation topic.

'Can many people in the Resistance drive?' I ask.

'Yep. We all drive.'

'All the adults?'

'All everybody.'

'The kids too?'

'Soon as they're big enough to see over the wheel.'

'Isn't that dangerous?'

Ven barks a laugh. 'They're in danger every minute of every day. And not from driving on empty roads. They need to be able to drive, in case of emergencies. And we've got a hell of a lot of emergencies just waiting to happen.'

I can't think of anything helpful to say so we don't speak for a while. I watch the sun coming up over the ruin-strewn Wilderness. Sometimes bomb damage has left roads blocked with piles of rubble. But Ven has clearly made this journey before; he always knows a way through even if it involves driving straight across a park. We drive under a flyover bridge with a hole blown through its middle. Ven steers expertly around the chunks of fallen concrete. I thought I was getting used to seeing the destruction caused by bombs, but I'm shocked to see such a massive strong structure in pieces. The slabs of concrete are so large that I can't comprehend the sheer force that must have been involved to blow them out of the bridge. Imagine your district being shaken by blasts that powerful every night.

As we're passing through another destroyed town, I ask Ven a question that's been scraping away at my insides.

'How are we going to get back to the other side?' I can't bear the thought of going back underground.

Ven turns to look at me with what seems to be a combination of irritation and disgust.

'I mean, I'm sure you know what you're doing,' I gabble. 'It's just that we came in a cable duct and that filled up with water – and I was thinking about those patrols that the guards do along the fence ...' I trail off.

'I know the timings of the patrols,' he says. 'And I know how to get to the other side without drowning.'

I remember the feeling of the walls of the tunnel constricting around me; I dig my nails into my palm and try to block out all thoughts of suffocating.

It doesn't work.

By the time the distinctive outline of the border fence comes into view on the horizon I'm light-headed with dread. I can see on the dashboard computer screen that we've travelled almost seventy miles. Ven has driven so fast that it has taken us less than an hour.

Ven stops in the remains of a street of shops and leads me into a collapsed shop. We have to crawl through a broken window and under a slanting steel beam. My shirt is stuck to my back with sweat. I suck in air. Ven's done this before and he's still here. It has to be safe. The shop seems to have sold appliances and, as we scramble under the caved-in ceiling, I see a collapsed shelf of kitchen gadgets in old-fashioned packaging and a row of ancient-looking washing machines. When we reach a doorway with steps leading down to a basement, it's a relief to be able to stand up again, but all hopes I had of avoiding going back underground die.

The basement is dank and crammed with mouldering boxes. My heart is beating so hard that my chest aches. I mustn't let Ven know I am afraid. We're going to find Janna and the password and then I can get back to Kay and make sure that she's okay. The fact that I'm a miserable coward afraid of small spaces is not going to stop me.

Beyond the rows of dead stock Ven opens a cupboard door. Inside the cupboard is the entrance to a tunnel. I let out my breath as quietly as I can when I see that it's big enough to walk upright in. Ven hands me a torch and I grip it hard as we make our way into the chill damp of the tunnel. I steel myself not to ask how far we have to go. I put one foot in front of the other. I don't look up to imagine cracks in the ceiling and I don't let my shaking legs break into a run. I am still afraid, but I am holding my fear instead of it holding me. We reach another door and I've done it.

We're in the basement of a house. The tunnel entrance is concealed behind a false wall. Ven moves it to the side and we tiptoe upstairs. We climb out through a back window and into an overgrown garden.

I'm thankful to be in the open air. 'Do the people who live here know about the tunnel?' I ask.

Ven looks at me. 'It would take a special kind of stupid to not realise that you had a tunnel to the Wilderness in

107

your basement. And since this place isn't inhabited by any relative of yours, yes, they know.'

As Ven closes the garden gate behind him I notice that the Resistance symbol is scratched into the paintwork beside the latch.

'Isn't it a bit dangerous having that there where anyone can see it?' I ask.

He narrows his eyes. 'How do you know about our symbol?'

'Paulo told me. And anyway, it's all over the hospital, I could hardly have missed it.'

Ven is already striding away.

I look at the gate again; I suppose that there are a lot of other scratches too. When I step away from the gate the symbol isn't so obvious.

We leave the residential area and take the metro. Our carriage is almost empty except for a few morning shoppers. I'm surprised when Ven swipes the reader with travel cards for both of us. I resist the urge to ask where he got them from because I know that he'll just give me a smart answer. But I am starting to think the Resistance might be better organised than I first thought. My heart starts to beat a little faster when I think about how they could help me stage a coup. How I could come face to face with The Leader and punish him for everything that he's done. I realise that I'm gripping the edge of my seat hard. I try to concentrate on reading a poster opposite me. I mustn't get ahead of myself. I need to get Ven on side and make sure Kay is safe first.

Janna's office is in the media sector of my old district. The train speeds across the district, passing so close to my Learning Community that I can almost see in the windows. What are they doing there now? What if I was still there? I feel an ache for something that's gone that I will never be able to get back again.

'That's my old school,' I say, almost to myself.

Ven looks out the window then back at me. 'That explains why you're all misty-eyed. Nothing like returning to the site of your childhood indoctrination of hate and bigotry to make you feel nostalgic.'

My jaw tightens. 'I'm not saying I want to go back. I know now that they taught us lies. But it was my home for most of my life.'

'Mmm, touching,' Ven says. 'Moving away from your continued self-obsession, what exactly did they teach you?'

I don't know if this is some sort of test. I don't know if Ven already knows what goes on in a Learning Community, but I'm trying to establish myself as trustworthy in his eyes so I tell him everything he wants to know about our school curriculum. He stares out the window while I tell him about the scientific research we conducted, but he sits up when I mention Future Leaders. 'Why do you think they taught you all that stuff about battle tactics and strategy?'

109

He obviously has his own ideas. 'They suggested that every good member of a government should be prepared for the most extreme eventualities.'

Ven says nothing. Does he think the Leadership are preparing for war?

'Was it just theory, these "how to be a general" classes?'

'No, we had weapons practice – nothing was real, just simulation stuff: guns, explosives—'

'You know how to make a bomb?'

'Well, in theory I do. I'm more of a book learner.'

Ven gives me that appraising look again. Have I convinced him that we're on his side yet?

We get off at the next stop and get into a lift by ourselves.

'Are we going to put the guard uniforms on?' I ask.

'Not yet.'

So Ven strolls down the street and into the newspaper building just as he is. I follow, trying to imitate his nonchalance. There's a reception desk inside the front door, but the receptionist is busy with two men in suits. Behind them a woman is waiting. Ven takes it all in without stopping. He keeps walking towards the stairs. I stick right behind him. Nobody says anything to us.

The journalists' office is on the third floor. When we reach the landing, Ven throws open a glass door and strides up to the nearest desk. There's an older woman with greying hair sat there.

'We're looking for Janna,' Ven says.

The woman looks up sharply. 'There's nobody working here called that.' She looks back to her computer.

Ven shoots an eyebrow up and moves to a man's desk in the centre of the room. I tail behind him.

'Can you tell me where I can find Janna?' he asks. This time the effect of her name ripples out to the surrounding desks. The typing and the chatter stop abruptly. 'I don't know anyone called Janna,' the man says.

'She works here,' I say. 'Or at least she did.'

'Nobody of that name has ever worked here,' he says.

A loop of fear tightens around my throat. He sounds like Facilitator Johnson did when he claimed never to have seen me before.

'What about you?' Ven says, looking at the woman at the next desk who is staring at him. 'Do you know her?'

'Never heard of her,' she says.

They've done something to Janna. No wonder she didn't come to the warehouse like she was supposed to. I bet they've made her disappear, just like they did with me.

'We should go,' I say to Ven in a low voice.

'What's going on here?' a voice behind me says.

I spin round.

It's Ty.

For a split second I'm pleased. He's the one that told us about the Resistance; he can help us. I expect him to take us to a private room or to tell us to meet him outside, but then I realise that he's terrified. Something bad has happened. He makes his eyes blank. 'We've got a busy newsroom here,' he says. 'I'm going to need you two to leave.'

I look between Ty and Ven, but if they recognise each other they're doing an excellent job of hiding it.

I almost appeal to Ty, but I know that he will pretend not to know me because he is afraid. I don't want to do anything to get him into trouble. And I'm afraid too. Are we being watched?

'We just—' Ven begins, but Ty is walking away towards a security man.

'You heard what he said. Get out,' says the woman with greying hair.

Ven turns on her and I know that he's about to launch into a caustic rant. I tug his sleeve. 'Come on.'

Before he can respond, the security man comes over and takes us by the shoulders. He propels us towards the door. I expect aggression, but he says, 'Come on lads,' in a not-unfriendly tone, 'no point in sticking around here. Like the man said, we've got no security jobs going here.'

'But we—'

'Take a tip. It's no good pitching up on doorsteps just asking for work. You've got to go through an agency.'

'Er, thanks,' I say. 'Could I just ask—?'

'Better shift it. He told me to get rid of you before the editor sees you. He said try the factory. Now clear off.'

'The factory?'

'He . . .' the guard gestures backwards with his head to

where Ty is hunched over a desk. His concentrated still-ness makes me think that he's listening to every word of this. 'He said get rid of them two and tell them there might be work going at the factory.'

'We want to see—'

'No, it's fine,' I interrupt Ven. 'We'll do as you suggest.' I walk through the door as fast as I can, pulling my collar up as I hurry down the stairs.

There's a pause before I hear Ven's footsteps join mine. Outside I don't speak until we're well away from the building.

'What was all that?' Ven asks.

'That was the guy I told you about. Ty, Janna's boyfriend – the one who said he knew the Resistance. I thought you'd know him.'

'I haven't actually shaken the hand of every person who sympathises with the cause. He certainly turned pale when he saw you.'

'He was afraid of something,' I say. 'He didn't want to see me.'

'I can understand that, but it's not a reason to run away.'

'No, I suppose if *you* respected the wishes of everyone who didn't want to see *you*, you'd never speak to anyone again.'

He doesn't seem to mind the jibe. He just says, 'That sounds peaceful.'

'What I mean is that they were denying all knowledge of Janna. And Ty, who was the one who suggested we go to the Resistance in the first place, didn't even want to acknowledge me. He was obviously frightened. I didn't think we were safe in there.'

Ven's eye's snap back to me. 'If you've led me into a trap—'

'I don't want anyone from the Leadership turning up any more than you do.'

We continue walking in silence. I think back over the last few minutes and remember what Kay said about someone shouting on the communicator to Ty. If Janna has been taken away, Ty must be terrified that he's next. I suppose I can't blame him for pretending not to know me, but I expected *something* from him.

It hits me.

'Janna's in the factory,' I say.

'Is that what all that nonsense the security guy was spouting was about? That was code from your Ty. Are you sure?'

'Yes, I am.'

I'm not really, but we haven't got anything else to go on and I don't want him refusing to come along. I've got to find Janna before anything happens to Kay.

It doesn't take us long to agree that since the factory by the river is the only one for miles it must be the one Ty was hinting at. We set off in that direction and I broach the question of security. Ven gives me a sideways look. He's still not sure about me. 'There aren't many people trying to break into a factory,' he says. 'Mostly they're watching for the ones trying to get out. The workers have all got chips fitted. It's largely an automated system. We put on the uniforms and everyone will believe we're Leadership guards.'

I'm amazed that he's shared this much with me. Maybe he's starting to believe that Kay and I aren't the pair of spies that they were tipped off about. 'How do you know so much about factory security?' I ask.

'It's interesting that every time I display knowledge you display surprise.'

Which doesn't answer my question, but it does tell me something about why he seems to dislike me so much. 'I appreciate you sharing information with me,' I say in what I hope is a placating tone.

'Oh no,' Ven says.

'What?'

'I can see where your tiny mind is going with this one. You're thinking that if I'm telling you what I know it must be because I'm starting to trust you.'

I try not to show annoyance at being second-guessed. 'Well, if you thought I was going to take it all back to the Leadership you wouldn't tell me, would you?'

He smiles. 'You forget there is always the option of rendering you unable to tell anything to anyone.'

Efwurding hell. He's still thinking about killing me.

He smiles again. 'Now that is a facial expression that conveys to me that you are remembering just how precarious things are for your pitiful existence, but I'm going to need you to wear your terror on the inside right now. The factory gates are around the corner.'

He pulls me down an alleyway to change into our guards' uniforms. I feel sick. If I'm not killed by the factory security there's a good chance that Ven will blow my brains out. And then what will happen to Kay? I struggle to get my buttons done up. We leave our other clothes in the bags, stashed behind some bins.

'Come on,' Ven says. 'Keep your head. Follow my lead. And try to look confident, idiot.'

It's true that it's not difficult to get into the factory. The security man on the gate waves us through as soon as he sees our uniforms. We get buzzed into the reception, but then the receptionist says something which sends a chill through me.

'You're a little earlier than we expected.'

Ven ignores the remark and signs the screen she holds out to him with a confident slash of the stylus, but my skin is crawling. There were already guards coming to the factory today. What were the guards coming to do? Surely we'll give ourselves away if we don't know?

The receptionist consults her computer. 'The worker you wanted to interview is on the factory floor. Straight down the corridor, just keep going all the way to the end. I'll let the foreman know you're on your way.'

Ven nods at her. She opens the double doors in front of us by clicking on her computer and I follow Ven through them.

117

The door swishes closed behind us. 'Ven,' I say under my breath, 'I've got a bad feeling about this. She said they were expecting guards. Real guards.'

He shoots me a stern look and keeps walking. 'Do you know? If I do end up believing your ridiculous story it will be because it's hard to imagine that when the Leadership were picking out spies they went with a coward like you.'

'You are so full of yourself,' I say, 'that you can't even listen to good advice. Let me put this in terms that you might understand. We should make this quick. Otherwise you might get caught.'

'I know that you're already trying to maintain a feeble pretence at being a man and I can appreciate that a further layer of deception might just flip your tiny brain right out of your oversized head, but is there any chance that you could try, just a little bit, to act like a guard and not a squeaking mouse?'

'Of course, it's not surprising that you've got no difficulty playing a conceited, arrogant bully.'

'Some of us are naturally gifted.'

I can't believe he's treating this whole thing like a joke. 'What are we going to do? If we don't do whatever it is they are expecting, they'll see through us.'

'Then we'll do what they're expecting. Follow their lead. Then when we've finished that, we'll find your friend. Keep your eye out for her.'

The corridor stretches on. The factory floor is a long

118

way from the reception and the other offices. As we draw closer it's easy to see why. It becomes louder and warmer the nearer we get. We go through a sort of air-lock of double doors and on to the factory floor itself.

It's like slamming up against a wall of noise. It smells of hot metal. It *sounds* of hot metal, of pieces of steel sheering against each other. It's a huge space with a high ceiling. There are many different types of machinery all being operated by navy-clad workers.

I expect to find dozens of pairs of eyes on me, but the workers remain diligently bent over their equipment. They're clearly trained not to be distracted.

Immediately in front of us are several large cutting machines. Watching the workers move this way and that, flipping over sections of casing, is hypnotic. It's only when I try to look more closely at what exactly it is that they're cutting that I realise that one of the operators is missing a hand. He flicks switches and pushes levers using the stump of his wrist.

I run my eye over the other workers in my line of sight. He's not the only one with a missing body part. There are two women with the sleeves of their shirts pinned up. They've both lost a whole arm. Further away from us, where workers are dipping circuit boards in acid, one of the women has a livid purple burn on one side of her face. In fact these workers have a rash of chemical burns and patches of melted skin on every exposed part of their bodies.

119

'How can they let people work in these conditions?' I say under my breath.

Ven raises a single eyebrow. 'What where you expecting? A spot of light basket-weaving followed by a tea break?'

What *was* I expecting? I should have known that factories run by the Leadership would be dangerous. 'But ... couldn't they use machines for some of these jobs?'

'Look around you, Blake. What you see are the most advanced and adaptable machines available. If you want a job done that requires judgement and flexibility, you want a human.'

I stare at the busy workers. One of them is drilling holes into metal shells. Her movements are smooth and repetitive until she spots that two sections have got stuck together. She stops and pulls them apart, then returns to her previous rhythm. Ven's right, there's no denying that human flexibility is extremely useful in any kind of production. 'But it looks so dangerous. And however skilled someone might be, humans make mistakes.'

'Which is where we come to the greatest advantage here of man over machine. Unlike an expensive imported piece of equipment, these workers are entirely expendable and totally replaceable. They have that special quality that ensures every factory manager is happy to use them: they're cheap.'

All the protests and exclamations I have about how

horrible and inhumane that is die on my lips because my words are pointless. Here they are; working in these conditions and suffering like this. 'It must be stopped,' I choke out eventually, but saying the words does nothing to lift the net of impotency and frustration that I feel myself caught in.

'Yes,' says Ven. 'It must.'

A man in the navy uniform with an orange stripe across his chest approaches us. Ven stiffens up.

'You've come for worker 136 from E section, sir?' he asks.

'That's right,' Ven says.

I have to supress a smirk at this poor man calling Ven "sir", but Ven's cool, authoritative face doesn't even quiver. He's probably enjoying it. I remember that I'm supposed to be looking for Janna. I go back to scanning the room.

'Lunch session has just begun for that section. I'll get security to take you over.'

'We can find our own way,' Ven says.

The foreman hesitates, bringing my attention back to him. 'You'll need security to locate the worker.' His voice rises at the end, suggesting that he is asking rather than telling, but it feels like a test. He's surprised because Ven has said something he wasn't expecting.

Ven senses danger and says, 'Of course.'

Which means we're stuck with a security guy leading us to the dining hall. I attempt to catch Ven's eye as we make

121

our way down another corridor, but he stares resolutely ahead. Goodness knows what he's going to do when we're presented with this worker. We turn on to another long corridor and the sound of the factory floor fades away.

In the dining room I expect to see rows of feeding pods like at the Academy, but instead the hall is filled with long tables and benches. The workers queue up around the room to be served from recesses in the wall. The recesses stretch the entire length of one side of the hall so the line moves briskly.

'I'll fetch the worker,' the security man says and walks away.

'Stop twitching,' Ven whispers.

I hadn't realised I was. I straighten my back and try to look like a guard. In the corner of the hall is a tower with two more security men sat at the top of it. They've got guns.

'Can you see her?' Ven asks without looking at me.

'No.' I scan the tables, but the hall is packed, it would be easy to miss her. 'Where's the security man?' I ask.

'Talking to another security guy, probably comparing the size of their hats. Either that or deciding which one of them is going to shoot you first.'

I squirm. I feel so exposed just standing here. We're at the very end of the line of recesses. All the workers have to pass us before taking their seats. Dozens have already walked by. I keep expecting one of them to say something to us, but most of them trudge along with their heads kept well down. When one of them does catch my eye he looks away quickly as if he's afraid of me.

I watch the next worker approach the recess closest to me, the last in the row.

It's a girl. Her shoulders are hunched over and she drags her feet, but she's young, it can't be long since she left an Academy.

"Remain still for retina scan," says an electronic voice in the recess.

The machine bleeps recognition. *"Sixty-four units completed."* There's a click and then a wet plopping, as whatever they're having for lunch is dispensed from a spout into a bowl. The girl lifts out the bowl, looking eagerly inside. As she passes me I can see that it's only half full.

The next worker, a thick-necked man, quickly takes her place. *"Remain still for retina scan,"* the machine repeats. *"One hundred and twelve units completed."*

I watch the same process several times, but it's only when a woman with her arm strapped up in a sling reaches the recess that I understand what's going on. *"Twenty-three units completed,"* the machine says, followed by a single wet squelch. The woman stares into her bowl with horror. As she passes I can see just a spoonful of food at the bottom of the dish. The workers' rations are in proportion to the amount of work they've done today. The more you work the more food you get. And if you've broken your arm then you're not going to get a lot to eat.

'That's pretty harsh—' I start to whisper to Ven.

'Sir,' says the security man coming up behind us. 'Here's the worker.'

I swing round. My mouth falls open.

It's Janna.

Horrible thoughts swarm in my head. This is some kind of a set-up. They're laughing at us. Fortunately, Ven is speaking so I keep quiet and follow him blindly out of the dining room, averting my eyes from Janna and trying to make sense of this.

The worker that the guards were coming for was Janna. It's not so crazy really. She's just been involved in an anti-Leadership punch-up at the Academy. Of course they want to talk to her. Maybe about me. I bite the inside of my cheek. This is all so dangerous. I just want to be out of here. We're lead back towards the front of the factory, past a couple of men in hard hats heading for the dining room, past a knot of people gathered outside an office, and past a man with a clipboard, opening the door to a yard with giant gas tanks in. I feel like each one of them is scrutinising me. I'm sweating again.

Finally, we go up a flight of stairs into a room with a

couple of chairs and a table. A breeze is coming through an open window. I take a gulp of fresh air.

'That will be all,' Ven says.

The security man obviously wants to stay, but Ven gives him his most impervious look and the man backs out of the room.

Janna turns to glare at me and takes in my face properly for the first time. She sucks in her breath.

'You! What the efwurd are you doing here?' she asks.

Before I can even open my mouth she goes on. 'I thought you'd still be at the warehouse.'

'Guards came.' I decide not to tell her anything else.

'But you escaped? Oh, that's just great. You're the one that started that riot at the Academy and I saved you, but it's me who's ended up in an efwurding factory while you manage to give the guards the slip. The next thing you tell me had better be that you're going to get me out of here. Did Ty send you?'

Hell, she thinks we're her rescue team. I look at Ven. He's watching me with amused eyes. I don't answer Janna's question. Instead I ask, 'What happened to you?'

'I was picked up by the guards the minute I walked into work three days ago,' she says.

Which explains why she never came back to the warehouse like she arranged. 'Why did they do that?' I ask. 'I thought you said that no one knew that you were at the Academy.'

126

'They must have scanned our press passes or something. They've clearly got a full list of everyone who was there.' She raises one of her extremely arched eyebrows. 'And it looks like they're determined to find everyone.'

'Do you mean that Blake really has got guards after him?' Ven asks, but he doesn't wait for an answer. 'I knew you were trouble,' he says to me.

He doesn't mention that he thought I was an entirely different sort of trouble. It seems that at least listening to Janna might have helped convince him that I was telling the truth about what happened at the Academy.

Ven jerks his chin up. 'Enough of the chat,' he says to me.

Janna is watching him closely. 'And who are you to be telling Genius Boy what to do?'

'This isn't about me,' Ven says in a low voice, 'it's about you. We need something from you.'

Janna stares at him from under her lashes. 'I'm not in the habit of giving away anything for free.'

I shake my head. We haven't got time for Janna's flirting. 'We've got to get a move on,' I say. 'Janna, we need the password for your AV bug.'

'The password for my AV bug? So that's what happened to that. I should have known. You thieving little brat!'

'Yes, sorry ab—'

'Sorry? I could really have done with that footage as a bargaining tool. Have you any idea what it's like in here? Do I look like the sort of girl who's suited to working

127

heavy machinery and splashing about in dangerous chemicals?'

It disturbs me that Janna seems to be suggesting that there is a kind of person who is suited to that stuff.

'You owe me,' she says to me. 'You're in no position to be asking favours.'

'There are some people,' Ven says, 'who might consider your little friend Blake here in an admirable position to ask you for anything his foolish little heart desires, since he's got the freedom to walk out of here and you've got nothing to look forward to but acid baths and amputation. I would put those guys in the category of people with a grip on reality, whereas you—'

'Have you actually got an escape plan?' Janna interrupts. 'One that involves me? One that we can carry out immediately?'

'Yes,' Ven says.

Which is news to me.

'If you'll just tell us the password then—'

'I'll tell you the password when you get me out of here.'

I supress a smile. Ven won't get far if he thinks that Janna can be fooled that easily.

She holds up her wrist. There's a raised red bump. 'There's a chip under there. If I try to leave these walls the external gates will be triggered. Have you allowed for that?'

'Of course,' Ven says.

I look out of the window in the hope that I won't give

away the fact I am almost certain that that is a lie. It's the narrow top section of the window that's open. It's no use to Janna with her chip, but maybe Ven and I could squeeze out of it.

'But I'm not prepared to assist you,' Ven says, 'unless you tell us the password first.'

Now they're in a deadlock. All this is taking up time. I need to get back to the hospital. I should have made Janna listen to me. If she won't give us the password, how am I going to free Kay?

A high-pitched beeping emits from a speaker in the corner of the room. I jump. They're on to us. 'Is that ...?'

'It's the end of the lunch period,' Janna says, and she shares a look of amused contempt for me with Ven. 'How do I know I can trust you?' she asks him in a low voice.

There's a tap at the door.

I twitch.

'Enter,' Ven says in his best commanding tone.

The receptionist peers round the door with a flushed face. 'Sorry to interrupt. It's just that ... Well, there are some of your colleagues here and they're saying ...' She flutters her hands about, trying to frame whatever it is she wants to say delicately. 'There seems to be some confusion over who is responsible for the interview with worker 136.'

Panic forms ice crystals inside my lungs.

Ven sighs as if he is put out. 'I'm sure this can be easily resolved,' he says ushering the receptionist out of the door before him. As he disappears he turns and gives me a hard look. But it's like he's said a foreign word. I have no idea what the look means. Does he want me to get the password out of Janna and fast? Or should I run for it? I stare after him. The door closes.

'Now you're in trouble,' Janna says.

I hardly even hear her. I need to think. What do I do? Eventually I say, 'I really need you to tell me the password.'

Janna snorts. 'Why would I do that?'

'So that I can bring down The Leader. Don't you care about stopping him?'

'What I care about is myself.'

That's when I remember that this isn't all about Ven. I don't have to try to second-guess what he wants. I can make my own decisions. What's important is that I get back to Kay. I open the door a crack and peer out. Two grim-faced guards are at the top of the stairs heading straight for us. I duck back into the room. What the hell has happened to Ven? I'm trapped. There's nowhere in the room to go . . . except out of the window. I push past Janna.

'What happened to the escape plan?' she asks.

I climb up on to the windowsill and look out. Below is the pavement at the front of the factory. It's not that high, I tell myself. Gripping the edge of the open top section of the window I scramble a leg up and over it.

'You have got to be kidding,' Janna says. 'What about me?'

I'm now straddling the top section. One arm and leg are

out of the building and the others inside. I work my other leg over. 'I'll get you out,' I say. 'I really will.' I manoeuvre on to my stomach so my upper body is sticking into the room while my legs are out in the breeze. 'Just draw the blind. Please.'

Janna pushes her tongue behind her teeth and shakes her head, but she reaches out and lets down the blind.

I ease backwards until my feet hit the outside sill. It's not very wide. I have to turn out my feet as far as I can to fit on it. I keep a tight grip on the edge of the window. I mustn't look down.

I hear the door crash open. 'Where the hell are they?' a man's voice asks.

I hear Janna's smooth, low voice but the wind is rushing around my ears and I can't make out exactly what she's saying. My fingers are turning white from gripping the edge of the window so hard. What the hell am I going to do? I won't be able to hold on like this for long and even if the guards leave, how am I going to get out of the factory without being noticed?

My view is mostly of green fabric, but when the breeze catches it, the blind sometimes puffs away from the window, and the back of one of the guards becomes visible.

I can't hear what is being said. But the guards have stopped shouting, so maybe that's a good thing. All I can hope is that Janna tells them I've left and that they go. My legs ache. My fingers are going numb. The wind cuts

131

through my hair and for a brief moment the blind is whipped further away from the window than before so that I can see right into the room. I don't like what I see.

Janna is shaking hands with one of the guards.

19

Kay was right about Janna. She's a self-centred back-stabber. But before I can start to imagine what Janna is playing at, the wind catches the blind again and rips it away from the window. This time one of the guards has turned around. He sees me. As the blind falls back he strides towards me. I choose this moment to look down. It's a long way to the ground. I stifle a retch. The guard tears down the blind, his face contorted with rage. King hell, don't let him push me off!

'What the devil are you playing at?' the guard barks.

The other guard brings a chair and the first guard climbs on to it and grabs hold of my wrist. It's almost a relief. Being hauled through the small window by two angry guards is extremely unpleasant, but at least I'm not falling on to the concrete. Even though I try to cooperate, my feet slip and slide and I'm mostly dragged in, scraping the skin off my stomach on the edge of the window.

The younger of the two guards lets go of me to return to Janna's side. The older one keeps a firm grip on me.

'What has she said to you?' I ask. Has she told them who I am? I try to twist away from the older guard.

'Settle down,' he says and handcuffs my right wrist to his left.

What are they going to do to me now that they've got me? What's going to happen to Kay if I don't get back to the hospital? Efwurd.

'Where's the other one?' the older guard says to me.

'I don't know.'

The younger guard and Janna are leaving. Her hand is on his arm. Surely she can't have charmed him into helping her escape?

'Hey!' I say, unable to form the questions I have for her.

Janna turns back and laughs, she actually laughs. My mouth twists in disgust. She looks at me full in the face. She is totally unabashed at colluding with guards. I channel my anger through my eyes and give her the filthiest look I can muster. She stares back at me.

'Say hello to your girlfriend for me,' she says in a singsong voice.

I stiffen. She's got no right to speak about Kay.

'Say hello and tell her . . .' She flips back her black hair. 'Tell her she's beautiful.' I can tell she's sneering at Kay.

'She's more beautiful than you!' I shout. 'She knew you for the back-stabber that you are!'

134

But she and the guard have turned away. She swings her hips as she walks through the door.

I lunge towards them, but the guard yanks me back.

'Traitor!' I shout at the top of my voice.

She doesn't even turn around.

That's when a grenade lands at my feet.

It must have come through the window behind us. This time, I know immediately what must be done. I reach down to take it, but the guard is quicker. He bends and scoops it up. As he draws back his arm, I see that instead of throwing it back out the window, as I would have done, that he is going to hurl it out of the still-open door. In the direction of the gas tanks.

'No!' I shout. But it's too late. We watch the grenade fly over the heads of Janna and the guard. It clatters to the floor of the corridor.

There's a moment of slow-motion where I see the wrinkles at the corner of the guard's eyes as his face stretches in terror, and Janna turns back in surprise. Then out of the silence comes an almighty bang.

It's all over.

The floor seems to ripple beneath me. I'm lifted off my feet and blown backwards into darkness.

*

When I come to, my head is throbbing. For a moment I think I'm in bed at the Academy and that I must have had a fight last night because my body is pulsing with pain. I open my eyes. It's dark. And dusty. My mouth seems to be full of grit. How the hell—? The factory. The guards. There was a noise. An explosion.

I'm on my back, enclosed in a tiny space. Oh God, no. This time I don't manage my fear. 'Help!' I scream. I claw at the stones covering my face with my left hand, but my right arm is stuck. My breath is coming in rattling gasps. I want to cry. I tense myself up and try to think methodically. I seem to be lying on rocks. I don't think I've broken any bones. Above me is a long section of something smooth. My fingers close on a handle. It's a door. The way it's landed means that it's created a space in the debris for me. I try to sit up but I can only get halfway up. My right arm won't come. I roll on to my side to use my left hand to help. There are pieces of rubble covering me from the right forearm down to the hand. I pull again but there is something around my wrist.

The handcuffs. I'm still cuffed to the guard.

'Can you hear me?' I shout.

Nothing. I stretch out the fingers of my cuffed hand. There's something sharp, some brick and ... something soft and warm. It's the guard's finger. I flinch back. But I can't move far because the metal of the cuffs cuts into my wrist.

I pull myself together and reach for his hand again. This

137

time I take hold of three fingers and give them a good hard squeeze. I wait. The fingers are still in mine. If he could feel me, surely he'd be squeezing back as hard as he could. Maybe he's dead. Maybe I'm trapped under the rubble handcuffed to a dead man. Panic threatens to suck me down into a whirlpool.

Efwurd. Kay. Is Kay all right? How long have I been passed out under here? Why has no one come to dig me out? Haven't they missed the guards? I cannot lose it now. I have to get back to Kay. I fill my lungs with the thick dusty air and shout, 'HELP!' as loudly as I can. The fingers don't stir. I start pulling at the pieces covering the end of my arm. The problem is where to put the junk that I move. I end up pushing it into the space behind my head. Actually, that isn't the biggest problem; what I'm really afraid of is that I'll start an avalanche of brick.

When I've moved the stuff off my arm, I twist my hand painfully in the cuffs so I can place two fingers on his wrist. I can't feel anything, but I can't be sure that I've got the right spot. Besides, my fingers are covered in filth and my own heart is pounding so loudly I don't know if I could detect another beat.

I keep using my left hand to move bricks away to uncover the guard. I'm getting close to his chest when I reach a chunk of something chalky that won't move. I rotate my hand to get a better grip and then pull hard. As soon as I've done it, I know that I shouldn't have. There's a terrible shifting. I've loosened something that

138

was holding up a lot of other somethings. I try to push it back but there's a sliding of bricks and a shower of small stones on my head. I pull away so I'm under the cover of the door. Stones, rubble, metal and wood scrape and fall around me. The door drops so that it's pressing against me. I tense my body, waiting for the air to be crushed out of me.

The rumbling slows to a trickle. I blink to get the dust out of my eyes.

I can see.

Not much, but I can see. That means that light is coming in from somewhere. I can't be buried too deep. That's good. I can also hear. Someone on the other side of this rubble is screaming.

The guard's arm is still exposed. I reach up to his shoulder and then scrabble through the junk to press my hand flat against his chest. There's no heartbeat. Before I can even really take that in, I realise that under my hand, in his breast pocket, is a key.

In that dusty, dusky space using only my left hand, it takes me a while to retrieve the key and then unlock the handcuffs, but finally my right hand is free.

I have no idea how much time has passed since the explosion. Ven told Alrye to kill Kay if he wasn't back by nightfall. There are trickles of sunlight in my tiny space. That means there's still time to get back to her.

I try to manoeuvre myself into a better position under the door. I push at the stones that have filled the space.

Something sharp spears me under the nail of my right index finger, but I keep clawing at the rubble. Finally, I can get my hands flat against wood of the door above and push. Things above the door are definitely moving, but then I seem to hit a barrier. I lower the door again. *Come on, come on.* Kay needs me. I squeeze on to my knees so that my back is against the door. I brace my legs, my right knee is pulsing with pain, but I bite my lip and push. There's a creaking and then once again things stop moving. I grit my teeth and give an almighty shove. The door flips off my back and suddenly I'm standing waist-deep in a pile of debris. I can hear the screaming loud and clear now, and there are voices shouting instructions back and forth, too.

I look around me. Even though the interview room was on the first floor I've ended up close to the ground. I try to take in the devastation. Where the front of the building was, there is now a pile of bricks. Where the gas tanks were a fire is raging. Further back, parts of the factory are still standing. There's a fire engine parked by the gates and a number of men are working through the rubble. A circle of people, lying on the ground waiting to be treated, surround a solitary ambulance. At least, I hope that they're waiting to be treated. Over to the left I see lines of navy-clad workers. They're upright and there are hundreds of them. The factory floor seems to be largely intact. It looks like most of the workers have survived.

'You all right?' One of the rescue workers is picking his way over bricks towards me.

'I'm fine,' I say.

He looks me up and down. 'You can walk?'

'I'm okay. Really.' I've got to get to Kay. How long will it take me to get back? What time does it get dark? I scramble awkwardly over the rubble until I'm on level ground.

'Someone will check you over,' he nods towards the ambulance. 'Might be a bit of a wait. He turns back to shifting rubble. 'It'd help if your lot would send more people,' he mutters.

I remember that I'm still in uniform. I wonder why the guards haven't sent reinforcements, but I don't have time to get into a discussion about why the hell there aren't more rescue workers at what is clearly a huge emergency.

'I'm fine,' I repeat, but he's not even listening. I look around me again. Everyone is stretched so thin trying to help the seriously injured that no one is paying any attention to me. I can just walk right out of here and that's what I need to do.

As I turn to leave, something protruding from under a pile of bricks catches my eye. It doesn't register with my brain until I've taken another step towards the gates. Then I stop. I know what I saw.

It was a human hand.

21

Part of my brain is screaming at me to leave anyway. Kay needs me. Time is running out. The rescue crew will get to the owner of the hand. They're probably dead anyway. But what keeps me from leaving is what I saw around the wrist of the hand. A flash of red. Whoever is under there is wearing a guard's uniform. Which means that either the hand belongs to the young guard, or it belongs to Ven.

I can't just walk away. I turn back. The person is actually barely covered, but a thick coating of dust and plaster means that they blend into the rest of the debris. As soon as I lift away a ripped piece of carpet I can see that it's Ven. I uncover the rest of him quickly. He looks terrible, but apart from blood trickling down his forehead, I can't see any obvious injuries. As I pull his arm free, his eyelids flutter open. He squints at me.

'What?' he says hoarsely.

'The factory, remember? There was an explosion. We can't stay here, they'll find us. We've got to get moving.'

His eyes come into focus as he reorientates himself. He nods. 'Let's go.'

'Can you stand?'

'I'm all right.'

He is far from all right. His eyes are glassy and he sways as I help him to his feet, but he doesn't complain.

I half drag Ven towards the exit. I expect to be stopped at any moment, but the place is in chaos. A woman sits on what remains of a wall, sobbing. Rescue workers are desperately raking through the rubble. Some of the walking wounded are drifting about. A man is bellowing something about contacting someone. We just limp right out of the gates. Ven insists that we go back to the alleyway and retrieve the backpacks so we can change out of our filthy uniforms before we start on the long walk back to the nearest metro stop.

'Can't you go any faster?' I ask Ven. This is a ridiculous thing to say. He's clearly very unwell. I'm amazed he can walk at all. But we've got to get back to Kay.

He looks at me sideways. 'I hope you're not thinking of rushing on ahead?'

'I'd quite happily leave you in the gutter, but you told them to kill Kay if you didn't come back, remember? I will be getting you home and it will be happening as fast as possible.'

He shrugs, but I notice that he picks up the pace as much as he is able. This doesn't make me feel any better because it just shows that he's worried that we won't get back in time either.

Eventually, we reach the station. I take the cards from Ven's bag and swipe them as we get on the train. I manage to find an almost-empty carriage where no one will stare at our dusty hair and dirty faces. Ven pulls up his hood and slumps in a seat. His breathing is shallow. He can die for all I care, but he'd better not do it before I'm sure Kay is safe.

When we get off the metro I check the clock by the exit. It's late afternoon already. We need to get a move on.

Getting back to the house with the tunnel in the base-ment is tough. Ven's head is bleeding again and, once, he staggers sideways and I have to catch him before he keels over. By the time we reach the house he is sweating and panting. I have to push him in through the window. He lands heavily. When I climb in behind him I discover that he's fainted. It's several minutes before I can wake him up. I don't even have time to get claustrophobic about the tunnel. I just grit my teeth and half carry and half drag Ven through to the other side. As I'm hauling him through the appliance shop I face the obvious: there's no way that Ven can drive in his condition.

The car is right outside the shop, exactly where we left it. I bundle Ven into the back. He flops down on the seat, breathing heavily. I locate the keys in the lower pocket of his trousers. His eyes are rolling back in his head. I shake him.

'Wake up! You've got to tell me how to drive.'

His head lolls forward. I lay him back on the seat. What

do I do? What the hell do I do? The sun is already lower in the sky and we need time to get back to the hospital. What's going to happen to Kay? I lift my hand and slap Ven hard across the cheek.

He snaps back into consciousness, tensing his body and raising his fist. 'Whatzit?' he slurs.

'The car. How do I drive the car?'

He frowns and fumbles in his pocket.

'I've got the keys. I swipe the key, then what? Then what?'

He grips my arm to steady himself. 'Accelerator on the right, brake in the middle, clutch on the left. Clutch to the floor. Put it in first gear. Start accelerating, bring the clutch up slowly. It's about the bite … you've got to make sure …' He stumbles to a halt and looks at me suspiciously. He lifts a hand to his forehead. 'I'm really hot,' he says and leans back in the seat, his eyes half open. I've lost him.

I scramble into the front seat. I can do this. Accelerator on the right, brake in the middle, clutch on the left. I put my left foot down on the clutch, then I find the key reader and swipe the key. The engine starts. That's good. Now I have to use the accelerator. I press it cautiously at first then more firmly. We jerk forward and stop, the engine stalls. *Come on, Blake, come on*. I start again. This time I bring the clutch up and push down on the accelerator at the same time and the car starts to move. I'm doing it, I'm doing it! I grip the steering wheel hard. We're not

145

moving very fast. That's okay, I don't want to crash. But we're really not moving very fast, I could walk faster than this.

'Handbrake,' Ven says from the back seat.

I pull up the handbrake and we speed forward.

'Efwurding idiot,' Ven says. Then he's gone again.

I'm concentrating too hard on not killing us to say anything back.

The first corner I take is terrifying. I have the entire road to myself and it's just as well because I make a huge curve. By the fifth or sixth corner I'm getting the hang of judging when to swing the steering wheel. After a while, I'm able to relax my shoulders a little. It's pretty straightforward really. The only thing I have to watch out for are obstacles on the road, mostly burnt-out cars and rubble, but also some random things like an armchair and a shopping trolley.

I understand the theory of changing gear, but I still make some terrible grinding noises. It could even be fun if I weren't so worried about Kay. There's no escaping the fact that the sun will soon be setting.

'Hey, Ven!' I shout.

Looking in the mirror I see his eyes open. 'They won't kill her, will they?' I ask. 'The people in charge of the Resistance won't authorise it, will they?'

'I'mincharge,' he slurs.

There's no point talking to him. He's concussed. I look at the road ahead of us. How quickly can I do this? I'm not going anywhere near as fast as Ven drove this morning. I put my foot down on the accelerator and lean forward. I've got to get back to Kay and it's got to be soon.

After a while Ven starts making grumbly noises in the back seat. I look at him in the mirror. His skin has a nasty sheen. He's dabbing at his wound and swearing.

'I'm going to die,' he says.

'We'll be back at the hospital soon then someone can take a look at your head.'

'It's not my head I'm worried about, it's your driving.'

'If you don't like it then you can drive.'

'My vision is blurred.'

'Then you're stuck with me.'

'I said my vision was blurred, that doesn't mean I couldn't drive better than you are.'

Despite his protests he slumps back on the seat and closes his eyes again. If he's recovered his sarcasm, he can't be too ill.

Finally, we reach the edge of the ghost-city where the hospital is, but my heart is pounding because the light is definitely going. I've got a very good memory. I know exactly the way to get back to the hospital and as we get closer I drive faster and get less careful. I swing round the last corner hard and the thing that I had been promising myself wouldn't happen, happens; I slam straight into another car.

'Efwurd!' Ven says as he's catapulted into the seat in front of him. I'm thrust forward and an airbag pops up in my face.

Everything stops.

My seat belt is digging into me. I struggle backwards and beat down the airbag so I can look out of the window.

The other driver is about ten years old. His mouth is stretched into an 'O'; he obviously wasn't expecting another car on the road either. He doesn't seem to be injured.

Behind me Ven is muttering, 'I should never have let you drive. How could you crash?' which suggests he's fine too.

I haven't got time for this. It's undeniably dark now. I have to get to Kay. The hospital is at the end of the road. I fling the car door open and start running.

My knee jars agonisingly every time my foot hits the ground. I screw up my face and push myself to keep up the pace. Is she all right? I can't believe it. I can't believe that idiot has put Kay's life in danger just because he's got some paranoid idea we're from the Leadership.

The hospital looms up in front me. *Don't stop, don't stop*, is all I have the energy to think as I force my leaden legs towards it. I fix my eyes on the space between the two buildings. There's nothing but the surging sound of blood in my ears and the alleyway in front of me. I power down the narrow space past the closed door that Paulo let us in last night and to the back entrance that we came out of this morning. I hammer on the door. *Come on, come on.* I shove past someone with a gun and I'm vaguely aware of someone else calling, 'Don't shoot him!' but my whole focus is on getting up the stairs. My breath is coming in gasps. I feel like my lungs are ripping. Please let her be alive. I run down the corridor so fast that I can't stop and I slam into the door of the lock-up room. I hammer with my fists.

'Kay! We're back! Don't hurt her!'

I reach for the handle, I don't expect it to be unlocked, but it is and the door swings open.

The room is empty.

22

I start throwing open doors all down the corridor and shouting Kay's name. I can't find her. When I get back to the top of the stairs, Ven is struggling up the last few steps.

'Where is she?' I say, grabbing him. 'What the hell have they done with her?'

Ven looks down at my hands on his shirt.

'If they've hurt her, I swear I will kill you.'

'Don't threaten me,' Ven says slowly.

He still thinks that he can intimidate me. 'I'll do more than threaten you.'

Ven pulls a face of tired resignation like I am a pestering little kid.

Rage explodes inside me and I spring forward and pin him against the wall. 'Listen to me. I know that when you look at me you see this gangly, cowardly boy, but let me tell you this: when it comes to Kay it doesn't matter how thin or how weak I am. I am quite capable of murdering anyone who hurts her. Do you understand? If someone has harmed her, I will kill you.' The words have come pouring out of my mouth. I am so blisteringly angry that time has slowed down while my mind gallops ahead. I see Ven in perfect clarity. I am going to make him pay and nothing will stop me.

He looks past me, over my shoulder. 'I think he likes you,' he says to someone behind me.

I swing round.

It's Kay.

She's all right. My Kay is stood with Paulo and she is most definitely still alive. Ven has a big fat grin on his face. He thinks it's funny. He has completely forgotten that I rescued him and he thinks nearly having Kay killed is funny. I thrust my face close to his.

'I'm not here for your amusement,' I say. 'I saved your life earlier. Only an idiot could still believe that we've got anything to do with the Leadership. We could help bring those bastards down, but if you don't start treating us with respect we're leaving.'

Ven wipes a fleck of my spit from his face and shrugs. 'Fine.' He sidesteps away from me. 'From now on I'll treat you the same way I treat everybody else in the Resistance.' He limps off down the corridor and mutters, 'Although I wouldn't exactly call that respect.'

'Bastard,' I say. 'Conceited, moronic, arrogant, heartless, bastard.' There's so much anger in me that I can't contain it. A red wave whips through me and I kick the wall. 'Bastard, bastard, bastard.'

151

'Blake,' Kay says.

With a huge effort I manage to relax my shoulders and look at her.

'What?' I say, but I can feel my venom ebbing.

'What happened?' she touches my face.

I must look a right state. My hair is full of plaster and I imagine there are bruises on my face. I don't know where to begin about the factory.

'I'll tell you later,' I say eventually.

Paulo clears his throat. 'You both need to come with me.' He looks apologetic.

'Are you locking us up again?' I ask. 'Because—'

'I thought maybe you should eat,' he interrupts.

'Oh. Okay.'

So we meekly follow Paulo downstairs. Solar lanterns are positioned on each landing, but they are far enough apart that at the mid-point between each floor the darkness takes over and I have to be careful not to trip on any of the pieces of plaster littering the steps.

'This place is a mess,' Kay says.

I can just imagine what Ven's response would be to that remark, but Paulo says, 'We move around a lot. Housekeeping isn't our top priority. Don't worry, the kitchens are clean.'

I'm so hungry I hardly care.

'Did you really save Ven?' Paulo asks.

'Yes, I damn well did. I could have left him. He'll have to give up on this Leadership spies nonsense now.'

'Did he say that?' Kay asks.

'Say what?' I ask. 'That he was an idiot? No, but he knows he made a mistake.'

'The thing is,' Paulo says, 'we were told a pair of spies, a boy and a girl, were going to turn up here pretending to be from an Academy. You can see why Ven was suspicious when you told us that's where you come from.'

I think of words other than 'suspicious' to describe Ven's behaviour, but clearly this is the closest to an apology that we're going to get.

Paulo leads us into the old hospital cafeteria. High above us, the ceiling sags in places, and dark stains crawl across the walls, but at least the hexagonal tables and plastic chairs look clean. Although the room is empty, the smell of cooked vegetables and the clanking of saucepans and chinking of crockery coming from the kitchen suggests that food is on its way.

'I just need a word with Ven about all this,' Paulo says, walking away. He sticks his head through the kitchen door, says a few words and then leaves the cafeteria. A serving hatch connecting to the kitchen slides open. We can't see anyone, but clearly Paulo has got someone watching us. It's so ridiculous that I laugh.

'This is crazy. After everything I've been through for that idiot today,' I say. 'I should have smacked him while my anger was overriding my natural cowardice.'

Kay smiles. 'You were going to do fighting for me,' she says.

'Of course I was.'

'You hate fighting. You must really big hate him.'

She looks at me. I thought she might be dead, but she's not, she's here, with me, her face all lit up. The curve of her bottom lip sends a jolt right through me. Without thinking, I wrap my arm around her waist and pull her gently to me. 'It's not about him, it's about you. I'll always fight for you.'

'You're nice.' She gives me a look that makes my fingertips fizz.

The kitchen door behind her swings open and someone comes out carrying a stack of plates. We separate. I can feel colour rushing to my cheeks. When they've gone back into the kitchen Kay touches my arm. 'You're nice,' she repeats, 'but when I'm there you should let me do the front fighting.'

I grin. 'Okay, I'll hang around in the background scorching people with my deadly wit.'

We're staring at each other again.

I'm going to kiss her.

My heart swoops around my chest. She smiles wide just for me. I lean towards her and our lips touch. Great bolts of happiness streak through me. I reach out and fit my hand to the nape of her neck. She presses against me. Our mouths open and when her tongue touches mine something cracks open inside of me and I want her so badly. I want—

A group of people come into the cafeteria. I break away

154

from Kay, my heart still thundering. Paulo reappears and ushers us to one of the tables which is laid with bowls, spoons and a basket of bread.

'Ven says you're on trial,' he tells us. 'You don't have to be locked up but . . .'

'You're watching us,' I finish for him.

Paulo shrugs.

'Blake saved Ven!' Kay says. 'It's not . . . It's not being . . .' Kay looks to me for the words she wants.

'It lacks gratitude,' I say.

Paulo snorts. 'This is as grateful as Ven gets.'

Which is the first thing he's said that suggests that he isn't entirely oblivious to the fact that Ven is an arrogant idiot.

Paulo goes to help distribute the dishes of food around the tables. I wonder what he really thinks of Ven. How come Ven gets to boss him about anyway?

'He should stand up to Ven,' I say to Kay.

'I think it was him who didn't let them kill me like you were thinking. I could hear some person saying, "It's getting too dark and you know what he said." And then Paulo came to that locking room and taked me away to another place. I think he was hiding me and then we heard you shouting.' She tightens her ponytail. 'So Paulo doesn't all times do the thing that Ven says.'

'Who is Ven to be telling people what to do anyway?' I ask.

'I think he's important,' Kay says.

155

'Do you think maybe he's the son of the man in charge?'

Kay catches my eye and I realise what I've said. 'Yes, okay, being the son of the man in charge hasn't exactly given me power and influence.' My lips twitch. 'And then there was the being shot at, the imprisonment, and that time they erased my life.'

Kay smiles. 'Yeah, I thought The Leader's son would be getting me all nice food and things to wear. But you get me crawling in a tunnel and chased by the guards.'

I shake my head in mock shame. 'I'm such a catch.'

Kay laughs and as she does she clutches my arm. Even after today, just being near her makes me feel good.

'You don't have to have influence. I like you with no influence.'

She makes me feel like the most important person in the world.

A boy with curly hair reaches between us to put a huge lidded tureen down on the table.

'Dig in,' he says pulling out a chair for himself and sitting down. 'You must be Blake and Kay. I'm Toren.'

I don't know whether to smile at him or not. I don't know where we are with these people. But Toren beams unreservedly at me while cramming a piece of bread into his mouth, so I manage a half-smile in return.

I lift the lid of the tureen and serve us a portion of the stew inside. After months of Academy slop I can't wait to eat a real meal. Kay is watching me carefully and I realise with a stab that she is used to eating at the Academy, where they expect the Specials to gulp down slop directly from a feeding nozzle. I lift my spoon and give her an encouraging smile. She follows my lead and we both take eager gulps of stew.

'I see you've made yourself at home.' It's Ven. His head is bandaged and he a little looks better. He sits down heavily.

'Shouldn't you be in sick bay?' Toren asks.

I don't hear Ven's reply because I'm watching the rest of Resistance swarm into the room. They chat and jostle as they take their seats and I can tell by the way that they attack their food that mealtimes are looked forward to. But something is weird. Something that's been bugging me since we got here.

'Where are the adults?' I say.

Kay breaks off talking to Paulo, who has sat down next to her. She glances around the room. The youngest person I can see is a little girl of four or five who is struggling to handle her cutlery, but even Ven can't be more than twenty.

'There aren't any,' Ven says, turning to face me. 'I don't know if you were born with this mistrust of what others say, or if it's a result of the shunning that you've doubtless experienced during your life, but I meant it in the car when I said I'm in charge.' He leans back in his chair. 'I'm the oldest person here.'

23

'What happened to all the grown-ups?' I ask. It crosses my mind that maybe Ven has led some horrible rebellion where all the adults were massacred.

Ven stretches his arms above his head. 'In your previous life as a Learning Community puppet, at what age do students leave the padded bosom of your luxurious existence?'

Why can he never just answer the question? And I notice that he now seems to have accepted that I really did come from a Learning Community. 'I don't see what that—'

'What age?'

'Twenty-one, but—'

He turns to Kay. 'And what about you, my elven friend? Remind us what age the Specials get shipped off to the factory.'

I know that Kay doesn't know what elven means, but her expression suggests that she doesn't like the sound of it. 'Seventeen,' she says with tight lips.

'What age do you think we start work here?' Ven asks.

I can see where this is going. There's no need for him to labour his point. All I did was ask a simple question. 'Eighteen months,' I say.

'Seven. Everyone here over the age of seven has a job to do. When you reach thirteen you can be sent on a mission – and from the fun we had earlier trying to prove your point, you'll remember that those can be life threatening.'

Trying to prove my point? Is he blaming me for everything that happened earlier?

Ven stabs a chunk of carrot with his fork. 'Thirteen, we send you out and expect you to stay alive.' He bites hard into the carrot. 'So don't tell me that there are no "grown-ups" here.'

'You know what I mean,' I persist. 'Why is there no one middle-aged here?'

'I find it odd that you're so concerned about the old folk. If what you've told us is true then you're not exactly one to recognise the authority of the elderly.'

I bristle at the 'if what you've told us is true'. But it's funny that he should think of me as a rebel. Until a few months ago I was a model student who did everything asked of him. I don't reply. I'm realising that the way to handle Ven is to wait. He'll tell you what he wants to tell you and nothing more. Everyone else at the table is waiting too.

Ven takes two more leisurely mouthfuls. 'The life expectancy of a Resistance member ...' he pauses to swallow '. . . is nineteen years. And that's not just because we tend to get shot or beaten to death when the Leadership catch us.' He leans close to Kay and says in a stage whisper, 'It's also because this place is slowly poisoning us all.'

'What?' Kay says.

My face is rigid with horror. 'Poison?'

'That's right. You didn't think that the Leadership would let us have this chunk of land unless there was something wrong with it, did you? Something bone-meltingly, lung-charringly wrong with it.' He slaps me on the back. 'Deep breaths, young man, deep breaths.'

I look to Paulo for an explanation.

He shrugs. 'The weapons the Greater Power used, they're still affecting the area. It's bad for your health.'

'That's horrible.' I find myself taking shallow breaths as if I can somehow avoid inhaling whatever toxins are in the air. We've got to get out of here and soon.

'Being at here is killing you?' Kay asks.

Paulo nods. 'We have to make the most of the time that we have.'

'Paulo's death sentence makes him want to stand about admiring sunsets,' Ven says. 'Personally, it makes me want to shoot stuff.'

'Why are you staying here when you know you're going to die?' Kay says.

Toren seems puzzled by her horror. 'This is our home,' he says.

160

'But there are other places to live,' I say. 'You could live on the other side of the fence.'

'I'd rather strive to do right for nineteen years than live a comfortable lie till I grow old,' Paulo says.

I watch Kay's face as she takes this sentiment in.

I'm surprised that Ven isn't spouting more of his opinions. 'You're strangely quiet,' I say to him.

'Couldn't speak.' He shakes his head. 'The emotion of Paulo's speech – it ...' he wipes away an imaginary tear '... it had me choking on my own vomit.' He pushes back his chair and stands up.

He really is nasty.

'I still don't understand why someone like you is even part of the Resistance,' I say.

He picks up his bowl and as he's walking away he turns back. 'Like I said, I like shooting stuff.'

24

I stare around at the others on the table. Toren watches Ven disappear. Paulo is staring into his stew. Kay widens her eyes at me.

'No adults?' she asks. 'No enforcer ones, or guard ones, or leader ones?'

'Ven seems to be saying that he is the leader one. Is that true?' I ask Paulo. 'Is Ven your leader?'

He shakes his head. 'We don't say leader. It has negative connotations.'

'We say captain,' Toren interrupts. 'He's our captain.' He takes another chunk of bread and tears into it cheerfully.

I stare at Paulo. He looks impassively back at me.

I suppose I'm not used to the idea of someone so young being in charge. I wasn't exactly comfortable myself when I was trying to lead the Specials at the Academy. And it's not just that he's young. He's so mean. 'Can you believe he's the boss?' I ask Kay.

Kay screws up her nose. 'Rex runned things.'

'Rex *thought* he ran things. And look at the horrible way he behaved with the little bit of power that he actually did have.'

Robin sits down in Ven's vacated chair, plonking down a half-full bowl of stew and a teddy bear on the table. 'Who's Rex?' she asks, as if she's been part of this conversation all along.

'A boy at the Academy,' Kay answers.

'Was he your friend? I bet he's not as nice as my friend.'

'He's not nice at all,' I say. 'He's an idiot.'

'Well, Ven isn't an idiot,' Toren says. 'You're eating food grown by the Provisions team, using a hydroponics garden updated by Ven. That shirt you're wearing was procured by another team, who source and catalogue items with a system designed by Ven. You're safe in this hospital because it's being guarded by the Defence team who are trained by Ven.'

I look back to Paulo.

'Ven's a genius.' He shrugs. 'Everybody knows it.'

I stiffen.

'He's not smarterer than Blake,' Kay says. 'No one is more clever than Blake.'

Toren grins. 'I guess we'll see about that.'

Robin gives me a look that is half sympathy and half contempt. 'You're more fun than Ven,' she says, as if that will comfort me. 'Ven is no fun at all. He stops people having nice times.'

163

'How long has Ven been your – what do you say – captain?' Kay asks.

'Since the last one died. She was the first ever captain,' Paulo says.

Finally, we're getting some information. 'How long has the Resistance been the Resistance?' I ask.

Paulo squints. 'Eighteen years. During the Long War this area was targeted by the Greater Power's bombing. They moved as many people away as they could and when the war was over they ordered anyone left to get out. They said they were going to "repair and regenerate" but some people refused to go.'

'Like my parents,' Toren says. 'They got together with some of the others who wanted to stay.'

I'm increasingly impressed by anyone who doesn't blindly follow orders from the Leadership, but I can't stop myself asking, 'Weren't they afraid to stay here in this mess?'

'They were more afraid of what it would be like living under the Leadership,' Robin says.

It's such a cynical, adult thing for a little girl to say that it makes me blink.

'Were those people Resistance?' Kay asks.

Paulo nods. 'They grew pretty rapidly from then on. The Leadership started dumping people here that they wanted to get rid of, including people who had once worked for them. Our first captain, Laurel, was one of them. When she arrived she had a lot of inside information. She joined the group Toren's parents started and told them that there were people on the other side of the fence who were against the Leadership.'

I've finished my bowl of stew and my stomach is aching. I'm not used to this much food any more, but I don't care because it feels so good to be full for once.

Kay is scraping up the last of her own stew. 'Do you go back to the other side?' she asks Toren.

'Sometimes we send trained people to pick up stuff, but it's quite dangerous.'

'We try to produce as much as we can ourselves,' Paulo says. 'We've got a hydroponics garden, like Toren said, and one of our cells is a farm.'

'Cells?' Kay asks.

Robin looks at Kay disdainfully. 'The Resistance isn't just the hospital. There are more Resistance people living all around the Wilderness. The groups are called cells. And one of them has got a farm. I might take my friend there one day.'

'You don't grow food in the earth, do you?' I ask. 'Isn't the earth ...?' I imagine my insides melting away. Who knows what damage has already been done?

'We can't steal food to feed the entire Resistance,' Paulo says. 'It's just not practical, besides there are areas of the Wilderness where the land isn't so bad.'

Which isn't the reassurance I was looking for.

'What about the water?' Kay asks.

'We filter water to a high level of purity,' Paulo says. 'We only go to the other side to get things we can't get here,' Toren says. 'Like technology, like the computers.'

'Where does the electricity come from for the computer?' I ask.

'There's a generator,' Robin says. 'Don't you know anything?'

'It runs on diesel,' Paulo explains. 'You'd be surprised how much diesel we've rounded up – and we're very careful with it. The computers only come on for vital stuff. Some of the lights even work. But usually we stick with the solar lanterns on dim setting because they're not bright enough to be noticed from a distance.'

'There've been rows about how we source things,' Toren says, going back to Kay's earlier question. 'There are people here who are really into getting stuff from the other side.' He exchanges a look with Paulo. They're obviously thinking of someone in particular. 'But I think we need to use what's here, you know?'

'Toren loves recycling.' Robin sounds so thoroughly disapproving that we laugh.

'It's true,' Toren says. 'The houses that still stand, and even some of those that don't, are like giant stores. We can salvage clothes, tinned foods, bedding, and candles. We're still finding new stuff.'

I remember the houses that we saw that had clearly already been stripped. 'It won't last forever,' I say.

'We're not going to be here forever,' Paulo says firmly.

Does he really believe that one day the Resistance will

triumph over the Leadership and then we'll all be living in harmony? It seems more likely that the resistance will all be dead before that happens.

Kay drops her spoon in her bowl with a clatter. 'What do we do now?' she asks.

'Hang on,' Toren says, waving a girl over. When she reaches our table Toren gives her a smile. 'This is Laurel's daughter, Tanisha.'

Tanisha nods at us.

'I have to get back upstairs,' Toren says to her. 'Can you show these guys to the recreation room?'

'Okay.' She looks at Paulo. 'You coming too?'

Paulo shakes his head and mutters, 'Work.'

'Why don't you ask me if I'm coming?' Robin glares at Tanisha. 'And why didn't you ask me to take them downstairs?' she says to Toren.

Toren raises his hands. 'Easy, Robin! I thought it was your bedtime.'

'It *is* her bedtime,' Tanisha says and she jerks her head to show that Robin ought to be going upstairs. Robin pushes back her chair and stomps away, gripping her bear tight. We can hear her muttering to herself even as we follow Tanisha out of the cafeteria.

'That's the main noticeboard,' Tanisha says, out in the corridor. 'Anything important goes up there. That's my office and that's Ven's. If you need anything, probably better off coming to me rather than Ven.'

We reach the stairs.

167

'You must get fit running up and down these all day,' I say.

'Quicker if you do this,' Tanisha says and straddles the banister. She pushes off and slides rapidly away from us. That explains why the hand rails are well polished.

Kay looks at me. 'Can we do it?' She glances over her shoulder. She's still expecting an enforcer to appear and start ordering us all around.

'Of course,' I say, and clamber on to show her. 'See?' I push off.

It's amazing how much speed you can gather and it certainly saves time. When I get to the bottom I shoot off a little too fast and almost knock over a young boy stood with Tanisha. Kay on the other hand zooms off and lands neatly on her feet like a gymnast.

'Nice,' the boy says and smiles at Kay.

'Amazing, isn't she?' I say. 'Small, but powerful.'

The boy's turns on me and his smile vanishes. 'I don't see why you find it amazing that she's both those things. You don't have to be lanky to be physically skilled.'

I take a second look at the boy. Even in the weak light of the solar lantern I can see his chin is covered in stubble. He's not so young, he's just short, and I've obviously annoyed him by mentioning Kay's size.

'I completely agree,' I say. 'Kay's a good example of how height doesn't matter. She's way stronger and fitter than I am.'

'That wouldn't be hard,' the boy sneers and turns back to Kay. 'Are you new?'

'They've just arrived,' Tanisha says.

'You should come and work with me,' the boy says. He leers at Kay in such an obvious way that I'm left open-mouthed at his lack of sophistication. Kay doesn't even seem to notice his ogling. 'See you.' He looks Kay up and down and saunters off without even glancing at me again.

'Who was that idiot?' I say in a voice that I hope is loud enough for him to hear.

'Nard,' Tanisha says. 'He's the captain of the Aqua team.' She leads us down the corridor in the opposite direction to him.

'Captain? I thought Ven was captain?' I say.

'Uh-huh, Ven is captain and Paulo is his vice-captain. Actually, I think that should be the other way around.'

I think I'm starting to like Tanisha.

'But everyone is all saying that Ven is a ... genius,' Kay says, stumbling over the unfamiliar word.

'Yeah, seems like that's just a way of saying somebody who thinks they're too smart to be nice to people.'

I can't help smiling at her.

'So Ven's the big boss,' Tanisha says. 'Then each of the teams has a captain. I'm Defence captain.'

'That's fighting, isn't it?' Kay asks.

'Surveillance, guard duty, weapons training *and* fighting.'

I feel Kay warming to Tanisha.

Tanisha stops in the doorway of a long room. 'Rec room,' she says.

By the soft glow of the solar lanterns I can make out a wall of sloping shelves full of books, and a motley collection of ragged chairs arranged in groups. Apart from the literature, it's depressingly reminiscent of the salon at the Academy. There's not much to do. The smallest kids have all disappeared; presumably they've gone to bed. The teenage members mostly sit in huddles, pouring over strips of paper.

I sit down gingerly on a beaten-up old sofa. It reeks of damp.

'What are they doing?' Kay asks.

'Making plans for tomorrow's work,' Tanisha says.

'What work?' I ask.

'Our jobs. Everybody works.'

'Ven did mention that. But what work can the little kids do?'

'The kids start with Basic Training. That's fitness, combat, weapons use, plus reading, writing, science and maths. Ven reckons you've got to be a smart soldier to be good soldier. When you hit seven there's not so much B.T. because you have to work in one of the teams. First off, I was a junior in Provisions helping to grow food, but then we had this Wilderness attack and everyone was saying I was brilliant at fighting them off. Which is true. So I got put on Defence and now I'm captain of the team.'

I don't know why I'm surprised that they're so

organised. Obviously organisation is necessary for a successful Resistance. 'If we stay, will Ven be expecting us to work?' I ask.

'Everybody works,' Tanisha repeats. 'You need to think about what skills you've got and what team you'd be good at, right?'

'Tell the teams to me,' Kay says.

'I told you about Defence – my team. Then there's Provisions – that's growing and finding food. Intelligence is . . . like finding out stuff about the Leadership. Medical is sorting the sick people. C.C. is looking after the kids, and Education is teaching them – you don't know enough about stuff to do to that.'

I consider explaining how highly educated I am, but I realise that she's probably talking about teaching children what the Resistance wants them to know.

'Catering and Housekeeping is mostly cooking and washing, and then there's Nard's team, Aqua—'

'Hey, Tanisha!' a girl shouts from the other end of the room. 'Ven wants you.'

'Sorry. Better go,' Tanisha says and hurries off.

Kay looks at me. 'What's the Aqua team?'

'Aqua will be getting hold of water.' I'm surprised that they've put that rude boy in charge of such an important job. But given that Ven is in charge of everything and he's no ray of sunshine, maybe it's not that shocking.

'Tanisha is talking like we're going to live here,' Kay says.

171

It nags at me that despite the fact that both Kay and I have been institutionalised and trained to obey orders, she's the first one to question Tanisha's assumption that we'll stay here. I want so much to destroy The Leader, but occasionally I suspect myself of a secret desire to just go back to being told what to do. I close my eyes. *No*. The truth hurts, but I am not going to hide from it any more. I've got to take control of my life.

'Do you think we *should* stay?' I ask Kay.

'There's food and water,' she says. 'That's good. But these people,' she leans closer to me and lowers her voice even further, 'do you think they want what you want?'

'They're a resistance; they want to stop the Leadership, don't they?'

'That's what Ty said.'

I sigh. I'm impressed with the set-up the Resistance have got here, but the fact that they've been around for eighteen years and the Leadership is still going suggests that they don't feel the same sense of urgency I do. I don't want to sit around waiting for action.

'We've got to find out what their planning is,' Kay says.

I nod. 'You mean what their plans are. Yes, and if they're no good, we'll leave.'

I don't know where the hell we would go, but the knowledge that we have a choice eases my mind.

Kay reaches out and smoothes my tangled hair away from my bruised face. 'You were brave today,' she says.

172

I rub my sore knee. 'I'm not really cut out for this action hero stuff.'

'It's not your skills, is it? Ilex would be laughing about your fighting.'

I nod, not trusting myself to speak. Ilex was my best friend at the Academy. I hope Kay was right when she said that he will have found a safe place.

'He'd laugh at another thing too,' she says. 'He'd laugh at you doing running for me.'

I manage a half-smile. 'I can't be doing that all the time. Let's agree to avoid any more hostage situations.' I shake my head. 'It was more hobbling than running anyway.'

She touches my arm and I immediately get a surge of desire. I want to pull her on top of me, I want to leave everything else behind and just be with Kay, like it was in the abandoned house – but she says, 'Tell me what happened today.'

I take a deep breath.

'Tell it from the start.'

'We went to Janna's office and I saw Ty, but he wasn't too keen to see me, I think because he was worried about getting into trouble. He did give me a cryptic – er, that's like secret – message to tell me that Janna had been sent to a factory. Ven and I went there, dressed as guards, to try and find her to get the password.'

'What was the factory like?'

If things had gone differently, Kay and I would have

been sent from the Academy to a factory when we turned seventeen.

'Oh, Kay, it was terrible.' I tell her about the injured workers with their burns and missing limbs. And how the workers are fed according to how much work they have done.

Kay's face turns pale. 'At the Academy there were Specials who were all saying that getting to the factory is great. Remember Carma?'

I nod.

'Carma was thinking that the factory is all food and that girls who made lots of babies like her get better things.' She rubs a hand across her face. 'I thinked, I mean, I thought it too. I didn't think it would be big nice all times, but I believed what the info said about the burgers for workers, didn't I?' She looks ashamed.

'It's not your fault that you wanted to think that you were going to a nicer place than the Academy.'

She sighs. 'What happened after you saw all the bad stuff?'

'We found Janna. She said she'd give us the password, but only if we helped her to escape.'

'I thought she would be saying that.'

'Then some real guards turned up. Of course Ven managed to slip away and just left me there. I ended up hanging out the bloody window.' It seems utterly ridiculous now. 'And I saw Janna ... making friends with the guards. She's was going to tell them everything, I know she was. Then there was an explosion—'

174

'Explosion? Like the bombs?'

'Smaller than the bombs, but—'

Her eyes widen. 'They explosioned you?'

I can't help laughing. 'It hit the gas tanks. Part of the factory fell down.'

Kay looks horrified.

I'm not sure now is the time to go into details. 'I was fine. And I found Ven in the rubble. I saved him.'

Kay grips my arm as she takes this all in. 'You're okay?'

'Yes, just tired. A bit sore.'

'What is it that you're saying about Janna?'

I shake my head. 'You were right about her. She's a traitor. I saw her shake hands with one of the guards.' Janna's smirking face comes back to me. 'In fact, we had a charming chat where she showed no remorse at all. The complete opposite.'

'What's chat?'

'Talk.'

'What's remorse?'

'Being sorry.'

'Janna doesn't do sorrying. What did she say?'

'To say hello to you.'

Kay's forehead creases. 'Me? That's not the meanness I was thinking she'd say.'

I drop my eyes to the worn fabric of the sofa.

'Blake? What more things did she say?'

'It doesn't matter.'

'Tell me.'

'She said to tell you that you're beautiful.'

'Oh.' She flinches ever so slightly, but then she covers it with her fighting face. 'That is mean.'

'No! Well, yes, but only because of the way she said it. Only because everything Janna says is mean.' I bite my lip. 'You *are* beautiful.'

'Oh, Blake.' She gives a half-laugh as if I have said something silly. 'Janna's beautiful.' She says it with undisguised envy and I'm filled with both sadness and anger. Why should someone as perfect as Kay ever want to be different? And why don't I have the words to make her see how perfect she is?

'You must think Janna is beautiful,' she persists.

I think back to when I first met Janna. She came to interview me and Wilson at the Learning Community when we won the Moritz prize. Wilson's eyes were out on stalks and I suppose that I thought that she was attractive too. She made me think about sex. But I don't think I liked her. I mean I don't really think that I thought about *her*. Since I've met Kay I've realised that it's horrible to judge a person by their body.

'Do you know what I like best about Janna?'

Kay rolls her eyes. 'What?'

'She's smart. She's really quick. Do you know what I like least about her? She doesn't care about anyone, but herself. What she looks like – well, it doesn't change either of those things.'

Kay nods slowly. I put my arm around her. She looks

176

up at me and I get that feeling again. Like something is peeling open inside me and there's this rush of sweetness and I want to hold her, touch her, be with her. She moves her mouth to mine. We kiss.

As we pull apart, I see Tanisha making her way back across the gloomy room.

'Ven said I have to show you where to sleep,' she says.

I exchange a look with Kay. This seems like another step towards Ven accepting us. My outburst must have had some effect.

Tanisha leads us back up four flights of stairs. We pass several wards before she says, 'This one.'

The ward is dark. There are a number of lumps in beds apparently already asleep. As Tanisha swings her torch around I see Robin curled up under a blanket clutching her bear.

'You've got the corner spot.' Tanisha points with her torch to a mattress covered with blankets.

'But there's no bed,' I say. 'Other people have got beds.' Actually, looking round the ward again I realise that there are some sleepers on mattresses in between the metal beds.

'You get a bed when you've done something. You know, like contributed to the Resistance. You haven't done anything.'

'I've just bloody well saved Ven's skin!'

Tanisha looks at me blankly.

'Well, yes,' I say. 'Obviously that's not much of a contribution.'

177

'Is it the bed for Blake or for me?' Kay interrupts.

'Both of you.' Tanisha smirks. 'Not getting coy now, are you? You weren't coy downstairs, I saw you, you were practically—'

'Thanks,' I say and walk away towards the corner.

Tanisha retreats out of the ward.

Even though we shared a bed in the abandoned farmhouse, I suddenly feel shy and hesitate beside the mattress.

'Come on!' Kay whispers and pulls me down and under the blanket.

She settles herself beside me with her arm around my middle.

I smile into the darkness.

In the middle of the night I wake up and all the fug of the explosion has melted away. My knee is throbbing, but my head is completely clear. I slide carefully away from Kay and stumble through the blackness, out of the slumbering ward. Out in the corridor it's much colder. I feel my way to the stairs and down several flights. I crunch along the gritty corridor to where Tanisha pointed out Ven's office. I can see a faint light leaking out under the door; I fling it open.

'You mother-efwurding bastard! It was you that threw that grenade, wasn't it?' I say.

Despite the late hour, Ven is working at a desk. He turns to look at me calmly.

'Wasn't it?' I demand.

He nods. His face still devoid of emotion.

'Don't you even feel bad?' I ask. 'People were killed in that explosion.'

'Not the workers. The workers were on the factory floor

179

on the other side of the building. I considered all factors, which, contrary to your opinion, is something that I always do with plans.'

'So it doesn't matter about the other factory staff?'

'They're part of the regime. If they end up on stretchers it's their own fault.'

'What about the ones that ended up in coffins?'

'The people we saw only had minor injuries.' He says it with such assurance that my temper flares.

'What kind of leader are you? You must have known when you threw that grenade you were risking the lives of innocent people.'

'What kind of leader would I be if I allowed myself the luxury of never taking any risks? I'd end up paralysed by inaction and indecision. Is that leadership?'

I look at him. He's only a little older than me and he's responsible for everybody here. In a way, he's responsible for trying to save the entire country, but surely he can't be a good captain if he doesn't care about people dying? Doesn't that make him as bad as the Leadership?

'I just keep thinking about those bodies,' I say.

'It was a contained impact grenade. There was no way I could have known that idiot would throw it into the gas tanks. It was designed to kill within a five-metre radius. It should only have killed the guards—'

'And me,' I interrupt, as everything clicks into place. Sweet efwurding efwurd. He was *trying* to kill me. I don't even know how I could have failed to see this before. 'You thought I was going to tell them about this place, didn't you? So you decided to kill me before I had the chance.'

'Oh, I'm sorry. Has my attempt to blow you up hurt your feelings?' He stands up. 'Do you want to get Paulo in here so that you two can sing me a little song about playing nicely with the other children?' He moves around the desk and steps towards me. 'Maybe we should all move away to the coast where we can settle down with the people we love and grow vegetables and educate the kids in something other than hand to hand combat and just give up on this whole crazy "let's get rid of the oppressive killing regime" idea, shall we?' He's right in my face. His skin is waxy. He's clearly still feeling the effects of the explosion.

I take a step back. 'I'm not saying that.'

'That's great. Try focusing on that will you? Try to *not* say as much as possible.'

He closes his eyes and tips his head back as he exhales. His eyes snap open again. He sits down, picks up his pen and carries on writing.

What the hell? '*Is that it?*' I ask. 'I saved your life. You tried to kill me and you think telling me that freedom is important is an adequate explanation? What the efwurd is wrong with you?'

He finishes his sentence and lays down his pen. 'A lot. A whole hell of a lot. You don't need me to tell you that I am far from perfect. I got you wrong. Based on the intelligence I had, I thought you were a threat, so I tried to kill

181

you. I was doing my job. I am attempting to overthrow a corrupt government. People are going to get hurt and some of them won't deserve it. If you don't like my methods, leave.' He goes back to his papers.

I stalk out of the room and stand in the corridor with my fists clenched and my face screwed up. My muscles are so taut with anger that I am quivering with suppressed rage. I want to wake Kay up and leave this stupid place, but I can't. A deep growl of frustration leaves my lips and I smack the heels of my hands against my temples. I realise my earlier conversation with Kay about whether we should leave was completely pointless. Even if I could figure out some other way of getting to my father, I just can't leave the Resistance now that we've found them. I have to stay. I want to help.

Which just goes to show that even when you think you're on the *good* side, the side that's fighting for people's rights, you're still not free to do whatever the hell you like.

182

26

The next morning after breakfast, Ven insists that Tanisha takes Kay and me through some Basic Training. We learn what we should do in the event of a Leadership attack and some rules about survival in the open Wilderness. She also tells us about the day-to-day routines of the hospital.

'Everyone starts with physical fitness before breakfast. After you've eaten, it's a work shift with your team. In the afternoon it's more team work or instruction classes. When you've had dinner, there a bit of rec time. You can only eat and drink at the set mealtimes. Water is pretty tight. Ven says you both had your wash allowance for the week, yesterday.'

I sigh. At least there was plenty of shower water at the Academy, even if it was usually cold. I remember the daily long hot baths I took at the Learning Community. I didn't know how lucky I was.

I turn to Tanisha. 'Can I ask a few questions?'

'Sure.'

'What exactly are the Resistance's plans?'

She gives me a long look. 'That's not the kind of thing Ven likes me sharing about.'

'But you don't always do what Ven tells you to, do you?'

Tanisha laughs. 'Listen, I don't reckon you're a threat, so I'll give you a rough idea. We want to get rid of the Leadership and replace them with elected representatives.'

'How are you going to do that?'

'There are a couple of different plans. Essentially, we want to create an inciting event where we show people all the nasty stuff the Leadership is up to so we can get them onside. We take the Leadership building by storm and cripple the infrastructure by taking out the power companies and then, when we've got them on their knees, we put in place emergency rule, because, you know, the elected representatives bit takes time.'

'What's emergency rule?' Kay asks.

'It's someone taking charge just for a short time,' I say. 'Who's going to do that? Ven?'

Tanisha snorts. 'No. Remember General Adil?'

'From the Long War? Isn't he retired?'

'Uh-huh, the Leadership "retired" him as soon as they realised that he wasn't going to go along with all of their nasty plans, but the public remember him and they love him and . . .' she grins, 'he's on our side.'

This is big news. Adil is a hero. 'Really?'

'Yep.' Tanisha's forehead creases. 'Anyway, that's probably more than I should have said. We've got plans, okay? That's all you really need to know.'

It's not all I need to know, but it will do for now. The Resistance have got definite plans and I want to be part of them.

Tanisha moves on to assigning us to a work team.

Fortunately, she seems happy to accept my assertion that I should be on the Intelligence team and Kay's that she should be with Defence. I was prepared to get into an argument about it, but Tanisha just nods and tells us to report to the captains after lunch and sends us off to the cafeteria.

When we're seated and attacking the salad that's been laid out on the table, Kay says, 'I've been thinking about Janna saying that thing about me.'

'What about it?' I don't want Kay being upset by Janna's nasty remarks.

'You were thinking that she was doing that thing when you're saying what you don't really think. Like, "Oh Kay, you are soooo beautiful."'

I laugh. 'You mean being sarcastic.'

'Yes. But after I had that fight with Janna she didn't do the sarcastic any more. She just said, "You're an idiot," and stuff like that.'

This is true. In the end Janna got so angry with Kay that she gave up making smart remarks and was just downright rude. 'But what difference does that make?' I ask.

Kay's face lights up. 'I don't think she said that thing to be mean.'

I can't help looking sceptical.

'I think she said it to help us. That's why she said that not-Janna thing. She was helping us.'

'What do you mean?'

'I think she told us the password. I think the password is "beautiful".'

I don't believe it for a moment. 'She was just being nasty.'

'Maybe,' Kay says. 'But can we try that word?'

'I don't know,' I say. I'm not sure that I can look at Ven without punching him – and he's the one with the AV bug and the key to the computer room.

'We need to try it. Are you thinking I'm wrong?'

'It's not really that . . .'

'What is it?' She looks at me and I can see that she really cares that something is bothering me. It's such a good feeling to know she worries about me, just like I worry about her. It makes me feel less alone. And I want to tell her what's wrong, but I'm pretty sure that if I told her that Ven tried to kill me that she would pulverise him. A smile escapes me.

'What?' she asks again.

'I just don't like Ven. But we should try out your idea.' I scan the room for Ven, but he's not here. I crunch my last piece of cucumber. 'Let's try his office,' I say.

We take our plates over to the kitchen hatch and leave the cafeteria.

'It's funny,' I say. 'We've switched positions on Janna.'

'What does that mean?'

'You hated her and I thought she was okay, and now I think what you thought and you—'

'I don't think she's okay,' Kay says.

'But you're the one suggesting that she's given us the password.'

'I don't like her. People I don't like can still do good things. She's probably not just bad and bad.'

I realise with a shock that we're talking about Janna in the present tense when in all likelihood she's dead. I don't know what to think about that. She shouldn't have died. She might have been a nasty piece of work, but she didn't deserve that.

We find Ven in his office dolling out orders to a queue of waiting kids. Thinking about Janna has brought back last night's rage. He shouldn't be allowed to go around blowing people up.

I move right up to the front of the waiting gaggle, but I know that if I speak to him I will lose it, which isn't a good idea. I have to work with Ven because he's in a much better position to overthrow the Leadership than I am. I have to work with him if I want to get at The Leader. So I let Kay do the talking.

'We know the password,' she says.

Ven doesn't react.

'We maybe know it,' she qualifies.

Ven looks at the long queue. 'Well, obviously I don't have anything else to do this afternoon other than check out the suspicions of a fairy girl.' He pushes his papers away. 'Come on, then.'

No one complains when Ven leaves the room, nor does he seem to think it necessary to explain where he is going or how long he will be. I notice that Paulo gets up from his own cramped desk and moves quietly into Ven's place. I don't know how he can stand working under Ven.

We head back up to the computer room. Even in the daytime the hospital is still dark and creepy. There are gaps at the edges of some of the window boards which allow shards of sunlight to slice through the gloom. On the stairs we hear a burst of laughter coming from one end of a corridor.

'What's down there?' Kay asks.

'That's the supply store.' He takes us both in with his dark eyes. 'We guard our supplies closely, so don't you get any ideas about helping yourselves. Only captains are allowed to access the supply room. So if you think you need something ask a captain, so that they can tell you that you don't.' He turns back to the stairs.

'What about down here?' I say looking down the left-hand corridor.

Ven looks grim. 'Don't go down that corridor.'

'But can't you—'

'Don't go down that corridor.'

'Wh—'

'Ever.'

I'm getting pretty sick of Ven ordering us about, but I'm determined not to show any curiosity about his stupid secret corridor, so I say nothing.

'Can I ask a thing?' Kay says to Ven. 'Do the Leadership know about the Resistance?'

Ven nods.

'If they know you're here, why don't they eliminate you?' I ask.

'Blake's got a lovely turn of phrase, hasn't he?' Ven says to Kay. He looks back to me. 'When you say "eliminate" you mean "slaughter", don't you?'

'I'm just asking a question. I'm not going to work my way out of this hideous ignorance of mine that you keep referring to unless I ask questions.'

'They don't see us as much of a threat. They keep an eye on us. When they catch us they usually kill us. But they think we're a bunch of kids. What could we possibly do to them?'

I don't tell him that the same thought had occurred to me.

'Also, we're useful to them. We give a face that they can direct people's outrage towards. If they want to blow something up then they can always blame it on us.'

I think about the newspaper article about the Academy

fire. And about the rumours I heard about terrorists when I was a kid. 'I suppose people are prepared to fall for that,' I say.

He narrows his eyes at me. 'Oh, you'd be surprised just how stupid people can be.'

'Anyway, couldn't they kill you all and still blame things on you?'

'They'd have to find us first. We're spread out on purpose and a lot of the cells are in remote locations. We rarely all meet up and when we do the location changes.'

In the computer room, Ven flicks switches in a manner that manages to convey his irritation and scepticism. He cuts in front of me and seats himself at the computer.

'Do you know what my problem is?' he asks Kay.

Kay flashes me a look. 'I know lots of your problems, which one do you want me to say?'

Ven makes a noise somewhere between a laugh and a cough.

'You're smarter than you sound, pixie girl. The specific problem I was referring to was how much I want this footage. I wanted it so much that I went off on that reckless trip with your boyfriend and now I'm wasting my time up here because you two think you've guessed a password.'

I'm not going to answer him. We don't have to keep defending ourselves to him.

'One of your problems,' Kay says, 'is that you do talking when you should do doing.'

Ven raises an eyebrow. 'Well now that I've reminded

myself what a charming pair you two are, it's assisted me in sufficiently lowering my expectations that's there's a hope in hell of this working, so let's give it a try.'

I straighten my back. He's never going to let us hear the end of it when it doesn't work.

'What's the magic word?' he asks.

'Beautiful,' Kay says.

Ven's lips twitch, but he holds back whatever it is he is thinking and lifts his hands to type.

It can't possibly be the password.

Ven's fingers move quickly.

Kay folds her arms.

The computer screen blinks.

The Leader's flushed face appears. *'Children need discipline,'* he says, slapping his hands together.

'I knew it!' Kay says. She grabs my hand and I squeeze it.

'You were right!' I say. 'Wasn't she, Ven? We got you the password after all, didn't we?' But it's stupid of me to expect gratitude. Ven isn't listening; he's studying The Leader's performance with rigid concentration.

We all watch The Leader's ranting for several minutes.

'Children must learn their duty and if we have to beat that into them . . .'

Then the Leader's aide shouts, *'CUT!'* and the image cuts to static.

Ven keeps staring at the screen. 'I might just be able to do it,' he says under his breath.

I don't ask him what he's talking about because I've just remembered who it was that actually gave us the password. I can't work out Janna at all. 'I thought Janna didn't care about beating The Leader,' I say. 'Why did she let us know the password?'

'It's a puzzler,' Ven says. 'I'd suggest that we sit around wasting time discussing it but a) I don't care and b) I'm trying to avoid all activities that bring me within three metres of you.'

He has got such a nerve. Kay shoots him a look of disgust. She takes my arm and turns me away from Ven. 'Maybe she was wanting to help us.'

'But she was with the guards.'

'That's why she said it in a they-won't-know way.'

'A secret way. But … she was *with* the guards. She seemed so cocky and glad that I'd been caught.'

'Did she want to go with the guards?'

'She looked pretty pleased with herself.'

'Janna is good at looking pleased. And she's good at doing the thing that helps her mostly.'

Janna is certainly one for turning things to her advantage. I suppose I don't really know exactly what the deal was with her and the guards. I was guessing that she offered them information, but there's no reason for me to assume that she was going to tell them the truth. I should just be grateful that she gave us the password – whatever her motive was.

Ven is thoroughly unpleasant, but there's no denying

he's decisive. He springs up from his chair, grabs several kids from the corridor and starts snapping out messages for them to take to the team captains.

'What's happening?' Kay asks.

'We're going to do it,' Ven says. 'We're going to cause a revolt.'

'Really?' I say. 'When?'

'Soon.'

When Tanisha was talking, I had assumed their plans were long-term. 'How soon? Don't you need time to prepare?'

'We've been preparing our whole lives. It has to be now. I can't wait.'

Certainly speed does seem to be of the essence because within minutes we're in a meeting room full of the captains and vice-captains of each working team. I'm surprised to see Toren here. I hadn't realised that he was a captain. Ven doesn't want Kay and me to be there, but I tell him that we want to help and I don't know if it's because he is grateful we got the footage for him, but he lets us stay. The room is buzzing. They can feel that something important is about to happen.

Ven doesn't even have to yell for quiet. He just stands really still in the centre of the room and the noise drops away.

'When you were a little kid,' Ven begins. 'You used to hear talk about the Big Day. For as long as any of us can

193

remember, the Resistance have been waiting for the right opportunity to start a revolt.' He pauses and sweeps the room with his dark eyes. 'Well, here it is. It's time for action. Five days from now we will strike with the Birthday Plan.'

There's a stunned silence.

Ven is unmoved. 'I'm going to choose to interpret your mealy-mouthed muteness as a soaring internal joy and a steely, but silent, determination to do your best. Let's get down to—'

'Five days?' Paulo asks.

'Yes. Don't worry, if you forget which day that is I'll remind you by handing you a gun and asking you to shoot anything dressed in red into a bloody pulp.'

'I'm not sure that we're ready.'

'We've been planning this for eighteen years. How much more ready do you want to get, Grandma?'

'But we always said that we needed something, a trigger—'

'And we've got it.'

'It just seems so soon,' Paulo says, almost to himself.

'The Leader's Birthday Plan?' Tanisha butts in. 'We're doing The Leader's Birthday Plan, yeah?'

'That's the one,' Ven says with faux patience. 'And yes, Paulo, it is soon, but The Leader's birthday, being a birthday, only happens once a year – why do I even have to explain this? We strike in five days' time.'

'So it has to be now because of the birthday?' Nard asks.

194

'Because of the birthday and lots of things. Now shut up and listen.'

I lean over to whisper in Kay's ear. 'That's what's great about the Resistance; it's not at all like the other side of the fence where everybody has to do what one bossy, crazy man says.'

If anyone has any further objections to make they keep them to themselves. Paulo adopts his harrowed expression and starts delegating tasks from Ven's long list.

Ven is on a communicator, talking rapidly to someone who I gather is the captain of one of the cells.

'Where did he get that communicator from?' I ask Tanisha.

'We, you know, "borrow" them,' she says.

'Don't you get in trouble for taking people's communicator things?' Kay asks.

'Not these people. They're dead.' She grins. 'Sometimes when someone dies they don't cut the account off for months.'

I'm trying to decide what I think about that when Ven shouts, 'Where are the happy couple?' He spots us. 'If you've finished smooching . . .' People turn round to stare at us. Kay and I shift guiltily apart, even though we weren't touching before.

'We need to make some adjustments,' Ven says, striding over to me. 'You claim your computer skills outshine the dim-wits I usually work with, so you can help with this.'

'If I'm going to help, do you think you could explain precisely what the plan is?' I ask.

'Am I not feeding you?' Ven glowers at me. 'I thought that maybe the provision of food and shelter might in some way place you in my debt.'

Oh that's rich. I saved his life. 'I find it sad that you value the bowl of stew and the blanket that you've given me more highly than the continued life that I've given you by pulling you from that rubble.'

He looks at me with mild surprise. I suck my lips in around my teeth. There's no point getting into a sarcasm war with Ven. 'Look,' I say, 'the more we know about what you're doing, the better placed we are to help.'

He gives a sigh like a growl and starts talking really fast. 'The Leader always gives some rousing little speech on his birthday, yes? This year, when The Leader's birthday message is supposed to go out on the Info, we're going to replace it with our own message featuring some scenes of what's really going on, including your shots of The Leader flipping out and some other pretty nasty images that we've captured on camera. We're going to trigger a riot. Specials, factory workers, the general masses, all of them will take a stand against the Leadership. Got it?'

The idea of everyone in the country rising up and

revolting makes me catch my breath, but I'm not entirely convinced. 'I've tried that broadcast thing, remember?' I say. 'They have a fifteen-minute delay on The Leader's "live" appearances.'

Kay nods in agreement.

Ven lolls his head back in undisguised annoyance. 'I know that, Blake. If I wanted to listen to someone who thought I was an unprepared idiot, I could talk to Paulo. Have you met Paulo? You two should form some sort of club for young men who sound like old women.'

I can feel my temper fraying. 'Are you always this obnoxious?' I say.

His impatient eyes slide off to watch what's happening on the other side of the room. He can't even be bothered to give me his full attention. 'No,' he says walking off to talk to someone else. 'Sometimes I'm asleep.'

It's my turn to make growling noises.

'We've got someone in the TV department of the Media Control Centre,' Paulo says, getting up from his seat and coming over to me. 'They can override the whole system and broadcast anything we want.'

I think about this. 'You're only going to be able to do that once, aren't you?'

He nods. 'They'll know it's him. He'll be busted almost as soon as it happens.'

'So we've got to make this count.'

'Which is why I'd really like to take our time over this.'

On the other side of the room Ven is stood over a frantically scribbling Nard shouting, 'Faster! Faster!'

Paulo shakes his head.

When the meeting disbands, Kay leaves with Tanisha to talk about fight strategies and I go with a boy called Jarit, who is the Intelligence captain. I've got to help him edit together the footage from the Academy with various pieces of film that they already have. The idea is to create something very short, yet convincing. Something which lays bare how evil the Leadership really is.

Jarit picks up everything I show him quickly, but he seems to be another one in the Ven fan club.

'I know he's prickly,' Jarit says, 'but you have to know that he has done great things for the Resistance. Before Ven was in charge we didn't have such clear aims. He's the one who made plans to remove the Leadership. Before that we used to gather bits and pieces of intelligence, but mostly we were working so hard to survive that we didn't get much time for planning. Ven's changed all that. He's made us efficient.'

'Yes, I'm sure the use of child labour does wonders for productivity.'

Jarit gives me a long look. 'You don't understand our way of life. We don't have decades to live. There's no long, innocent childhood for us and there's no gentle decline into old age. We work towards the cause. That's the way it is. At least now Ven's in charge we have enough to eat and we have time to rest.'

'I saw enough of children being exploited on the other side of the fence. I hoped things would be different here.'

'They *are* different. Everyone here chooses to work. At least now we can hope that it's going to get us somewhere.' He looks back to the computer. 'Hope is almost as important as food,' he says in a low voice. 'And you can say what you like about Ven, but we don't go without either any more.'

Jarit and I don't chat much after that.

We work right into the night. When we've finished editing the incriminating footage, we move on to trying to access the Leadership's celebration plans for The Leader's birthday. The solar lantern has faded before we're done, so we work in the black room with only the computer screen for light. Finally, Jarit suggests that we get some sleep.

On my way along the corridor to bed I see Nard pinning something to one of the numerous noticeboards around the hospital. Even though I have to pass him, I keep my eyes fixed ahead of me.

I stumble forwards.

When I look round, I realise that Nard has tripped me up. He smirks into his shoulder. What the hell is his problem?

'Jumped-up water-carrier,' I mutter.

He takes a step towards me. 'Water-carrier? What the efwurd are you talking about?'

'You fetch the water. You're the head of Aqua, aren't you?'

He bursts out laughing. 'Oh that's good! I thought you were thick, but I had no idea you were this stupid. It's not Aqua as in water, it's Aqua as in *Acquisitions*. I get the things that the Resistance needs.'

I look him up and down with what I hope is undisguised disgust. 'You mean you're a thief.'

'I acquire things. And I'm good at it, too. Don't look down your snotty nose at me. Where do you think your clothes came from? This place wouldn't survive without me.'

'I can only hope that we get the chance to see if that statement is true,' I say. And then I turn away before he can have the last word.

Kay is already in bed. She rolls over to smile at me when I climb in.

'How was your day?' I whisper.

'Fighty.'

'Oh.'

'What was your day doing?' She's leant right up against me, her mouth almost touching my ear, so that she can keep her voice right down. Her breath tickles. I like it.

'I was doing stuff on the computer all day.'

'Oh.'

'I guess it's nice that we've both been doing something we enjoy,' I say. 'Why have you been fighting today? Surely you should be saving that for the Big Day?'

'We've just been trying some moves and talking about . . .' she hesitates and I know a new word is coming. 'Strategy.'

'Strategy is good. I'd hate to think that this rebellion was just something Ven had quickly cobbled together.'

'What's cobbled together?'

'Something that hasn't been thought about properly.'

'They've been . . . How do you say it? Planning it for a big long time.'

'That doesn't mean they're ready.'

'What did you do on your computer?'

'We edited together our footage of The Leader with some recordings they've got of conditions in the factories and Academies. Then we hacked into some Leadership files so we could see what they're planning for the celebrations.'

'How can you be looking at what's on the Leadership computers when you're here in the hospital?'

'It's the way they store the information. All their records are stored in remote government data stores.'

'What's remote?'

'It just means that you can get hold of that information from anywhere. If you know how.'

'Do you know?'

'A bit. We found a few things. Actually, most of the afternoon was taken up by a lengthy discussion about whether the Resistance symbol should feature in the film or not.'

'Why would you not be putting the thing in it? It's for the Resistance, isn't it?'

'Yes, but at the moment it's sort of secret; now Ven says that the time for secrecy is over.'

'So it is in?'

'After several hours of discussion, it is.'

I must sound deflated because Kay squeezes my hand. 'The film thing is important like the fighting,' she says.

And she's right. Words and images and symbols mean just as much as any punches you throw. I promise myself that I'll stay positive tomorrow.

The next morning I get to work straight away. In order to get into the central square where The Leader is delivering his birthday speech, Ven has got one of his contacts on the other side to persuade some people with tickets to part with them. I don't know if they used money or threats or a combination, but they've already managed to get us three tickets. Ven wants me to see if we can forge some more. I slide the tickets out of an envelope. I can see straight away we've got no chance of reproducing them. They're chipped and each one has the name, age and occupation of the holder printed on – it's a typical security measure for Leadership paperwork.

My mind shifts to my own plans for the Big Day. If I want to kill The Leader, my best bet is probably to get into the square, too. I'm going to need one of these tickets. I glance sideways at Jarit, who is hard at work on the computer next to me. I wonder if I should take it now or try to find out where they're kept.

I'm interrupted by Ven striding into the room. 'Stop fiddling about with whatever you're doing,' he says, as if he didn't know that I'm doing the job that he gave me. 'Blake, I need you to find some information for me.'

'Well, I didn't think you'd brought tea and biscuits,' I say.

'Steady on, let's not waste your limited capabilities on sarcasm; you're going to need all three of your brain cells to hack into The Leader's itinerary.'

He takes the tickets out of my hands and replaces them with some details. I can't think of a reply vicious enough so I just slap the papers down on the desk. Ven has already switched his attention to Jarit, who is grinning up at him.

My anger towards Ven starts to smoulder. He's still completely ungrateful for what I did for him at the factory and he can't even acknowledge everything that I'm doing for him now. There's no way the Intelligence team would be able to access half of the stuff he wants without my help. It was me who exploited the fact the Leadership's authentication mechanisms are susceptible to a buffer over-run, me who used it to gain elevated privileges, and me who gained access to their system. Jarit would never have been able to do that.

I set my teeth and get to work.

By the time I'm sat in the cafeteria eating lunch with Kay, my resentment has reached a good rolling boil. Who does he think he is, bossing me about? I don't have to follow his stupid rules. I lean over to Kay and whisper.

'Let's check out the secret corridor.'

'Ven told us not to go there.'

'Kay, when have you ever been the kind of person who does what they're told?'

'You want Ven's help so that you can get The Leader, yes? He's not going to help you if you make him angry. And it's not big hard to make Ven angry.' She takes a bite of bread. 'Sometimes I think you do it just by being there.'

'Okay, okay.' I tear my eyes away from her full lips. 'Do you know that you've developed this really annoying habit of being right all the time?'

But right or not, as soon as I get the chance, I'm going down that corridor.

The afternoon is more of the same. I have some success at spoofing addresses and joining the Leadership's internal administration network, which is the first step in gaining access to their messaging service. By the time I meet Kay for dinner my vision is fuzzy from staring at a screen for so long.

'Look at this,' she says, holding up a silver chain necklace with a gleaming stone hanging from it.

'Where did you get that from?'

'Nard gave it to me.'

Why is that creep giving Kay expensive jewellery?

'Where did he steal that from? I don't think he should be using his position to get you sparkly presents.'

Kay beams. 'It is present, isn't it? Nard told me about presents.'

It was almost me that gave Kay her first present. When I got excluded from the Academy I gathered up a whole load of shiny shrap for her, but then I threw it at those boys when they were chasing me and Wilson. I could kick Nard for getting in before I found something else to give Kay.

Kay spins the necklace so that the stone catches the light. 'I'm going to wear it all the times, it's shinier than any shrap!' she says.

Lying in bed later, my annoyance melts away. I remind myself how grateful I am to be alive, lying here, with Kay.

I think of Ilex. I hope that he and all the other Specials are somewhere safe and warm now. Even Ali.

Especially Ali.

At breakfast the following day I notice that Ven has got all his captains gathered around him. He's clearly having a meeting. I know we're not part of the management here, but I can't help wanting to know what's going on. I sidle up to the table in the pretence that I need a knife from the nearby cutlery tray. Of course, Ven spots me straight away.

'Thank you, Blake,' he says. 'I'll have a cup of tea. Anyone else?'

I let that remark go. 'Everything okay?' I ask. 'Anything important happening today?'

'It's no concern of yours.'

'I just want to help.'

'Persistent, aren't you?' He shakes his head. 'Like a tapeworm.'

'Some people are going out to the Wilderness today,' Tanisha says.

I smile at her. It's nice that someone knows how to communicate politely. 'And why's that?' I ask her.

'Recruiting.'

I blink. 'Really? The Wilderness people we saw didn't look like they'd take orders.'

'Reminds me of someone,' Ven mutters.

'It's only some of the Wilderness people who are violent and crazy,' Paulo breaks in. 'Some of them are perfectly reasonable.'

'*We're* Wilderness people,' Tanisha says to him. 'I don't know why you're always talking about them like they're aliens. We're all from the Wilderness too.'

'Don't say that!' Nard says. 'I'm Resistance. We're a different gene pool. I am not Wilderness. I'm not some filthy nutter digging around in the dirt.'

'That's enough, Nard,' Ven says, without looking at him. 'Well, Blake, it seems that once again you've been attempting to apply your limited life experience to a broader situation. I'm sending a team to try to recruit some of our very pleasant Wilderness neighbours to the uprising. So if you could just give us your approval then we could get on with it ... Oh, no, wait – I don't actually require your approval for anything. Ever.'

I ignore his childish insults. 'Sounds interesting,' I say.

'You can't go. You've got work to do here.' He pushes back his chair and turns back to the rest of the group. 'I'll see you all at the meeting this evening.' He picks up an apple and leaves.

I didn't even say that I wanted to go. Ven is so controlling. What if I did want to go? Why shouldn't I?

'When is this recruiting happening?' I ask.

'I don't think that you—' Paulo begins, but Tanisha cuts him off.

'Ten o'clock. Main exit.' She winks at me.

We'll see who makes the decisions about where I go.

Just before ten, I tell Jarrit that Tanisha needs me for something and run down to the main exit, where Tanisha is organising about a dozen Defence team members. Kay is one of them.

'Does Ven know you're here?' Kay asks. She can tell by my face that he doesn't. 'I don't think you should go with us,' she says.

'Why not? Tanisha doesn't have a problem with me.'

'Isn't there a thing that you have to do with Jarit?'

'Since when have you become such a stickler for the rules?'

'I'm not a rule sticker. Isn't your computer things for the Big Day more important than going to the Wilderness?'

'A few hours won't hurt.'

Kay gives up her protests and we leave the hospital and climb into a minibus. We head off in the opposite direction to the one Ven and I took to the border.

Driving through the empty city gives me the creeps. All these offices and shops and houses and schools and restaurants and playgrounds should be full of people. It's like the end of the world.

The walls of buildings are streaked grey and mottled

with black. If this is what the atmosphere does to concrete, how is it affecting our lungs?

'Why are all the buildings standing up here?' Kay asks Tanisha.

Tanisha wrinkles her nose. 'No one really knows. We've come across other areas that didn't see much damage, but it's pretty incredible that this entire city never took a hit.'

'Do you think they just got lucky?' I ask.

'Maybe. Of course Ven reckons there's something sinister behind it. He says there's a reason the Greater Power didn't drop bombs here.'

'Doesn't surprise me to hear that Ven's always looking for the dark motive.'

Tanisha laughs.

Once we're out of the city we see more bomb damage. We pass a row of bungalows. One has a massive hole in its front. Furniture and belongings pour out of it into a heap in the garden, as if the house has vomited its contents. I flinch when I see a man and a woman picking through the junk.

'Are these people safe to be around?' I ask Tanisha.

'Of course.'

'It's just the last lot we met weren't very friendly.'

'I don't think you get it about out here, do you?'

'Get what?'

'Most of the people in the Wilderness are all right. They're just trying to survive. There are some weird ones. But if I'd been messed up by the Leadership I might lose my marbles.'

I blush. It had never occurred to me that the Leadership might be responsible for the state those people who chased us were in.

We drive for fifteen minutes to a small town peppered with the terrifying craters like the one Kay and I saw when we were hunting for water.

'What did that?' I ask Tanisha, pointing out the window.

Her forehead creases. 'Don't you know? What do they teach you at school?'

'Big lies,' Kay says.

I nod. 'I mean, I knew there was bomb damage, but ...'

'T-eight-threes,' Tanisha says. 'The energy involved is so extreme that you end up with a superheated plasma, which leaves nothing recognisable behind. That's how the houses disappear.' She wrinkles her nose. 'Something like that. Ask the Education captain if you want a better explanation.'

I press my lips together. That's one hell of a nasty weapon. I hope we never get into an argument with the Greater Power again.

Our driver stops the minibus at a car park at the edge of the town. There's a weather-beaten sign swinging in the breeze. *Underground Caverns.*

I've got a bad feeling about this.

'Do your friendly types live in the caverns?' I ask.

Tanisha nods. 'Didn't I say?'

She did not say. Kay looks a question at me.

A gate slams down on the brave part of me. I just can't

go underground again. I can't bear the way it makes me feel, like the earth is going to close around me and suffocate me. I feel like an idiot because I invited myself along and now I don't even want to go with them – but I just can't force myself. Not this time.

'Maybe I should wait outside and keep an eye on things,' I say, trying to sound as casual as possible.

'Really?' Tanisha asks, but her attention is already distracted by the driver turning around to ask who their contact for the day is.

'I'll wait, too,' Kay says to me. 'If Tanisha says it's okay.'

I protest, but it turns out that Tanisha was planning to leave two people to keep guard on the minibus anyway, so Kay stays with me while the others walk into the visitors' centre where the entrance to the caverns is.

'Sorry,' I say to Kay.

She dismisses my apology with a shake of the head. 'I don't mind it.'

'Why would anyone want to live underground?' I shudder.

'Maybe they're coming out lots. It wouldn't be nice to not see the sky and all things.'

Kay looks up at the clouds. She spent so long cooped up in the Academy that just being in the open air makes her face light up. 'Tanisha told me these people are working all together. What's that thing when you get stuff and all the people have some of it?'

'Sharing.'

'She said they do sharing all the time. That's good, isn't it?'

'I can't imagine that they've got a lot to share. They'd be better off joining the Resistance.'

'Yes, but—' Kay breaks off. She's staring behind me. I turn around to follow her sight line. Coming down the path to our left is a woman. Her clothes are in tatters and her hair is long and matted.

'Don't panic,' I say to Kay in a low voice. I try to remember what Tanisha said about Wilderness people. Just because she looks odd she might not be aggressive. I hope she might turn off before she reaches the car park, but she carries on, heading straight for us, and there's no misunderstanding the expression on her face. She's angry.

'Inside,' I say, grabbing Kay's hand.

'But the bus . . .'

'I don't think it's the bus she wants.'

Kay lets me pull her towards the entrance to the visitors' centre. Before we reach it the sound of someone clobbering a saucepan rings out from behind the open door.

'What the hell?' Kay says.

I look back at the Wilderness woman; she's stopped dead in her tracks, wincing away from the noise. I'm rooted to the spot. The clanging gets louder and closer. I don't take my eyes off the Wilderness woman. She cringes and then, slowly, turns and creeps away.

'Thank you,' I say, turning to face our rescuer, but I don't get any further than that because when I see who is holding the saucepan, my mouth falls open.

It's Ilex.

'Ilex!' Kay shouts and throws herself into his arms.

I can't believe he's here. When I first arrived at the Academy, Ilex was the only one who would even speak to me. We lost him when we escaped, and all this time I've been wondering if he made it out alive. I slap him on the back.

'It *is* you,' Ilex says, pulling back from Kay to look at me with his eyes wide. 'They said they had Academy Specials with them and I ... Blake, where's Ali?'

It's like the air has been punched out of me. I look at Kay. Ilex doesn't move, but his face changes. He knows. His eyes turn glassy.

Kay eases Ilex into a sitting position on the doorstep. He stares unseeing at the ground. She takes both his hands in hers. 'I'm so sorry,' she says. 'Ali is dead.'

He blinks.

'She was amazing,' I say. 'She saved us. We were trapped in the lift and she climbed out and went to get the

key and stood up to The Leader's aide, but . . . he shot her.'
I remember Ali's body crumpling when the bullet hit her.
All I can say is, 'She was so brave—'

'I don't want to know it,' Ilex says. He twists his head
away as if to avoid hearing. 'It's not good. She
shouldn't be saving you.' He looks back to me, raw
grief contorting his face. 'You're the big good, Blake;
you're the one with the thinkings and the words. *You*
should have saved you. Why did you get Ali to do it?
She was a little girl. She was mine.' A sob tears from his
throat. 'I loved her.' He puts his head in his hands and
weeps.

I don't know what to do. I don't know what to say. I
don't have the right words to make things better.

Kay pulls Ilex to her and wraps her arms around him.
She doesn't speak. She just makes noises like a mother
comforting a baby.

Kay sits with Ilex like that for a long time. In the end
Ilex lifts his head and rubs his face with his sleeve.

'I have to go now,' he says.

'Ilex, wait,' I say, but he's already gone back into the
visitors' centre. He disappears down a corridor marked *To
the Caverns*.

I don't know if I should follow. I desperately want to
talk to him. I want to make him feel better. I'm afraid
that I've lost a really good friend. Tears prick at my
eyes.

Kay sees my indecision. 'We have to wait to talk to him.

216

He loved Ali so much. He wants to think about her, he doesn't want to talk to us.'

She's right. Ilex needs time. I can't force him to understand just because I feel terrible.

A man comes towards us along the corridor Ilex disappeared down. I tense.

'You the Academy kids?' he asks.

'Yes,' Kay says.

'Ilex's friends?'

I don't feel like a very good friend, but Kay nods.

He sighs. 'No Ali, then.'

'She died,' I say. 'We tried to look after her, we really did, but there was this man—'

'Terrible places,' the man interrupts. 'Academies. Terrible.'

'Yes,' Kay agrees.

'Been looking for her since he got out,' the man explains. 'When he heard you were here . . . well, suppose he hoped one of you'd be Ali.'

The guilt of being alive when Ali is not fills my throat.

'Is Ilex all right?' Kay asks. 'I mean, is he okay here? Is it a good place?'

The man's face darkens. 'Don't believe everything the Resistance say about us. We know how to look after kids. And we don't send them off to get shot.'

The muscles in his neck have tensed up.

'The Resistance didn't say anything bad about you,' I

217

say. 'Honestly; they told us that you were good people.'

'Good, is it? Normally, we get called shirkers.'

'What's shirker?' Kay asks.

I look at the man, but he obviously isn't going to offer an explanation. 'It's, er, someone who doesn't do the thing that they should do,' I say.

'Should do?' The man's face darkens. 'You think we should go interfering on the other side of the fence, do you? Then what happens? My kids'll end up in an Academy. Thought you ran away from one of them.'

I feel like we're caught in the blast of his rage towards the Resistance.

'I don't want anyone in an Academy,' I say quietly.

But the man isn't listening; he's off on his own train of thought. 'Coming round here, asking for help! What about what you could do for us? Do you think sticking a bit of food our way is enough? If you've got such big ideas about making things better for Wilderness people, you could start with us.'

'Maybe—' Kay begins.

'Do you think we like living down there in the dark and the dirt? Do you think we don't wish it were different?'

'It must be hard,' Kay says gently.

'That's why the Resistance are so tough on their kids.' And as I say it, I realise that I'm becoming more sympathetic to their methods. 'They're fighting to make things better. That's why they want your help.'

He gives a gusty sigh. 'No use fighting. This isn't the

nicest way to live, but you've got to accept things. Do the best with what there is. It's no good dreaming. That's what you are: load of silly kids dreaming. You'll never change a thing.'

I might be a kid, but I refuse to accept that there is nothing we can do.

'We've got to believe in a better world if we want to bring about change,' I say.

The man tuts.

'It is hard to keep on fighting,' Kay says, and I'm not sure if she's talking to me or the man.

The man gives Kay a long look. 'We'll take care of Ilex,' he says, and he walks away.

When Tanisha and the others return, she doesn't look too happy. We board the minibus and she throws herself back in her seat.

'It's just stubborn,' she says, more to herself than anyone else.

'Did they say no?' Kay asks.

'Yeah, they said no.' Tanisha blows out a breath. 'Most of them anyway.'

Kay shoots her a commiserating look. 'Are there lots of people down there?'

Tanisha nods. 'There used to be a whole lot more of them when they lived in the school.'

'What happened?' I asked.

'Leadership pounced and took a load of them away. I reckon they're in factories now.' She frowns. 'If they're lucky.'

'They just took them away? Has that ever happened with the Resistance?'

'They manage to pick off a cell occasionally. Us central lot move around a lot. We've got strict security. We don't normally let in anyone we're not expecting.'

'I thought that was because of this boy and girl Ven was told would be posing as Academy students,' I say.

'Trust me; Ven's suspicious of new arrivals even when he's not expecting Leadership spies.'

I look out the window. What happened to the boy and girl? Was the information wrong, or are they still wondering about in the Wilderness? They must have been around my age; did they want to spy for the Leadership or were they forced into it?

'Do they ...' Kay nods back in the direction of the caverns, 'have guards?'

'Uh-huh,' Tanisha nods, 'for what it's worth.'

I catch her meaning. 'They're kidding themselves thinking they're safe down there, aren't they?'

Tanisha shrugs. 'It's not a bad place to hide.'

'But if anyone ever finds them and wants to catch them, they'll be like rats in a trap.'

She shrugs again. 'We don't try to tell them how to live. In fact, we've tried to help them. You'd think they'd want to give something back.' She grips the seat in front of her. 'It's not even *for* us, it's for everyone. They're too damn scared, that's what it is.'

I remember what the man said. 'I think they're so beaten

down that they're afraid to even imagine that things could be better,' I say.

'Hmm,' Tanisha says. I think she feels it's got more to do with straight-up cowardice.

'So no helpers at all?' Kay asks.

'A few of them said they'd come. Out of the adults. They didn't even give the kids a choice. I bet they would have come if they'd had the chance.'

I'm not so sure. Part of the reason this country is in such a mess is because it's really hard to trust any other way than the one you've grown up with.

For the rest of the journey all I can think of is Ilex's face falling from hope to grief.

All through the afternoon I keep running over what happened at the Academy. It's my fault that Ali's dead. I want to scream *I didn't mean it*.

All these things that I've done. All these people who have died. Ali, my mother, Wilson, Scarface. I didn't mean for any of this to happen. How have I become a murderer? It doesn't feel like I had any choice. I don't want to be where I am. This has to end soon. This revolt has got to work.

That night, Kay is upstairs working and I'm still lost in my thoughts, staring at the feathered paint peeling off the rec room walls, when a whispered word from Tanisha's conversation with a boy with dreadlocks pierces my bubble.

Assassination.

Without turning my head or changing my posture, I tune into Tanisha's low voice. At first she says a lot of things about timings that I can't follow, but then the boy talks. His voice is louder and I distinctly hear an occasional word drop like a penny.

'Rifles ... square ... The Leader ... assassination team ...'

I catch my breath.

They don't just want to remove the Leadership from power. They want to kill The Leader. I'd assumed that they wanted to imprison him, maybe put him on trial. But they want to kill him, just like me.

Tanisha and the boy are interrupted by Robin. 'You were talking to those cave people today,' she says to Tanisha accusingly.

'Yep,' Tanisha agrees.

'You were trying to get them to help.'

'That was the plan.'

'I could ask my friend Jed to help you.'

'No point, we can't take any of the Wilderness children unless their parents agree.' Tanisha catches hold of Robin's arm to ensure she has her attention. 'And Robin, you'll be in trouble if anyone finds out you've been roaming about playing with kids in the Wilderness.'

Robin pouts. Tanisha placates her by saying she'll play a game of cards before Robin goes to bed. The boy moves away.

The word *assassination* is still flashing like a sign in my mind. All this time I've been thinking that I'd have to steal one of the tickets that Ven has got hold of for the celebrations in the central square where The Leader is going to speak, so that I would be able to get close enough to him to kill him. And even though I knew that every Resistance member will be given a gun, I was panicking that Ven would try to make me an exception. But now it's all being made easy for me. Ven will have planned how to get as close as possible to The Leader. All that weapons practice in our Future Leaders sessions on warfare is finally going to be some use. All I've got to do is get on that Assassination team.

I just have to persuade Ven.

30

Ven has come to check on my progress in the computer room, but I've got more important things to talk about.

'I want to be on the assassination team,' I say.

'And I want to work with monkeys because I think they would better appreciate the concept of secrecy. How the hell do you know about the Assassination team?'

'It doesn't matter. Can I be on the team with you?'

'Touched as I am that you've formed some sort of attachment to me, I think you'd be better off away from weapons. I haven't seen you actually do anything useful with your brains, but I'm guessing you'd miss them if you accidentally blew them out.'

I'm not going to react to his jibes, this is too important. 'I just really need to do this.'

'I see, you think you're going to be the one to fire the golden shot. Fancy yourself as a hero, do you?'

'It's not about being a hero. It's personal.'

Ven bursts out laughing. 'I'm running a revolution here,

not a girls' slumber party. If I take you you'll only end up getting yourself shot.'

'I'm fairly certain that you feel able to spare me.'

'And just what is it about you that makes you think I should choose you to kill The Leader over my highly-trained Defence team?'

'Because I want The Leader dead.'

'We all want him dead.'

'That man has ripped apart my life. He is responsible for the death of my mother and my best friend. I've seen the terrible things that happen in his Academies and his factories. I don't just want him dead, I want to annihilate him.'

'If you could shoot him through the heart with sheer willpower and vitriol then I would certainly take you along, but as it is I'd rather have someone who shoots real bullets, not ones made of teenage angst.'

'I can shoot a gun.'

'Hmm, it's cute when you lie. You blink too much. No, wait, only one of those statements is true.'

'I've spent plenty of time shooting. I told you before, we had training with simulation weapons at the Learning Community. Come on, Ven, you've got to take me.'

'They call them simulation weapons because they're not real. I want The Leader to watch an actual bullet speed towards his face, not a toy one.'

I'm getting nowhere. I decide to hedge my bets.

'Even if you're not going to let me be in the Assassination team with you, you should probably let me have a go with a real gun. Wherever I am on the day I'm going to need one, aren't I?'

Ven shrugs. 'All right, Blake, even I enjoy a good laugh occasionally. Let's take a look at you.'

The Resistance practice their shooting in the vast underground car park. When Ven and I arrive, there are already several groups of people, including Nard, aiming at plastic barrels and shop mannequins. I enjoy watching Nard miss a couple of times and then I'm alarmed to see a small girl loading a rifle.

'Is it safe for her to do that?' I ask.

Ven scowls at me.

I know Ven thinks I'm too protective of the kids, but I can't stop myself from saying, 'I just think that when I was that age I probably wasn't careful enough.'

'When I try to imagine the skinny parcel of pomposity that you must have been as a child, I'm fairly certain that you were incapable of following instructions because firstly, you'd already embarked on the erroneous path of considering yourself better than anyone else and secondly, you knew efwurd all about how dangerous the world can be. These kids have been trained. They have learnt the hard way. They remember the girl who shot herself in the leg. They know that they have to learn how to survive. They're not ordinary kids; they're members of the Resistance.'

Someone fires a machine gun and I twitch with surprise.

Ven smirks. I really hope that I'm not going to make an idiot out of myself.

Ven strides over to a well-built boy. 'I know what you're thinking,' he says to the boy, not bothering with a greeting. 'You're thinking that Blake here looks like a book-loving, weak-wristed asthmatic, but apparently he fancies himself as a sniper, and you know me, I don't like to grind a young man's hopes and dreams beneath the sturdy heel of realism – well, actually I do, but today I'm so full of love, or possibly gas, that I want to make a wish come true. Give him a rifle.'

The boy turns to me. 'Hi, I'm Eame.' He holds out his hand, which is something no one has done to me for a long time. It takes me a second to remember to shake it. 'I'm Defence vice-captain,' he says. 'So are you here for a brush up or ...?'

'He's here to shoot a damn gun, as I already wasted valuable breath telling you. Maybe we'll get lucky and he'll turn it on himself. Who can know? Nobody can know until you give him the efwurding gun.'

'Just a second,' Eame says to me and he walks over to a locked trunk.

Is he deliberately ignoring Ven? It's nice to see someone making a point. I don't know why so many of them tolerate Ven's rudeness. Ven doesn't seem at all bothered. He goes over to Tanisha and starts hectoring her about something. I'm left with the others behind a safety line.

'Getting some practice in before the big day, huh?' a girl with a drawling voice says to me.

'Something like that,' I reply.

'Yeah, it's pretty good to get the feel again. I mean, I know that they have to be careful with the ammunition supplies, but it's been months since I've used actual bullets.'

'Months, you say?' I wonder what she'd think if I told her that I've never held a real gun in my life.

Eame comes back and holds out a rifle. 'Do you need me to . . .?'

'Lend him your spine?' Ven says, reappearing. 'Yes, that would be useful.'

I decide to try Eame's technique and ignore Ven altogether. I look at the gun. 'If you could just jog my memory,' I say.

'Okay, come over here.' He leads Ven and me to a platform made of bricks and planks, where another boy is already lying on his stomach shooting at shop dummies set up some distance down the concrete space.

'Lie down,' Eame says.

I get on to my front.

'Hold it like this. Take your aim; get the target square in the cross-hair. Then you need to relax.'

Which is exactly what they told us in the Future Leaders gun training sessions. I remember this. I can do this. My shoulders are up around my ears. I swallow and try to let the tension go.

'Before you shoot, let out a breath. Then squeeze. There's going to be some recoil, okay? The mannequin with no arms is yours.'

I take my aim, blow out a breath and squeeze the trigger. The gun kicks. The plastic dummy falls backwards. Yes! I can still feel reverberations through my hand.

Eame raises his eyebrows. 'You've done this before.'

'Sort of.'

'Go again. Next mannequin along.'

I focus on the dummy. Down it goes. And the next one. And the next.

'Let's, uh, let's try a little more distance shall we? See the next set of targets? Try them.'

I don't think. I don't hope. I don't even look at Ven. I just breathe and shoot, breathe and shoot. Every time I take a dummy I imagine Wilson beside me in the simulation room, punching the air. I hit target after target. Gradually the sound around me falls away and when I knock the final dummy flying there's a great cheer. I realise that everyone else in the car park has stopped what they're doing to watch me. I allow myself a smile. I look around for Ven, but I can't see him.

'Ven had to go up to sick bay,' Eame says.

What the hell? That's just typical. I bet he had to leave right around the time he realised that I was going to prove him wrong.

'You'll tell him that I'm a good shot, won't you?' I ask Eame. I really have to get on that team.

229

'Sure will. Reckon you're one of the best.'

I notice one person hasn't joined my admirers. Nard has turned his back on the crowd and is reloading his gun.

'What about him?' I say, nodding towards Nard. 'Is he any good?'

Eame grins. 'Nope. He ought to be, spends enough time down here. But he's never quite got the knack.'

My smile returns.

Kay appears from the back of the crowd. I'm so hyped up by success that I pull her into an embrace. I feel amazing. Kay feels amazing.

'Are you doing something important?' I ask. 'Do you want to come and see the film we've put together?'

Her eyes twinkle. 'It's lunchtime for me. I can come there for a time.'

We leave the dispersing crowd and head back into the hospital proper.

'I didn't know you did shooting,' Kay says.

'I haven't done it like that before.'

'How did you do it?'

'It was a simulation.'

Kay gives me her questioning look.

'A pretend gun and pictures of people to shoot on a computer.'

Kay nods slowly.

'It was a pretty good simulation. The facilitator always told us it was just like the real thing. I wasn't entirely convinced, but I guess they were right.

Everything was just like the practice gun. The muzzle flash, the recoil—'

'That recoil is like a punch in the shoulder,' Kay says, showing off her own newfound experience.

I laugh. 'I never thought we'd be having a conversation about our shooting skills.'

'We have to learn it before the Big Day,' Kay says with a straight face. 'I'm just hoping I've learnt it good enough.'

Which isn't so funny, but I push down any worrying thoughts because I've just shown Ven up and Kay is holding my hand.

We start up the main staircase and my cheerful mood bubbles up again. I'm pretty pleased with myself. No wonder guards always look so cocky. Being able to shoot straight is a surprisingly good feeling. As we ascend I realise that I'm walking tall with my shoulders back and my chest out. I really am feeling quite smug and also sort of . . . manly.

Then there's a piercing scream and I almost wet myself.

'What the hell was that?' I say.

'I don't know. Maybe some Defence team are doing fighting?' Kay says.

She's trying to fob me off. 'Most of the Defence team are in the car park. That scream came from over there.' I point down Ven's forbidden corridor. 'Let's take a look.'

'No, Blake. That's a bad-shouldn't.'

'Come on. Someone was screaming, really screaming.'

'Ven will be cross.'

But I don't care what Ven thinks; I've just proved him wrong and I'm so pumped up I'm convinced I can do it again. 'Are you just going to do whatever he tells you?' I ask.

'I don't want trouble.'

'If Ven is doing something bad then I don't think we can just ignore it.'

She looks up and down the stairs. There's no one coming. She tilts her head on one side. 'Okay, one quick looking.'

In the first ward we peer into, the metal framework used for hanging curtains to separate the beds has been torn away from the ceiling. It lies on the floor in twists and coils like toy train track. The next room is smaller with a porcelain sink covered in scales of filth. There are streaks of something green down the tiled walls.

As we duck back out I realise I'm holding my breath, maybe because the whole corridor is so quiet. Unlike the other floors, where there's plenty of activity, there's no one walking about or working away in rooms. Halfway down the corridor we side-step an abandoned green fabric screen on a bent metal frame and find a door with a sign saying *ISOLATION UNIT*.

'What does that mean?' Kay asks.

'It's where they kept people who they didn't want to give their illnesses to others.'

The skin on my scalp tightens.

'Do you think it's safe?' Kay asks.

I'm not sure it is safe, least of all when Ven finds out that we've disobeyed him, but if he's doing something horrible then I have to know. 'Just . . . be ready,' I say. Kay tenses up and raises her hands.

There's a soft sound from behind the door and finally I can bear it no longer. My blood pumps hard and I take a deep breath.

I fling open the door.

And there is a room full of the absolute last thing I ever expected to find.

Babies.

The clean and tidy ward is filled with sleeping infants. Down one side are the smallest babies, in tiny cribs like clear plastic boxes on legs. On the other side are older babies and toddlers in metal cots.

'I thought it was going to be bodies,' I say. 'Or something horrible that Ven had done, but not . . .'

'Babies.'

I peer into the plastic crib nearest to me. The baby is pink and chubby and has fuzzy blonde hair. 'It looks healthy,' I say.

'Blake, where have all these babies come from?'

'Oh hell.' My face crumples in disgust. 'Do you think they've got something like the Making Hour?' One of the horrible things that I discovered at the Academy was that the Specials were encouraged to get pregnant so that their babies could be taken away to be raised as Specials and then factory workers themselves.

'We would have heard talking about it, wouldn't we?' says Kay. 'And where are the baby-bellies?'

She's right. I haven't seen a single pregnant girl in all the time that we've been here.

'So where have they come from and what the hell are they planning to do with them?' I have a nasty vision of Ven leading a tiny army into battle with the guards.

One of the babies starts to whimper.

Kay looks at it like it's an unexploded bomb. 'That is going to do big crying in a minute. Do something.'

I don't have a clue what you do with a crying baby. 'Like what?'

The baby stops whimpering and lets out a wail.

'Let's go,' Kay says.

But before we've gone two paces, a door at the back of the ward swings open and the boy with curly hair, Toren, comes out.

Kay shoots me a horrified look.

Toren scoops up the squalling baby and makes a shushing noise. He rocks him back and forth. 'Can you keep it down?' he says to us.

I wait for him to shout at us to get out or to say that he's going to tell Ven that we came into this secret place. But he doesn't.

'Er, okay,' I whisper.

'It's just I've only just got him to stop screaming.'

I manage a nod.

'They always have a nap after their lunch. If you want to visit, it's best if you come back at playtime.'

I nod again. 'So . . . you look after the babies do you?'

'Mmm-hmm. I thought you knew that. I'm captain of C.C.'

He sees my blank look.

'Child Care?'

I had noticed that Toren was a captain, but no one ever mentioned what of.

'I thought Tanisha was saying C.C. is education,' Kay says.

'We're sort of linked. We start teaching them early. But we play too.' He smiles down at the baby, who has drifted back off to sleep.

'That's . . . great,' I say. 'Come on, Kay, we should go.'

Back out in the corridor I struggle to keep my voice at a level that Toren won't hear. 'What the hell is Ven playing at? Those kids aren't a secret! He was just messing with me.' I gesture a hand at the door. 'The door isn't even locked! He just wanted to wind me up. Stupid jerk.'

Kay tuts. 'That Ven, he likes playing with you. He likes thinking that he is cleverer than you.' She looks at me sternly. 'And you . . .'

'And I get drawn into the battle.' I rub my face. 'I know; I've got to stop giving him a reaction.'

We go back to the stairs, heading towards the computer room, but my good mood has disappeared. Why does Ven have to keep playing mind games? And what the hell are they doing with all those little kids?

Nard spots us from the landing above.

'Hi Kay,' he calls, deliberately ignoring me. 'I've got something to talk to you about. Do you think you could come to the Aqua office later?'

'Okay,' Kay says, beaming at him like he's a really great guy.

Nard continues up the stairs without even glancing at me.

'He is so rude,' I say loud enough for him to hear.

Kay rolls her eyes.

'What? You know it's not really your opinion that he's interested in.'

'Stop it. Stop this jealous.'

'Jealous? I'm not jealous. Do you even know what that word means?'

'Yes, I know it. Tanisha told me it. Do you know when she told it? When she was talking about you.'

'I'm not really interested in your bitchy chats with the girls.'

'Don't do that!' she snaps so fiercely that I flinch.

'What? Don't do what?'

'Don't do that girls-are-bitches thing. I hate it. I thought you weren't a person that's all saying girls are like this and boys are like that. If you don't like me, don't like me because of me, not because I'm a girl.'

I feel ashamed of talking in stereotypes, but I'm too wound up to admit it. Things were going so well and now everything is annoying me.

Kay storms off, but I'm too cross to follow her. It's not my fault that she's too naive to see Nard for the creep that he is.

I slink down to the rec room, where I spot Paulo sat on a corner table surrounded by pieces of paper. Maybe he can give me some answers about the babies. He looks up as I approach.

'Can I sit down?' I ask.

He piles up some papers to make a space. 'Sure.'

'Can I ask you something?'

'Go ahead.'

I open my mouth and close it again. I'm not really sure how to phrase the question.

'Kay and I just saw the babies napping.'

'Yeah?' he smiles. 'Did you see Nell? She's my niece, my sister's little girl.'

'Er, I don't think I met Nell. I don't think I've met your sister either.'

'She died.'

'Oh. I'm sorry.'

He shrugs. 'She was twenty-one. That's longer than most people get.'

I struggle to adjust to the idea that twenty-one is a good innings.

Paulo smiles. 'I got on really well with her. She was brilliant; kept telling me what great things I was going to do.' His smile fades and he looks down at his hands.

I don't know what to say. Have I made him sad by

bringing up his sister? 'Well, she was right, wasn't she? Here you are, vice-captain of the whole show.'

He nods vaguely.

I should change the subject. 'Do all the babies belong to people who, um ...' I nearly say 'died' but the word doesn't quite come out.

'A few of them. It's been a while since there's been anyone here who was in a position to want a child. After the war it was the adults who died of the Sickness first. We didn't really understand what was going on till a doctor from the other side came to join us. He realised how the aftermath of the T-eight-three bombs was destroying our health. And it was pretty clear that older bodies are more quickly affected.' He pauses to make sure I'm listening. I don't know what this has to do with the babies, but I nod to encourage him to continue.

'As the years went on, younger people started dying from the Sickness, and of course some Resistance members were lost in missions. Tanisha's mum and her captains could see that if they allowed things to go on as they were the entire Resistance would be wiped out.'

My mind swings to what a bleak and lonely experience that would have been for the last handful of survivors. Efwurd, imagine being the very last person left.

'They knew that we needed to keep our numbers up. It seems reproductive organs suffer in the Wilderness too, plus most of us are too young for kids anyway. So, not many babies have been naturally conceived out here.'

'So . . . where do the babies . . .?'

'Babies?' Ven has crept up behind me. 'Are you asking about babies, Blake?'

To my shame I feel myself blushing. 'I—'

'Are you asking about Resistance babies?'

'I just wonder—'

'Resistance babies who live upstairs? On the corridor I told you not to go to?'

'Well, yes but—'

'Let me just get this straight, you deliberately disobeyed me? Me, the captain of the Resistance. The group of people that you are hoping will accomplish what you'll never manage on your own.'

Annoyance prickles over me like a rash. 'Shut up, Ven. No one else has said anything about the babies being a secret.'

'They're not,' Ven says. He snaps off his pretence at being angry and gives me an amused sneer.

'King hell, you're infuriating. I just wanted to know where they came from.'

'I'm sure Paulo is doing a good job of giving you a history lesson. He's always happy to get involved after the event. Go on Paulo.'

'The babies are the future of the Resistance,' Paulo says.

It sounds like a slogan, but I can see from the way he says it that he believes it.

'You know that life expectancy for us is nineteen years,' Paulo continues, 'which means we need new blood, all the time. Before a Resistance member dies they are expected to deliver someone to replace themself and, in order to increase our numbers, an additional person.'

'What do you mean by "deliver"?' I ask.

Paulo's eyes flick to Ven. 'We bring them through the tunnel.'

I stop still. 'You steal babies?'

'The younger the replacement, the longer they'll live in these conditions,' Paulo says.

'*You steal babies.*'

'Oh, Blake,' Ven interrupts, 'you seem fixated on the idea of theft. Is this your criminal background coming out again?'

'Kidnapping isn't something to joke about,' I say.

'No,' he says and his smirk disappears. 'You're right, it's not. A child's future is a very serious thing. What if your tiny-hipped girlfriend ever managed to push out a baby? What would you want for your child? Would you want them shunted off to an Academy – where you assure us no one is having much fun – or would you want them out here? Free and fighting for others to be free—'

'And soaking up the toxic atmosphere so they can die before they've really lived,' I finish.

Ven pulls his lips tight. 'Sacrifices have to be made.'

'Where exactly do these babies come from?'

'I'm sure you're indulging your hysterical side and imagining us plucking them away from the loving bosom of their families, but actually they're all the children of

241

Academy Specials. They would have been shoved in a state nursery anyway.'

'So that makes it all right for you to play God, does it?'

Paulo goes on about how they've got a doctor working for them, helping them get babies out of the maternity homes, and something about the terrible conditions in the state nurseries, but I'm hardly listening. Ven makes me so angry, I want to smash something. I want to kick his stupid head, but there's no point in even letting him know he upsets me. I press my tongue hard against the back of my teeth and clench my fists under the table.

The silence stretches taut.

'So . . .' falters Paulo, 'I heard that you're really something with a rifle, Blake.'

I suck in air through my nose and relax my hands.

'That's right,' I say turning to Ven. 'I hit every target.'

'That's nice,' he says.

I'm waiting for him to say something about the assassination team, but he doesn't.

'I took out every single dummy, ask anyone.' To my annoyance, I sound like a sulky child.

'I don't need to ask, I already know. Just like I know that you've got no experience of gunfights or assassinations. And that you've never had any stealth training and that your physical fitness is atrocious.'

'But . . . surely . . . I mean, doesn't it count for anything that I'm a brilliant shot?'

'Like I said, it's nice.' He turns back to Paulo and I know that's his final word.

That night I'm back in the rec room, with my head in my hands and wondering how the hell I'm going to get close to The Leader, when Kay walks in. I stiffen and resolve not to look at her, but my eyes betray me by flicking sideways. She meets my gaze. I can't help it, my lips twitch. She laughs and shakes her head at the same time. 'Don't be mad at me,' she says sitting down.

'I'm not mad at you. I'm mad at that sleaze Nard.'

She touches my arm. 'Don't be all cross if I'm not being rude to the people you're rude to.'

I make a decision to stop telling Kay what an idiot Nard is. It's not up to me who she is friends with. 'Okay,' I say. 'Let's not fight.'

Then she kisses me and I remember how happy I am that it's me she wants to be with.

There aren't many people in the recreation room. Ven has still got a lot of teams working on his plans and those who aren't working are so tired that they've gone to bed. I sit on a sofa with Kay and relate what Paulo and Ven said about the babies. Her mouth drops open when I describe how they steal them away from the other side, but when I've finished she doesn't explode with outrage as I expected.

'Don't you think that's terribly wrong?' I ask.

She rubs her eyebrow. 'I don't know if we should be saying it's right or wrong.'

'And what would happen if no one said that the Leadership is wrong? What if I'd never said that Academies were wrong? It might not be easy to decide if something is wrong, but that doesn't mean that we shouldn't bother.'

'Okay, okay. I'm just thinking if someone had stealed me away when I was a baby and I had lived here and not in the Academy. If I could have had the choice, I think I would have choosed to come here.'

'You might have, but you can't make that decision for other children. That's what it's all about isn't it? People should be able to choose for themselves.'

'But it's not like that. And if you can't choose for yourself, then you want someone to do a good choice for you.'

I'm unreasonably irritated by Kay saying this. I have to stand up and go and look at a stack of books on one of the many shelves. The soft glow of the solar lamp doesn't reach this far into the darkness and I can't make out the titles. I don't want Kay to see how cross I am because I know what she's saying makes sense, but it still makes me angry. I know that we don't live in a perfect world. Far from it. I know that if I want it to change then I've got to work with the Resistance, but part of me feels like a little kid. I want to throw myself down and hammer my fists on the ground and ask why is it so unfair? I don't want it to be.

I take a few deep breaths.

'I'm thinking,' Kay says to my back, 'about what Ven

said, that before Resistance people die they have to get the babies.'

'What about it?' I tug at the bottom book in the pile.

'How do they know? How do they know when they're going to die?'

I remember what Paulo said about their short lives being purposeful, and before the books come crashing down I know the answer to that question.

They know when they're going to die because they kill themselves.

'Why? Why would anyone kill themselves?' I ask.

We're in Ven's office. Kay marched straight here to ask him to deny my suspicions, but instead he calmly tells us that it's true.

'We don't all kill ourselves. Some of us die on missions.'

'But a lot of you do,' I say. 'Why?'

'Plenty of reasons for someone to kill themself,' Ven says. 'They might be you, for starters. Or they could be in crippling pain. Or they might have realised that man is essentially alone in an uncaring universe. But if you want to know why Resistance members kill themselves, it's pretty simple. Dying of the Sickness is slow. Slow and messy. You need a lot of care. We don't have time to nurse the sick; we're trying to start a revolution.'

I suck my breath in. It seems so callous. 'So they kill themselves to avoid being a burden?'

'Yes.' Ven goes back to his papers.

'That's taking self-sacrifice a bit far, isn't it?' I say.

'Those who aren't cut out to be noble,' he turns to give me a significant look, 'can always choose to do it to avoid that crippling pain I mentioned.'

There's no point in discussing it any further with Ven, so we leave him and go up to bed.

'I just don't understand him,' I say to Kay. 'It's like he deliberately sets out to shock us.'

Kay nods.

'Anyone would think he didn't want us to like him.'

'He doesn't,' she says.

'And he really doesn't like me.'

I tell Kay about the assassination team. Her face clouds over when I tell her that Ven said no. That's one of the things I love about Kay, she knows me and she understands what things mean to me. It looks like I'm back to stealing one of the tickets to the celebrations in the square, so that I can get within range of The Leader while he's making his speech. It's not going to be easy.

'What kind of guns are they going to give out to everyone on the Big Day?' I ask Kay.

She looks over her shoulder and lowers her voice. 'I heard that maybe there isn't guns for everyone.'

That's not good news. 'So what are my chances of getting hold of a rifle?'

'Those ones are for the top Defence people.'

I was afraid she'd say that. 'What am I going to do?'

'You'll think of something.'

Kay doesn't seem to want to discuss it any more, so I wait till we're in bed to think it through.

I lie awake most of the night. I keep perfectly still while my mind scrambles for a solution. By morning I've come up with a plan. With The Leader's personal security team I won't be able to get really up close to him, which means my weapon of choice has got to be a rifle – and if I want a rifle I'm going to have to get it from Nard. He's the one who 'acquires' things around here.

My breakfast sticks in my throat while I try to bring myself to a point where I am prepared to ask Nard for help.

I manage to get Nard alone after breakfast. When he hears what I want, he laughs. 'I've got strict orders from Ven to hand over all weapons to him. You know how Ven loves to give out orders.'

'I'm sure that someone as resourceful as you could get me a rifle, couldn't you? If you wanted to?'

'Why would I want to?'

'I can pay.'

'What's it for? Are you going to shoot anyone Kay gets friendly with?'

I bite my tongue. 'I want it to kill The Leader.'

Nard hoots with laughter. 'If you want to do that, maybe you should get on Ven's little squad.'

'I wanted to. He won't let me.'

Nard laughs again. 'And you think you'll be more successful striking out alone?'

· 'I've got to try.'

'Of course you have,' he says in a supremely patronising tone. 'What's this all about? Are you trying to set yourself up as Ven's replacement?'

I frown. 'What's this got to do with replacing Ven?'

'Whoever gets rid of The Leader will have secured themselves the captaincy, won't they?'

He's such an idiot. 'I'm not trying to be captain; I just want to kill The Leader.'

Nard gives me an infuriatingly knowing look. 'Of course you do.'

'So will you get me a rifle?'

'No.' He laughs and walks away.

I have to put my problems to one side for the rest of the day because Kay and I have decided that we must see Ilex again. I work quickly through my list of tasks. Halfway through the morning I've completed all my jobs and I slip away to meet Kay by the exit before Ven can give me any more.

The Resistance have salvaged a number of bicycles, which they use as much as possible to save on petrol. We take a couple of these from the ambulance shed because I don't want to risk helping ourselves to one of the cars. Even though I'm constantly scanning for Wilderness people or wild animals, I still find the ride strangely enjoyable – and when we arrive in the town where the caverns are after an hour's cycling I'm not even tired. I'm fitter than Ven imagines I am.

'Do you think they'll let us in?' I ask Kay. I'm not sure that these people's relationship with the Resistance was left in the best shape the last time we were here.

But there's no need to worry about getting access to the caverns, or steeling myself to go underground, because as we approach the visitors' centre I spot a group of people spilling out of the door. One of them is Ilex.

He stops dead when he sees us.

'Ilex,' I say, asking for forgiveness with that one word because I'm afraid it's the only one I'm going to get.

But instead of running away from us, Ilex says something to an older woman and then makes his way towards us.

He takes a deep breath. 'It's good you're here,' he says. 'I wanted to say to you my thinks about Ali.'

I nod.

Ilex leads us back into the visitors' centre. The three of us sit down on creaking chairs in a tiny office.

'I'm sorry,' I say. 'I'm really sorry about everything that happened. I shouldn't have let Ali try to save us.'

'I'm sorry, too,' Kay says. 'I wanted to keep Ali safe.'

Ilex is biting his lip. 'I was big angry with you. I had the think that if Ali wasn't all brave and fighting the guards that she could be here. I wanted that she didn't do all those big good things. Then she would be here with me.' He grips his knees. 'But that's not right. When I want like that it's taking away Ali. Because Ali was them things. She was brave and good and fighting.

250

When she died she was being big-all Ali. And that's a good thing.'

He's crying again but this time the tears just flow down his face. He isn't racked with sobs. It's a relief.

'We loved Ali,' Kay says, squeezing his arm. 'I wish she was here.'

Ilex wipes his eyes on his sleeve.

'Ilex, can I tell you something about Ali? Something amazing?' I ask.

He nods.

'She did a really good thing. I don't think that everyone believed me when I tried to tell them about how terrible things in the Academy were, so . . . Ali told them.'

'What do you mean told them? Not talking telling?'

'Yes,' Kay says. 'She talked. She was doing lots of talking. It just came out.'

Ilex blinks. 'Talking? I didn't hear Ali talking for a big time. She didn't do talking all the times we were at the Academy.' His face crumples. 'I wish I heared it! I want to hear Ali talking!'

Kay puts an arm around him. We exchange a look because someone has got to tell him what Ali said about him. I wait for his sobbing to subside again.

'She told me to tell you that you're the best brother,' I say.

'Oh!'

And we watch Ilex losing Ali all over again.

After a while he gives a watery smile. 'She was joking.

She was always joking me. But she was a big good sister.'

'And you are the kindest, gentlest, most loving brother I've ever seen.'

Ilex pushes back his shaggy hair and sits up straight in his chair. 'I want to be in your Resistance,' he announces.

My eyes find Kay.

'Really?' she asks.

'Ali would be in your Resistance. I want to do it.'

I hesitate. 'Well . . . that's great, isn't it, Kay?'

Kay doesn't look so sure.

'Big lots of people here said no they are not helping the Resistance, but some ones said yes. I'm going to come with them,' Ilex says.

Kay tries to tell him that he doesn't have to join us. She's interrupted by a group of teenage boys coming back through the door carrying baskets of skinny carrots with the dirt still on them.

The tallest takes one look at us and scowls.

'Resistance,' he mutters to his friends. They head straight for the caverns' entrance but as they move away, out of the corner of my eye, I see one of them gesture to another. My head whips round. 'Do that again,' I say.

'What?' the boy demands. The rest of them stop. Squaring up for a fight.

'I don't want trouble,' I say. 'I just want to see what you did with your hands.'

The boy smacks a balled fist into his other hand and then points downwards with two fingers.

Kay looks at me.

The boy does it again. 'It's to say—'

'Loser,' I interrupt. 'I know what it means.' I know because I remember little Ali making the same gesture when she was fighting that horrible rat-faced girl. But how did Ali know?

I turn to look at Ilex.

There's a strained silence.

'You all right, Ilex?' one of the boys asks.

Ilex nods. 'You go,' he says to the boys and they do.

'Ilex?' I say. The colour has drained out of his face; I think he knows what I'm going to ask. 'Are you and Ali Wilderness?'

Ilex looks at the desk in front of him and gives the smallest of nods.

Whoa. I never would have imagined it. But it explains why Ilex and Ali came to the Academy late and why he was so cagey that time I asked him about how he knew that Ali was his sister.

'It's not like they said at the Academy,' Ilex bursts out. 'Wilderness aren't all mad and killing. The people here are good. My family is good,' he looks down again. 'My family *was* good.'

'You don't have to explain,' I say. 'All that stuff that people said about the Wilderness, I've realised that it was rubbish, I mean, there are all kinds of people here, aren't there?'

'I thought Ali might be here,' he says, twisting his hands

253

together. 'When it went all bad at the Academy I couldn't find her. I couldn't find you. Some Specials made a hole under the thing – you know the thing to stop you getting to the Wilderness?'

'The fence,' Kay supplies.

Ilex nods. 'I thinked that maybe Ali is going back home to here. So I came to look. But she wasn't here. And my mother . . . they telled to me that she died.'

I think of my own mother and I reach out a hand to squeeze Ilex's shoulder.

'I don't get it. Why did you and Ali go to the Academy?' Kay asks gently.

Ilex breathes out slowly. 'It was hard in the Wilderness. All the times my mother was . . . she was . . . feeling a bad thing because it's hard to get food. And she doesn't want Ali and me to get taked away by the Leadership like my father.'

'They took your father away?'

'When I was big small. They comed sometimes to take away people when we lived in the school. They don't come now we're here.' Ilex leans towards us and says in a low voice, 'They're thinking it's because this is a big good safe place, but I think the Leadership doesn't care any more because it's not so big lots of people down there. And a lot of them are sick.' He smiles sadly. 'My mother didn't want that Sickness to get us either, so she thinks it's gooder if we can get to the not-Wilderness place, and she gets a man to take us.'

254

'What happened when you got to the other side?' I ask.

Ilex screws up his face trying to remember. 'It was cold. I wanted to be good for Ali, but there was no things and we were not in any place. Then some men like enforcers came and took us to the Academy. I told Ali it was good because our mother wanted us to be in that place.'

I bite my lip. The thought of any mother wishing her child into an Academy because the alternative was even worse sickens me. They would have ended up in the factory anyway, which is where I suspect Ilex's father was taken. It's just too sad.

'But you talk like a Special,' Kay says.

Ilex nods. 'I was small when we comed. I forgotted lots of words.' He gives a half-smile. 'But not Ali, all the times in her head she knowed all the big words, didn't she?'

It's true that even when she was only using sign language Ali's vocabulary was always better than Ilex's.

'She was really smart,' Kay agrees.

We talk about Ali for a while. Then Ilex tells us how the cavern people are obsessed with guarding the two entrances to the caverns. He says the best thing about them is how kind they are. Apparently they even try to help the crazy Wilderness people sometimes.

'What's it like down there?' Kay asks.

'It's cold, but we have blankets and those things that you put in the sun and then you get light.'

'Solar lanterns?'

'Yes, and we have people going all the times to these broken houses and getting all the things they can.'

I have the same thought that I did about the Resistance scavenging: these pickings won't last forever.

'So I take it your lot aren't too fond of the Resistance,' I say.

Ilex shrugs. 'Most times they say the Resistance are okay. But they get scared. They don't want to fight. They lost a lot of people. I hear the Resistance is good to us. They got us some things. Medicine and a making-water-clean-thing and all stuff like that. Your leader is a good one.'

I snort with laughter. I've never thought of describing Ven as a good one.

'Are you going to stay here?' Kay asks.

'Now, yes. But when the people that said yes to helping the Resistance come, I'm going.'

When we leave, Kay embraces him and I see her whisper in his ear.

We don't talk much on the way back.

33

That night I can't find Kay at dinner and when she finally comes into the recreation room her face is creased into a frown.

'What is it?' I ask.

She shakes her head and smoothes her hair back towards her ponytail, but her lips are still puckered.

'What's wrong? I can see you're cross.'

'It's okay,' she says. 'It's not a big bad thing. I was just . . . How do you say it? Shocked. Nard—'

'Nard? What has that creep done?'

'Nothing, I mean . . . He wanted to kiss me.'

I knew it.

'Where is he?' I'll kill him. I make for the door.

'No, Blake.' She pulls me back. 'Don't go to him. It's okay. I told him no.'

'Did he try to force you?'

Kay puts on a more Kay-ish expression.

'Do you really think Nard could be forcing me to do a thing?'

I step back from the door. I need to remember that Kay can look after herself. 'But still, how dare he?'

'He was angry. That was the bad bit. He was big angry when I said no.'

'It's not your fault,' I say.

Kay gives me an incredulous look. 'Why would it be my fault? He's the stupid one. I'm not feeling bad for me. I'm feeling bad for him. If he keeps being like that he's going to get his head kicked in.'

And I'd be quite happy to do the kicking.

'I told you he was an idiot; I don't know why you thought he was so great.'

'Stop it, Blake! I don't know why you were thinking that I was thinking he was great, I never said that.'

'You were pretty friendly.'

'I wasn't big friendly. You wanted me to be rude, like you. When I meet people I don't say "You're all bad" before I've even talked to them.'

'And that's what I do, is it?'

'Yes.'

Which I think is harsh. Just because I recognise an idiot when I see one. But I don't want to fight with Kay. Maybe I am too quick to judge people. 'Let's get out of here,' I say.

Kay shakes her head. She's still cross.

'Just for a while. This place is claustrophobic. Let's get some air.'

'We can't go out now. It's dark out there.'

I look at the feeble glow of the solar lantern nearest us. 'It's dark in here!'

'There will be the bad Wilderness ones. And animals.'

She's got a point, but now that I've thought about getting out I don't think I can sit in this gloomy closed-in space any more.

'I've got an idea,' I say. 'Come on.'

Kay shakes her head again, but she comes with me anyway. We go all the way to the top floor of the hospital. Even super-fit Kay is panting by the time we make it.

'There must be access somewhere,' I say.

Kay tuts. 'What are we doing?'

'Aha.' I've found a door. It's not even locked. Behind it is a short flight of steps and then another door, which *is* locked, but only from the inside. I unbolt it and we're out on the roof.

'Oh,' Kay says.

I almost trip over a row of solar lanterns, obviously put up here ready to catch the early-morning sun. I steer around them and take a deep breath. It's good to feel a breeze running through my hair after the dank air of the hospital. I look at Kay. She's got a strange expression on her face.

'Are you worrying about what Ven would say?' I ask.

'Efwurd Ven,' she says.

I almost laugh, but I can see that Kay still isn't in a laughing mood. She walks away from me, towards the edge.

Over a low wall we can see the whole shadowy city.

I look over to the right in the direction of the caverns.

'Ilex will be here tomorrow,' I say.

'I told him not to come,' Kay says slowly.

'What do you mean?'

The stiff mask drops from her face and she catches hold of my hands. 'I told him to stay where it's safe. And we could go there too, Blake, and stay with Ilex's friends.'

My jaw drops. Where did that come from? I know that Kay isn't as committed to the Resistance as I am; I know that I've annoyed her over Nard, but I'm still stunned. 'What about the revolt?' I finally ask. 'What about getting rid of The Leader?'

She turns her head and I realise that she doesn't believe that I'll ever kill The Leader, or that the Resistance will ever change the way this country is run. It's like she's kicked me in the face. 'Don't you care at all?' I say.

'I do care, Blake, of course I care. I know how big you want to make it right and show your father—'

'How much *I* want it? Don't you want it?'

'I did think so but ... I've been thinking about all things.' She lays a hand on my shoulder. 'When you want things and you don't get them ... it's hard. It's very hard. I wanted to be Dom.'

'You can be something better than the head girl of a pack of Specials.'

She sighs. 'You're such a believer, Blake.'

'What's wrong with that?'

260

'Nothing. It's a good thing. I just … I'm tired. All my life it's been the fighting and the being tough and then you came and there was more fighting and running and thinking and I'm tired.'

I remember the look she shared with the man at the caverns. 'That man who said the Resistance were silly dreamers – you agree with him, don't you?'

Kay stares out over the city. 'I look at those Wilderness people and they get to be living with their families, like you said people should be, and I think how it would be to be safe and happy and quiet.'

'Kay, Ilex's mother sent her children away because she wanted them to have a better life. *She sent them to an Academy*. Their life wasn't safe or happy or quiet.'

'Ilex said they do sharing and they're kind and the Resistance helps them. We could do it, Blake, we're smart.'

I catch my breath. She's talking about us being together. I should be so happy to hear her suggesting that we could become a family, but a terrible heaviness has come over me. She wants to be with me, but it's all wrong.

'I have to be here,' I say. 'I have to fight. People need me.'

'And what do you need? I thought you needed me.'

'I do need you. You mean so much to me … but I have to help the Resistance.'

Her anger from a few minutes ago comes rushing back. 'It's not about the helping!'

261

'What's that supposed to mean? I'm trying to make this country a better place.'

'That's a lie. The only person that you care about is yourself. All you want is to kill your father because he hurt you. I don't think you care at all about anyone else or the things that happens to them. Until you had to live in a horrible Academy you didn't think about the way people were treated.'

I can't believe she said that. 'I didn't know then. But now I'm trying to do something!' I say. 'Can't you see that I'm trying to change things?'

'You're trying to kill your father. You're trying to get what *you* want.' She turns away from me and runs back to the door and down the stairs.

I stay exactly where I am.

When I finally stomp down the stairs, someone flashes their torch in my face. I swat it away. It's Ven. He raises an eyebrow.

'I'm not in the mood for a lecture,' I say. 'I wasn't doing any harm up there.'

'Well, it's certainly true that you have a limited ability to impact on anything. I just came to tell you there's a planning meeting for captains, their vices and the assassination team tomorrow morning at eight. Don't be late.'

'What?'

'Let's hope your reactions are a little quicker when you're trying to shoot The Leader's head off, shall we?'

'I'm not on the team. You told me I wasn't on the team.' What the hell is he playing at?

'If I can tax your feeble brain just for a moment and ask you to access your memory – I appreciate that it's not something you do often and that it may cause you some pain – now think; did I actually ever say you couldn't be on the team?'

'Yes, I mean . . . well, you said that I didn't have all the necessary skills.'

'Come on, Blake, if I only allowed you to do things you were fully qualified for you'd never do an efwurding thing. You're on the team. Make sure you're at the meeting.'

I should be happy, but I'm not. 'Why have you always got to play mind games, Ven?'

Ven smirks. 'Why do people normally play games?'

He thinks he's so clever. 'In psychological terms,' I say, 'play serves a purpose in preparing immature minds for real-life situations. I hope you've learnt something from messing with my head, Ven.'

Just for once it's nice to walk away having had the last word.

As I reach the landing of the next floor down I see the glow of a solar lantern and hear voices. I give into my curiosity and take a closer look. Paulo, Robin and a dark-haired girl are sorting through piles of clothes. I stop in the doorway.

'What are you doing?' I ask.

'Something very important,' Robin says smugly.

'Clothes for the Big Day,' Paulo explains.

Robin holds up a frilly dress against herself. 'I would look good in this, wouldn't I?' Without waiting for an answer she puts down the dress and tries on a smart jacket instead. It's much too big for her, but she twirls around anyway.

'Robin . . .' Paulo warns.

I take a look at the heaps of clothes. Someone has done an excellent job. There are a number of uniforms, some for guards, others for delivery people or event stewards. They've also got some smart outfits for children. The sort of thing that kids from a Learning Community might wear on The Leader's birthday.

'This is good stuff,' I say. There must be clothes for every member of the Resistance here. 'Where did it all come from?' I ask.

'Not telling,' Robin says.

'The Aqua team,' the dark-haired girl says.

'Nard,' I say.

She laughs at my tone. 'Are you not a fan? He is a bit . . . you know, but he certainly gets his job done.'

'Here,' Paulo says, 'take the labels off these.' He pushes a bundle of clothes across a table towards me. I start pulling tags off jumpers. My eyes widen when I see the prices. I wonder if Nard actually steals things from shops or if someone else does it for him.

I turn back to the girl. 'If by "a bit you know" you mean he's an utter jerk, then I agree.'

Paulo just blinks, but Robin throws down the hanger she is holding. 'Why are you being mean about Nard? Don't be horrible. He's nice. He gave me Bear. That's not horrible, is it?'

I'm surprised to hear that Nard has done anything for anyone.

'She's his little pet,' the dark-haired girl explains to me. 'Calm down, Robin, you can't deny that your Nard is a bit intense. And he loves his guns, doesn't he?'

He loved them too much to let me borrow one, anyway.

'So? I like guns, too,' Robin says.

'Everyone in the Resistance spends time with guns.' Paulo is playing the peacemaker as usual.

'Not as much as Nard,' the girl insists. 'And it's not just guns, is it? I got stuck on guard duty with him once and I had to hear all about his knife collection.'

'You're all just jealous,' Robin snaps.

'Robin, have you got a pair of size four boots over there?' Paulo is trying to change the subject.

'You lot never like anyone I like. Nobody likes Nard. Nobody likes my friend Jed. You think the people I like are stupid.'

'That's enough, Robin.' He leans over to take the boots and speaks into her ear. 'Stop making a fuss or I won't let you out to play with Jed.'

I don't think the dark-haired girl hears, but I do. I feel perversely pleased that Paulo is going against Ven and letting Robin play with her little friend.

Robin looks thunderous, but says nothing and we all sort the clothes in silence for a few minutes.

'Are you on the Assassination team, Paulo?' I ask.

'Blake, you know we're not supposed to discuss our individual roles for the Big Day.'

Another one of Ven's stupid rules.

266

'All right, I won't discuss that. I've just been wondering whether you've ever tried it before, the Resistance I mean – surely you could have killed The Leader before now?'

'Nard says that. Nard says shoot him quick.' Robin looks thrilled that she's found something that Nard and I agree on.

'It's not that simple,' Paulo says.

'You'd only need one volunteer,' I say.

'One volunteer to get around The Leader's bulletproof car or to take out the pack of bodyguards he travels around with?'

'There must be times when a sniper could get a single headshot. That's all it would take.'

'That's all it would take to kill The Leader. It's not all that it would take to kill the Leadership. If we'd killed him before now, we'd have been the bad guys. We have to get people to understand that he's the enemy before we kill him. Then they'll know that we've done the right thing.'

'We could have done Nard's Plan Scarlett,' Robin says.

'You're not supposed to know about that,' Paulo says.

'Everybody knows about it,' the dark-haired girl says. 'It just blowing the Leadership up, isn't it?'

Paulo pushes more clothes at the girl. 'We really shouldn't be discussing any of this. Let's concentrate on getting this done so I can get half an hour's sleep before I'm expected to organise something else, shall we?'

*

267

All through the night I can't stop imagining that single shot to The Leader's head. Which makes me wonder about what Kay said. What do I care about destroying more – the whole oppressive government or just my father?

Kay never comes to bed.

Even though I get very little sleep, I make sure I get to Ven's office early; I'm not giving him any excuses to take back what he said about me being on the team.

By the time Ven waves us into the room, there are more than twenty of us waiting. That means I'm not the only one here who isn't a captain or a vice. I only recognise a few people.

We sit on plastic chairs gathered around several tables pushed together. I'm next to Tanisha.

She leans over and says, 'I hear you're on the assassination team.'

I nod.

'So's he.' She nods towards a boy with long blond hair. 'And me and Ven.'

'Is that it?'

'That's it.'

'Right,' says Ven. He looks shattered; I wonder if he's

slept at all since I saw him last night. 'Let's establish something now before I waste the limited moisture in my mouth. This meeting is not about taking requests or hearing stories about the cabbage you almost ate last Thursday. It's about the uprising.'

'I think you ought to listen to what the other captains have got to say,' Nard interrupts.

Ven closes his eyes and makes a growling noise. 'I'm already running dry, Nard, so I'm going to resort to gestures.' He shakes his head vigorously. 'Now, no more interruptions or I may be reduced to another kind of gesture altogether.' He sits down heavily and nods towards his deputy. 'Paulo.'

Paulo stands up and leans over the table to unroll a map.

'This shows the focal points of our attack. As you can see we're going to hit the central district hard. The media centre, the Leadership building, the communications tower – but we've also got targets in outlying districts like the power company and the guards' barracks.

'What about weapons? What about the assassination?' Nard asks.

That girl last night was right – he is obsessed.

'You know I can't bring myself to give a compliment,' Ven says to Nard, 'but I will say this; despite rumours to the contrary, you have ensured that we are in possession of adequate numbers of firearms. They will be distributed to teams as they leave the hospital. As for the assassination, I will discuss that with the assassination team.' Ven

270

leans towards Nard and whispers, 'The clue is in the name.'

Nard sniffs. 'Just because I don't spend my time shooting plastic dolls, it doesn't mean I don't have anything to contribute to the plans.'

I give him an incredulous look because Eame said he spent plenty of time shooting. He's just trying to be patronising because he's not very good at it.

'We're going to shoot The Leader,' Ven says. 'That's all you need to know.'

'Shoot him? How do you know you'll get a chance? Why don't you use a bomb?'

'We've considered explosives. Too many innocent people would die.'

'So? If that really bothers you then don't do it in the middle of an efwurding picnic! You should think about using Plan Scarlett.'

'We've considered an alternative location and dismissed it, Nard. We've also previously considered your suggestion that we use Plan Scarlett.'

'Many times,' Tanisha whispers to me.

'It's crazy to rely on a few idiots with guns,' Nard says, looking at me. 'Let's just blow The Leader up.'

'Let's just shut up,' the captain of the Provisions team says, and Tanisha and I burst out laughing.

'Let's grow up,' Ven says, eyeing me coldly. 'Diverting as your endless questioning and joking may be to people with reduced mental capacity; it's not an efficient use of our time. We have our plans, Nard, and we will not be altering them at this point.'

Nard looks ready to throw a tantrum.

'How are the ticket purchases?' Tanisha asks.

'What ticket purchases?' a girl with freckles asks.

'If you remember,' Ven says with a face that suggests he doesn't expect anyone around the table to be capable of remembering anything useful, 'previous versions of the Birthday Plan relied on us highjacking one of the official snack vans in order to gain entrance to the central square. This time we've decided instead to procure legitimate tickets to get in. One of our contacts on the other side has been paying good money for unwanted tickets. He's passed five to us so far.'

'Five isn't very many,' Nard says.

'Five is plenty when you only need four,' Paulo points out.

Nard doesn't even acknowledge that she's spoken. 'So it's just the Assassination team that get to go into the square, is it?' he says to Ven.

'It's an extremely dangerous mission, Nard, not a special treat.'

'So we've definitely got tickets for the Assassination team?' Tanisha asks.

'Not quite,' Paulo says. 'There are three tickets in the names of Learning Community boys which are perfect for Ven, Blake and Kurt.' He nods towards the blond boy Tanisha pointed out.

'What about a ticket for me?' Tanisha says.

'We're working on it,' Paulo says. 'The fourth ticket is for a woman in her sixties – I don't think anyone here can pull off looking that old – and the fifth is for a Girl Guard.'

'What's a Girl Guard?' Toren asks.

'It's like a club,' I say, 'for little girls. They do sports and raise money and take a pledge to serve The Leader. I guess it's another way for the Leadership to get children thinking their way.'

'How young are the girls?' Nard asks, looking at Tanisha in an appraising way.

'The ticket is for an eleven-year-old,' Paulo says.

Kurt bursts out laughing. Tanisha would never pass for eleven.

'I'm sure Paulo will ensure Tanisha has the correct ticket,' Ven says. 'Moving on, we need a lot of team captains for this. Vices will all have to lead their own teams and I'll be discussing with captains other suitable candidates to lead a group. We've got people arriving from the cells from now on and also a number of Wilderness people who want in. It's up to you lot to make sure they know what they're doing. Are you all clear on which area your teams are attacking? I'm going to speak to each team in private later.'

Nard rolls his eyes. 'Do we really need all this secrecy?'

'Yes, we do, Nard. You won't know what other teams are doing and they won't know what you're doing. And that is so that when your inability to follow commands

273

gets you caught and the Leadership start pulling your nails out and you start squealing and tell them everything that you know, you won't know much. Understand?'

Nard glowers.

'I'll brief the assassination team first. I'll see the rest of you later.'

Ven waits for the others to go till only he, Paulo, me, Tanisha and the boy called Kurt are left.

Paulo pulls out a plan of the central square and points at it with a pencil. 'We've chosen this building as most suitable for the assassination team to work from, as we've discovered that the entrance will be obscured by a display of children's artwork.'

Actually, I discovered that by accessing the planning committee's records, but I've given up ever expecting my efforts to be acknowledged.

'Weapons went into the building yesterday,' Ven says. 'When we arrive we'll post someone on the main entrance and we'll take up position. As soon as our special film has run, we shoot The Leader. Actually, the film may not run all the way through and even if it does, The Leader may not stick around for all of it, so let me put this another way, as soon as The Leader runs, we shoot him.'

We stare at each other. He makes it sound so simple.

'That's all you need to know.' He dismisses us with a nod of the head.

As the others are moving out I say to Ven, 'Nard seems keen on using a bomb.'

'Mmm,' Ven says, still looking at his papers.

'Have you even got that kind of thing?'

Ven's head jerks up. 'We're a Resistance movement; of course we've got explosives.'

'Here?'

'Most of it is in a store just the other side of the fence. Nard keeps a lot of stuff we wouldn't want anyone to find here, over there. You know, he might be annoying, but he's pretty good at his job. He's the one that acquires explosives.'

I really don't want to hear how great Nard is. 'He doesn't seem to be bothered by the idea of casualties,' I point out.

'He wants this revolution to happen. I can understand that.'

But I'm not so sure. Does Nard want revolution or just death and destruction? There's no denying that Nard is passionate, but I'm not sure that his fervour is really connected to the idea of changing the government. It strikes me that Nard would be just as determined to wreak havoc if he belonged to the guards instead of the Resistance.

Maybe some people are looking for a cause and it's just a matter of which one they find first.

I see Kay across the cafeteria at lunch and I'm glad that she keeps her distance. I'm still upset. Even if it is true that I've got a personal grudge against my father, I don't think it's fair of her to suggest that I don't care about

275

what this uprising could mean for everyone. She's supposed to be on my side. It hurts that she thinks so badly of me.

In the afternoon a steady stream of people from the cells and a few from the caverns arrive. I'm in Ven's office when Ilex walks by, but I barely have time to greet him before he's taken off for briefing. The next opportunity I have to speak to him is at dinner. When the Wilderness people come in, I wave him over to my table.

'Everything okay?' I ask.

He nods. 'Yes, things okay. I'm a watcher. I'm on the ... team of this Patrick boy.' He points across the cafeteria to a boy that I recognise as the vice-captain of Catering. I've got no idea whether he's qualified to lead a team into a revolution. I run a hand through my hair. If I'm realistic, surely none of us are qualified. We're all just kids. What can kids do to change the way things are?

'What is it, Blake?' Ilex asks.

'Nothing. That's a good team. Be careful tomorrow, won't you?'

'Careful?'

'Don't get shot.'

Ilex looks at his hands. 'Blake, I am scared.'

'That's okay. I'm scared too. You know, you don't have to do this.'

'I want to. But I don't want to be the person who is getting it wrong and making it all efwurded up. I'm not a brainer.' He leans towards me. 'Some of the things that

276

Patrick is saying; I don't know what they are. I'm scared I'm big stupid for this.'

'Ilex, you're not stupid. You've never had anyone to teach you things and show you stuff. I think it's amazing how much you do know. You want to do this, don't you?'

He nods.

'That's the most important thing. It doesn't take geniuses to tell a government that they're wrong. It just needs ordinary decent people to stand up and be seen.'

'Yes.' He lets out a breath and looks around the room. 'Where's Kay?' he asks.

I feel my face tighten. 'I don't know.'

He looks at me for a moment. 'I have to go to Patrick, but I want to say it that you are a good friend, Blake.' He smacks me across the back affectionately. His eyes meet mine again. 'And tomorrow is going to be a bad hard time. You have to talk to Kay.' He squeezes my arm and heads over to the table where Patrick is sat.

I sit down and try to think about anything other than Kay.

36

When Ven arrives in the cafeteria, people turn around to get a look at him. Paulo walks behind him with a face like he's in a funeral parade. The talking dies away as Ven climbs on to a table. He looks terrible; he seems to have aged in the last few days.

'You know what you've got to do,' he says. 'And I'm sure no one wants to end up in the hands of the guards because they couldn't remember the plan, do they, Paulo?'

'Just get on with it, Ven,' Paulo says. He sounds exhausted too.

'Departures will be staggered between now and tomorrow. Each team has a prime target. You know what yours is. At twelve, The Leader will make his speech, but instead of that parcel of lies, our man will be playing our footage of what is really going on. At the very moment it finishes we set off a chain of explosions which will help let everybody know that we really do mean business and that now is the time to join us. You'll all be issued with weapons.

Aim for Leadership officials and guards.' He pauses for breath.

His clothes seem loose on him. It looks like he's been skipping meals as well as sleep.

A dozen or so hands go up.

'If you have questions, I suggest you save them for afterwards.' He turns away and mutters, 'By which time I'll probably be too dead to be bothered by them.'

Paulo watches him leave the cafeteria and looks up at the ceiling. He seems to have realised that that speech was not what this bunch of frightened kids needed to hear.

Paulo waves his arms. 'We can do it,' he says without conviction. 'If we stick together and fight hard, we can do it.' But his feeble voice is lost in the nervous chattering of the Resistance.

Someone has got to say something.

I find myself climbing on to my own table. I put my fingers in my mouth and whistle. The noise stops and people turn around to stare up at me.

I don't have a clue what I'm doing.

'Tomorrow,' I say, 'will be difficult. There will be bloodshed. We all know that our lives will be in danger.'

Frowning faces look up at me. Most of them don't even know who I am.

'But I won't be thinking about that tonight,' I say. 'Tonight, I am going to remember my mother and my best friend. Those people are the reason I want to free this country. They both died because of The Leader's actions.'

279

The cafeteria has fallen silent. Everyone in the room is staring at me. I swallow. 'I know that you have lost people, too, and we all have so many reasons to want things to change. I am going to think about how much I loved my mother and Wilson, and you should think of your lost family and friends, because then we will remember why we're prepared to face the guards' guns tomorrow, and why we will keep fighting until nobody has to lose someone they love to the Leadership because we'll all be free.'

There's a storm of clapping and cheering. I'm shaking. But this is what they need to hear. Not Ven's tough attitude or Paulo's terror. They need to remember what we're doing this for. We all do.

A group of kids come over to tell me it was a good speech, and around me I can hear people talking about their parents and others discussing how life will change for the better after tomorrow.

When things settle down I take my seat again and try to enjoy what may be my last decent meal ever, but Robin plonks herself down next to me and starts babbling in my ear.

'I hate Ven.' She scowls. She doesn't even bother to keep her voice down when she says it now. 'He says all these things about doing stuff for the Resistance, but he never does anything for us. He won't even listen to what we want.'

I close my eyes and picture my mother. I want to keep her memory with me tomorrow.

'Not even if you ask nicely—'

I think about the last time that I saw Wilson as he really was. He was joking about on the metro.

'You'd think if a Wilderness boy needed medicine for his sister that Ven would let them have it. He says no to everything.'

A girl on the other side of Robin says something about how sick kids should go to the Medical captain, but I'm hardly listening. I'm remembering how Wilson was after we were attacked. I've got to take this feeling and use it.

'He just always says no,' Robin moans. 'I don't think we should let him be in charge.'

Her whining is breaking my concentration.

'I should tell him,' she says, slapping a hand on the table. 'I should say "No, Ven, I don't want to do a stupid rebellion," and I could tell him that Jed says—'

'Go on then!' I snap. 'Say no. Stay here. Just shut the hell up.'

Everyone at the table is staring at me. I'm almost as surprised as they are by my outburst.

Robin glares at me, open-mouthed. She doesn't reply because I've called her bluff. We all know that she can't bear to be left out of anything. She's got no intention of telling Ven that she won't be coming. She pouts and stalks off with her bear to join a different table. Halfway across the room, she turns around and gives me such a menacing look that even though she is only eight years old, I rather wish I hadn't shouted at her.

I push my half-full plate away. Even with Robin gone I

281

can't concentrate. My mind keeps coming back to Kay. She might think I'm a selfish judgemental loser obsessed with my father, but I can't leave things as they are. For once in my life I have to tell someone how much they mean to me before I lose the chance. I told everyone else to remember the reason why we're doing this. Kay is just as much my reason as my mother and Wilson. I've been so pig-headed.

Kay isn't in the cafeteria, or the rec room or Tanisha's office. I scour the hospital and finally inspiration comes and I try the roof. She's there looking out over the district.

'I'm sorry,' I call.

She turns around.

'I'm sorry that I'm an idiot and that I don't give people a chance,' I say, walking towards her. 'And I'm sorry that I'm so wrapped up in what I want and how to get it. And you're right that I'm selfish. And you're right that I've just been thinking about paying my father back.' I'm standing in front of her now. 'Kay, I love you so efwurding much and I can't bear for tomorrow to happen without me telling you.'

She looks at me and there's something shining out of her eyes that fills me with light.

'I love you too, you idiot.'

She reaches out and pulls me to her. Her lips are soft, but then she presses her mouth against mine and soon we're kissing so hard that it almost hurts. She puts her hands in my hair and pulls me to her – because she wants me. I'm so happy that she wants me.

When we finally stop, I'm out of breath. There's a bubble of joy inside me that makes me feel so light I could float away.

'Kay, do you really not want me to go tomorrow?' I ask.

'No. You have to do it. We both have to do it. It's the right thing. I just … When I wanted to be Dom I said I wanted to help the little kids, and I did want to, but the thing I wanted was for me. I wanted to be top.'

I see where she's going with this.

'It's not wrong to want things for yourself, Blake, but you have to know what they are and you have to think about if it's going to be good for you to get them. Or all that wanting can make you crazy. You have to know yourself, Blake. And you have to tell it true to me. I've had the lying all my life. I don't want lies from you.'

I hold her gaze and nod my head. She's right. I want to be the best I can be for her. And I'm going to be.

'I want to kill my father,' I say. 'I want to hurt him because he hurt my mother and because he was no efwurding good as a father.' I take a deep breath. My lungs hurt. 'And I want to kill The Leader because I want to stop him from destroying any more children's lives.'

We stare at each other for a moment. Kay nods slowly. She reaches out for me.

'You're cold,' she says and wraps her arms around me.

I close my eyes. I want to catch and keep this moment of

283

being here, of being honest and being accepted. I want to remember what it's like to feel safe in Kay's arms because I don't know if I'll ever have a moment like it again.

In the end I draw back because there are more things I need to tell her.

'You're on Nard's team, aren't you?' I say.

'Yes, but—'

'No, I'm not going to get jealous. Nard's team are going to be monitoring the guards' communications, aren't they?'

Kay looks at me.

'And you'll be just outside the central square, won't you?'

'We're not supposed to talk about it,' Kay says.

'But I already know, don't I? And you know that I'm going to be nearby, don't you? For the assassination.'

She nods.

'I'm going to be in the Atterling building. It's the second tallest building in the square. If something goes wrong …'

'Blake, it will be okay.'

'But … just remember that I'm in the Atterling building if you need to come.'

'Okay.' She touches my face. 'Let's not talk that. Let's talk about you and me.'

The way she says 'you and me' sparks a glow in me that radiates out to my fingers and toes.

For a while we don't do any talking at all. When we stop kissing, Kay asks, 'Are you afraid?'

I *am* afraid, but not in the way Kay means. I haven't allowed myself to think about how dangerous tomorrow

284

will be. What I'm afraid of is that I might fail. After everything that has happened, I've been holding myself together with the thought that it will be all right if I can succeed in killing The Leader. I just hope that I can do it.

'No,' I say. 'You know me – I love all that violence stuff.'

Kay laughs.

We stand there till late, looking into the dark night. What's going to happen tomorrow? Are the Resistance going to change everything? Or are we going to be slaughtered?

'Are you really sure you want to do this?' I ask.

'Yes. I don't want to be living like that. I don't want to be living in an Academy and I don't want to be living underground or in this hospital. If you want a thing to be a different thing you have to change it. You taught me that.'

It amazes me that I could have taught anything to someone as smart as Kay.

'I can't tell you how many things you've taught me,' I say.

'Like what?'

'Like how to be a better person and what it feels like to love someone.'

And then we kiss until I feel like my edges have blurred and melted into the darkness.

37

I wake up very early and go to the window that has a hole in its board, so I can look out at the bright blue sky.

I remember this time last year. The Leader's birthday is a public holiday. I used to look forward to it at the Learning Community because we'd get the day off from studying. It was one of the few days that we'd be taken out. Last year we went on a picnic. I sat with Wilson and he drank so much lemonade that he couldn't stop burping. It feels like something I read about now. I can't ever get back to that time.

Kay rolls over and looks around for me. She pushes back the blankets and pads across the ward to wrap an arm around me.

'What are you thinking?' she whispers.

I tune out of my memories. 'Did you celebrate The Leader's birthday in the Academy?' I ask.

'What's celebrate?'

'Like marking a special day, remembering it by having

a good time.' The further I get into that sentence the less likely it seems that there were any celebrations at the Academy.

'The Leader's birthday was a more food day.' She thinks harder. 'And maybe on this day Enforcer Tong is not big mean.'

I laugh. I guess in an Academy that would pass as a good time.

Kay puts a hand on my cheek. 'Be good,' she says. 'Be good at fighting and running and don't be killed.'

I press my face into her hair.

'I won't die if you don't,' I say.

And I hold her so tightly that my fingers ache.

The teams are scheduled to leave at different times. Some left yesterday and others through the night. We have to time things carefully to avoid guard patrols along the fence. Also, there are a limited number of tunnels from this side of the fence to the other and we don't want an obvious stream of people appearing. Kay leaves before me. I keep my eyes on her until she's disappeared from sight. I refuse to look at Nard's smirking face.

The assassination team are one of the last to leave. As we drive away from the hospital, I wonder if we'll come back in one piece. Do the Leadership have any idea of the chaos we're going to unleash today? Did I leave any trails on their computer system? Have they found any of the guns we've planted? What if those spies they were supposed to have sent have been watching the hospital the whole time? There's so much that could go wrong.

Ven drives us to the border in his favourite car. We go to the appliances store with the same tunnel that we used to go and see Janna. Janna. Another life The Leader has claimed.

I'm so full of adrenaline that while I feel hyper aware of everything around me, I'm also strangely calm. I walk right through the tunnel without imagining it collapsing once. What we've got to do today is so big that everything else seems to fade into insignificance.

On the other side a car has been left for us. Ven already has the keys. The windows are tinted dark so that you can't see inside. I think Ven's hoping that people will assume that it belongs to someone important and leave us alone. I sit in the front with Ven. He looks terrible. All the stress of planning really seems to have got to him.

We set off towards the central district where The Leader will be appearing in the main square. I know I should be channelling my anger and picturing a positive outcome and all that kind of mental management stuff that they taught us in our Future Leaders sessions, but I feel like there's something I've forgotten. I clear my throat.

Ven takes his eyes off the road to look at me. 'What's the matter with you?' he asks. 'I'd say that you look even more dim-witted than usual, but let's face it, you've already set the baseline pretty low. You've got to focus, Blake.'

I shake my head to clear it. There's something nagging at the back of my mind. I keep trying to reach it, but the more I pursue it the further away I push it.

Kurt and Tanisha are talking in low voices in the back of the car.

'Why are you two whispering?' Ven snaps. 'Anyone would think that I was some inapproachable monster. If you've got something to say, say it out loud. Only, do remember that stupid remarks trigger an uncontrollable flow of sarcasm from me.'

'Yeah, we know,' Tanisha says. 'We're just talking about the kids. Kurt's worried about the little ones.'

'Don't worry about that lot,' Ven says. 'They're tough. One of them kicked me in the shins before we came out.'

I bet I know who that was. I wonder if Robin treated Ven to one of her rants about how he always says no and how her friend, Jed—

Oh no. Oh no, no, no.

The weight of what I've just realised is so enormous that my brain fails to come up with an effective way of communicating it. Attempted words clog my throat. But I have to tell Ven, and fast.

Ven turns to say something to me and does a double-take. I must look horrified. 'What?' he demands.

'Robin,' I say. 'How much does Robin know of the plans?'

'What's Robin got to do with anything?' Tanisha says.

'Who's Robin?' Ven asks.

289

'The kid that kicked you. The difficult one. The one that always wants something, attention mostly.'

'Well, you know that all plans were supposed to be on a need-to-know basis, but she's a nosy kid. Blake, you've turned an even less attractive shade of pale than usual. What is it?'

'Last night, at dinner, she said a Wilderness kid wanted medicine for his sister. She must have meant that boy that she's been seeing, she must have.'

'She's been seeing a boy?'

'Playing with a boy. I thought that he was a little kid. A Wilderness boy, but yesterday she talked about him having a sister. She must have meant Jed. He's all she ever talks about. She never said he had a sister before.'

'What does it matter if some kid's got a sister?' Kurt asks.

'Because it means there were two of them. Two strangers. A boy and a girl. Wanting Robin to take them to the hospital.'

Ven brakes hard. 'Are you serious?'

I nod. 'A boy and a girl, just like your insider told us the Leadership were sending.'

'What boy and girl?' Kurt asks.

'When I first arrived at the hospital, don't you remember how Ven tried to have me shot because he thought Kay and I were spies from the Leadership? You said your guy had told you the Leadership were going to send a boy and a girl pretending to be from an Academy, didn't you?'

Ven nods.

'But it might not be them,' Tanisha says.

I try to fight down the fear that's battering about in my chest and be sensible.

'Okay. How long has Robin known this boy?' I ask.

'I know you believe me to be omnipotent and omnipresent, Blake,' Ven says, 'but I haven't got an efwurding clue.' He pulls over into a space in front of some houses. 'You know who stores up boring details about boring people? Paulo.' He pulls out a communicator and stabs at the buttons.

'About Robin,' he says without salutation when Paulo

picks up. 'Her Wilderness friend—' He looks at me questioningly.

'Jed,' I say.

'Jed. How long has she known him?'

There's a pause. I can just imagine Paulo's creeping fear that he's about to get into trouble for letting Robin out to play.

'Think hard. How long has she known him?'

'Not long,' Paulo says on the other end of the communicator. 'What's happened?'

'Did she meet him before or after you got the tip off about Leadership spies?' I say loud enough for him hear.

There's an awful pause

'It was right around the time we got that information.'

I put my head in my hands.

'It's them,' Ven says. 'It's the pair of kids they told us would be sent, but they weren't pretending to be from the Academy – they were pretending to be from the Wilderness. I assumed that they would approach me. I didn't even consider that they would target one of the kids.'

'It can't be them.' Paulo's voice breaks. 'It was just a boy. Just a little boy.'

'Did you see him?'

'No, but—'

'Did she tell you he was a little kid?'

There's a pause.

'No, but—'

'What's she told them? Never mind. Where is she? Which team is she in?'

292

'She's with Patrick.'

That's Ilex's team.

Ven cuts the connection and hits buttons on the communicator again.

'Whoa,' Kurt says, sounding more awake than he has all morning. 'You mean that that little Robin girl has been hanging out with some Leadership kids? Ones that were sent to ... What were they sent to do?'

Nobody answers him.

'Patrick, let me speak to Robin,' Ven says into the communicator.

'What's go—'

'*Now*,' Ven says.

There's a pause while Patrick finds Robin, and I wonder if she has told the Leadership spies all our plans. It can't all be over before we've even started.

'What?' Robin's sulky voice comes over the communicator.

'Robin, it's Ven.'

'Are you going to tell me off for kicking you? Because—'

'Listen to me. That boy, Jed, how old is he?'

'He's a big boy. As big as you, he could beat you up if I wanted him to.'

'What did you tell him about us? Did you tell him where the hospital is? Did you show him the hospital?'

Halfway through this sentence I know that Robin will kick off.

'Why does everybody hate my friend? You just don't want me to be happy!'

This isn't the best way to get information out of her.

'Robin! Did you show him the hospital?' Ven repeats.

'No! I know the stupid rules about keeping where we are a stupid secret.'

'Did he ask you to tell him where we were? Did he ask you anything about the Resistance?'

'So what if he asked me things? He's my friend and I can tell him about what we do if I want to!'

Ven's jaw tightens and I know that he is about to explode right back at her. If he keeps making her angry she will clam up all together and we don't have time for that.

I snatch the communicator out of his hand, but then I recall that the last time I saw Robin I shouted at her. She's not going to want to talk to me either. I look around desperately. I hand the communicator to Tanisha.

She opens her mouth to talk, but hesitates. She's thinking. That's good. Robin needs careful handling.

'Robin, it's Tanisha. I'd like to meet Jed.'

'He wouldn't like to meet you,' Robin answers. 'He only likes me.'

Ven is gesticulating angrily. 'Do they know? Do they know about today?' he says in a whisper so harsh that it must hurt his throat.

Tanisha turns away from Ven. 'I bet he does like you. I bet you talk to him a lot. Did you tell him about today?'

'I know what you're doing,' Robin says. I can picture the scowl on her face. 'You're trying to be nice.'

'We need to know, Robin. We need to know that everybody is still safe. Did you tell him?'

'Stop asking me. Stop asking me things!'

'Did he ask you questions about the Resistance?'

'You think he's only my friend because he wants to know about the Resistance. I don't care if I told him things; he's nice, but you can't believe that he's nice and he gave me this bracelet and—'

'What bracelet?' I say.

No answer.

I yank the communicator out of Tanisha's hand. 'Robin, what bracelet?'

But the connection is dead.

'Well, it's a good job that we asked her all the important stuff before we got cut off, and didn't waste time trying to butter the brat up,' Ven says. 'Oh, no, wait, I've got that the wrong way round. Oh, no, wait; it wasn't me who got it the wrong way round.' He glares at Tanisha.

'Efwurd off, Ven! Screaming at someone isn't always the way to get what you want.'

Ven blinks as if blown backwards by her volume. 'As you're demonstrating right now.'

'Shut up!' I say. I stab every button on the communicator, but the screen is dead. I shake it and smack it against the steering wheel. It's gone. The connection must have been switched off. This is the problem with using dead people's communicators. 'We've got to get hold of Robin again. We need another communicator.'

'Ven's got a spare, haven't you, Ven?' Tanisha says.

'Yes, Tanisha, I've got a spare. I would have mentioned it earlier, only I was too shy and polite to speak up. No, I don't have an efwurding spare.'

'Why not? You're always telling us—'

'Well, I haven't!'

'I can't believe it,' Kurt says in genuine surprise. 'You always have everything we need. You're the captain.'

'Yes I am, so less abusing me and more obeying me.' He starts the car up and pulls back on to the road. 'Can you see anyone using a communicator?'

We all obediently crane our necks, looking up and down the street, even though I've got a nasty idea about what will happen if we do see someone.

'Can't see anyone at all,' Kurt says.

'Everybody is at The Leader's birthday celebrations,' I say.

'We could break into a house,' Kurt says.

'What about Nard's cache?' Tanisha asks. 'That's near here, isn't it?'

Ven swings the car straight into a turn. 'Good idea.'

Nobody speaks for a moment.

'Are we . . . are we maybe panicking too much?' Kurt asks. 'I mean, what exactly do you guys think is the problem?'

'We're not panicking,' Ven says. 'We're reacting to a life-threatening situation. I don't know about *you guys,* but when people are about to die, I don't think you can react too much.'

The fact that Ven is being even more of a sniping bastard than usual makes me think that he must be worried.

'It seems pretty likely that because of Robin the Leadership know at least some of our plans,' I say to Kurt.

'You really think some random guy she met in the Wilderness is a Leadership agent?'

Ven takes a corner at such speed that I'm thrown up against him. 'Would you talk to Robin unless someone was paying you?' he says.

'She said he was as old as Ven, why else would he be interested in Robin?' Tanisha says.

'And he'd been asking her questions about the Resistance,' I add.

'I just thought that it could all be a coincidence,' Kurt says.

'I used to be surprised that you're good with a gun, Kurt,' Ven says, 'but I'm rapidly coming to the conclusion that it's because tuning everything else out really isn't a task for you because you're never really tuned in, are you? Which alternate plane of reality were you on when our insider told us that they were sending a couple of teenagers posing as someone else to cause trouble?'

'Okay, okay, man, you are tetchy.'

'I'm trying to save hundreds of lives. It makes me a little tense.'

'It's the bracelet I'm worried about,' I say to Kurt. 'If she's wearing a bracelet this Jed gave her, she could be bugged. At the very least, I bet you there's a tracking device in it. If the Leadership know where she is, they'll see that she's crossed over to this side and they'll realise that something is up. The guards will be on that team any second now.'

'How do you know she's wearing it?' Tanisha asks. 'Maybe she left it behind.'

This idea doesn't seem to have occurred to Ven and a look of horror soaks across his face. He's worried about the babies that have been left behind with the C.C. team in the hospital.

'No,' I say, putting a hand on his arm because I'm afraid he's going to crash the car. 'I'm sure she was wearing it. She said "*this* bracelet" like she was looking right at it.'

This seems to calm Ven, or at least he goes back to looking furious instead of horrified. I don't know what would have happened if he'd thought that the bracelet was back at the hospital with the babies.

Ven drives at top speed for a few minutes.

'Here we go,' he says and shrieks to a halt.

We get out of the car and Ven leads us down an alleyway. He looks behind us before he stops at a heavy metal door and presses his fingertip to the reader on the frame. It clicks and the door swings open. I take one look inside and what I see freezes my heart.

I thought things were bad before.

They're a hundred times worse now.

'What is it?' Tanisha says.

Ven pushes past me and looks into the storage room himself. Sitting next to a pile of boxes, with her hands tied and a gag in her mouth is a small girl in her underwear. Her eyes blaze with fear.

'Who the hell is that?' Tanisha asks.

'I've got a pretty good idea,' I say.

I bend down to the little girl. She flinches away.

'I'm not going to hurt you, I promise. Just answer a question for me. Are you in the Girl Guards?'

Her eyes widen even further. Slowly she nods.

'How did you know that?' Kurt asks.

Ven is rubbing his forehead with the heel of his hand. 'Nard.'

'Of course,' I say.

'Nard what?' Tanisha clutches her hands in frustration. 'Will someone tell me what the efwurd is going on?'

'Remember the tickets for the celebration in the central

square that we got hold of?' I say to Tanisha. 'We swapped the old woman's one for yours. The only one we didn't use was for a Girl Guard. Nard obviously decided that he was going to use it. And he needed a Girl Guard uniform. This is where he got it.'

Kurt approaches the girl slowly and reaches to untie her hands.

'Don't,' Ven says. 'And don't take her gag off.'

'That's a bit harsh.'

'She'll scream. We'll have to leave her for now. She's a security risk.'

Kurt shakes his head at Ven, but he lets go of the cord, sits down and pats the girl's arm instead. At first she stiffens, but Kurt keeps smiling and patting.

'Isn't Nard a bit old to pass as a Girl Guard?' Kurt asks, still smiling at the girl. 'And, er, the wrong sex.'

'I don't think he was planning to wear it himself,' I say.

Tanisha draws in a breath. 'You mean he's taken this girl's uniform and put one of our little ones in it? Why?'

Ven and I exchange looks. Ven walks to the back of the store and starts tapping at the electronic lock on a reinforced door.

'I can't be sure,' I say, 'but at the planning meeting Nard was very keen on using explosives to take out The Leader.'

The lock beeps. Ven walks into the cupboard and starts searching for something.

'I don't get it.' Tanisha shakes her head. 'He's got a ticket to the celebrations for a Girl Guard, so he's going to send a little kid dressed in the uniform into the square, and then what does he think he's going to get them to do? '

'Well, Tanisha,' Ven says, 'there's a bloody great gap on the shelf where a whole load of explosives used to be. Do you think that could be a clue?'

'C'mon,' says Tanisha. 'Does he really reckon he can get a kid to hide a bomb?'

'I think it's worse than that,' I say. 'I think the kid *is* the bomb.'

Tanisha and Kurt stare at me in horror.

'Do you mean he's sent one of our tinies on a suicide mission? I don't believe it. None of our kids would agree to do that,' Tanisha says.

'I doubt he's asked them,' Ven says.

'Ven's right,' I say. 'He's not going to tell the kid his plan, they might blab or screw it up. He's just going to use them as a carrier.'

'That guy is seriously wrong.' Kurt's forehead crumples. 'Why would he turn a little kid into a bomb?'

'Because it was the only idea his feeble brain could come up with that seemed to guarantee success.' Ven rifles through a shelf of equipment and locates a bashed-up communicator. 'It's almost as if the universe thinks that solving one life-threatening situation would be too easy for me,' he says. 'So now we've got two major problems.' He passes the communicator to me. 'You're the technology expert. Can you fix that?'

I take a look. 'I can try.'

'Do it.'

'I still don't get it,' Kurt persists. 'We were planning to get The Leader and the Leadership anyway, why is Nard trying to do a new plan?'

'Because he wants to be the one to kill The Leader. And he wants to do it his way.' Ven rubs a hand across his face. 'We need to split up.'

I nod.

'Blake, you come with me to sort out the huge mess that Robin has caused and you two can deal with Nard's explosives obsession.'

'What do we do?' Tanisha asks.

Kurt is slack-jawed, looking between us and the girl.

'Maybe I should go with Tanisha,' I say.

'Because you'd be great at spotting the girl with the secret bomb? How many of the Resistance girls aged seven to eleven do you think you would recognise, Blake? Can I suggest for not the first time in our acquaintance that you remember that all of my decision-making is based on reason, and that if you feel the need to reverse one of those decisions you should assume that you are wrong and shut the efwurd up.'

'I just . . .' I look at Kurt.

'Kurt is going to be fine, aren't you, Kurt? Kurt has had years of training, all of which is going to inform what he does next. Kurt and Tanisha are going to the square now. One of them is going to watch the gate and the other one

304

is going to patrol the square until they find the Resistance girl. Remember that, Kurt, you're looking for one of our girls around this high.' He gestures with his hand. 'When you find her you take her to the nearest quiet space – off the top of my head I'm going to suggest a toilet stall – and you deactivate that bomb.'

'I can deactivate a bomb,' I say. 'At least, I think I can. We learnt about it in our Future Leaders sessions.'

'Tanisha can do it. She's practised on the real thing.'

Tanisha makes to speak but Ven cuts her off. 'If you really can't do it, then get it well away from the crowds of people.' He looks at his watch. 'The Leader isn't scheduled to speak until twelve, so I think we can assume that if Nard has made a bomb it won't be programmed to go off until around that time. You've got less than two hours.'

'We need a car,' Tanisha says.

'The entire district is busy celebrating. If you can't steal a car in these conditions then you're not the girl I thought you were.' Ven dismisses her with a nod.

'Let's go, Blake.'

'But what about the girl?' Kurt asks. 'Can we let her go?'

'I told you, she's a risk.' Ven moves to the door.

I follow him. I'm sorry for the little girl, but no harm is going to come to her in the lock-up.

'Then I'll stay here with her,' Kurt says.

Ven spins back round. 'The hell you will. Listen to me, Kurt, there's another sweet little girl out there and, unlike this one who is safe in a storage unit, she's got a ton of explosives strapped to her. I'm not losing you to babysitting duty.'

'Okay, okay.' Kurt takes the girl's hand and starts whispering to her rapidly, telling her not to worry and that he'll come back and set her free. Then he follows Tanisha down the street and Ven and I go back to the car.

He accelerates away so fast that I'm thrown back in my seat. I prise open the back of the communicator and take a look.

'The failsafe fuse has blown,' I say. 'I need something metallic to bypass it.'

'I don't know if you've noticed,' Ven says, 'but my hands are pretty full with keeping us on the road while we travel at high speeds. You're going to have to find your own something metallic.'

I poke about in the storage section of my door. Nothing useful there. In the glove compartment the first thing I notice is a gun, but since that's no use to me at the moment I keep looking. I find a ballpoint pen, which I take apart and, using the little metal spring inside, I manage to get the communicator working again.

I try to call Patrick over and over, but either something has happened to prevent him from answering, or their communicator has now been cut off too. I have to hope it's the latter.

Robin's team were heading for the media sector of the central district. We have no choice but to chase after them.

'What the hell was Nard thinking?' Ven snarls.

'It's just like you said, he wants to be the one to kill The Leader.'

'We're *going* to kill The Leader and we're going to do it in the most effective way. We're not going to murder innocent children at the same time. Do you know how powerful the stuff Nard took is? Powerful enough to take out far more than that square. Does he think anyone will have any sympathy with the Resistance if we kill a load of families on their day out? And what about our message? What about the uprising? The celebrations will be called off and we'll have lost the chance to make our point.'

It's all true and I haven't got anything helpful to add.

Ven is curled over the steering wheel, radiating anger and tension. I can almost hear his mind whirring through possibilities. In the middle of my swirling despair I try to hold on to Ven's brilliance. His and mine. Between us there must be a solution.

'We can fix this,' I say.

And for the first time I'm glad that we're on the same side.

It doesn't take us long before we reach the main road into the central district, which Robin's team must have taken to get to their destination. When we hit it, Ven really puts his foot down and we burn along. There's very little traffic. Everyone will be at home or at parties. We're travelling much faster than the bus carrying Robin's team could; we should be able to catch them up. And then what will happen? Are the guards already on the tail of the bus? Have they caught them?

While I'm trying to prepare for the various scenarios that might greet us, I continue to try to reach them on their communicator. I'm still dialling when we turn a corner and Ven sucks in his breath hard. As I look up, he swerves violently to avoid a stationary red van in the middle of the road, which almost sends us into a skid. I twist around to look at the van; there's a red-clad guard slumped over the wheel.

'Driver's dead,' I say. Then I notice that his passenger has fallen out of the van on to the road. The wind catches his jacket and it flaps about like a broken wing.

'Do you think they were after our lot?' Ven asks.

I spot another body not dressed in red. Instead, she's in a black uniform. But her face with its blank staring eyes seems too young to be a real delivery person.

'Yes.' I point towards the girl. 'I think they had a shootout.' I look around to see if there's any sign of the bus or more Resistance members.

'They can't be far away,' Ven says. 'We've got to get them off that bus before every guard in the district shows up.'

'And get rid of the bracelet and find out if they're missing a small child who may now be an unwitting suicide bomber,' I say.

'Yes, thank you, Blake, I am so glad that I brought you along. You always know just how to lift my spirits.'

The road starts an ascent and I turn around to look back at the bodies behind us. I try to picture what happened. The guards appearing behind the bus are starting to shoot. The team leaning out of the windows to retaliate ... Are there casualties on the bus? Please let Ilex be all right.

We approach the brow of the hill and I sit up straight, ready to scan the road running down in front of us.

The car reaches the top and there, at the bottom, I see the bus.

Consumed by flames.

42

We're too late. Please don't let it be their bus. But it *is* their bus. I recognise it. The flames are climbing. Black smoke swirls upwards. Don't let Ilex be dead. But he must be. Everyone on that bus must be charred to their bones.

'Can you see any guards?' Ven says, looking over his shoulder. His voice sounds strange, as if I'm in a cave.

'I . . .'

I can't speak. I can't think. They can't be dead. Ilex and Robin and all those kids.

Ven pulls on to the grassy bank a short distance behind the burning bus.

I fumble to open the door. My hands are shaking so badly that I can hardly grip the catch. I turn to the bus; can we put the fire out? What good would it do anyway?

'Ven! Blake!' someone shouts.

I turn around and there at the edge of some trees is Ilex waving his arms. He's alive. And he's not alone. Emerging from between the branches are more Resistance members. Thank God. I struggle to catch my breath.

I see Robin at the same moment that Ven does. We both sprint towards her; Ven gets there first.

'Where's the bracelet?' he says.

'He made us get off the bus,' Robin says, pointing at Ilex who is striding in our direction. 'And then . . .' her eyes blaze '. . . and then he *stole* my bracelet and threw it away.' She looks at us to share her outrage.

'Blake!' Ilex says.

'Ilex, how did you know?'

'I listened to you talking to Robin about that shrap – that . . . bracelet and I knowed you were thinking it was bad. I gived it to Patrick and he looked and seed the thing, that tracker thing, and we . . .' He mimes throwing the bracelet away.

I'm beaming. 'I told you you're smart. Where did you throw the bracelet?' I ask.

'On to a lorry!' Robin snaps. 'He shouts and bosses me about just like the rest of you and—'

'Be quiet,' Ven says in a dangerously low voice. He takes Robin by the shoulders and looks her in the eyes. 'You were very nearly responsible for the death of everyone here – and you still might be. Shut up and think about that.'

Robin looks thunderous, but she closes her mouth.

Patrick jogs up behind Ven.

'Patrick said to do the burning of the bus,' Ilex says.

311

'When guards come they'll maybe be thinking we're all dead.'

'A guard van started shooting at us,' Patrick says. 'We lost Hannah. What's going on, Ven?'

Ven's eyes flash. 'What's going on? I was hoping that on account of you being in charge you might be able to tell me that, but perhaps you consider your title of captain of this team to be a merely decorative one.'

Patrick colours. 'We found a tracking device in Robin's bracelet and—'

'I know they were tracking Robin. *I* knew that despite the fact that I was miles away from you, and despite the fact that apart from her torrents of abuse aimed at me, I have rarely spoken to Robin; the question is why you, the captain of her team, who was sat on a bus with her, did not.'

'I didn't—'

'No, you didn't and *that's* the problem. This is an efwurding shambles! I should have worn a paper bag over my head while I was delivering those lectures on looking after your team because then you wouldn't have been mesmerised by my good looks, which you clearly were, because I can think of no other good reason why someone who calls themselves a member of the Resistance would fail to listen to the basic rules of leadership.'

Patrick looks like he's going cry.

Ven lifts both his fists and for a moment I think that he's going to strike Patrick, but then he throws his hands to the side in a gesture of frustration.

'Tell them what to do,' Ven growls at me as he turns away. 'I need to think.' He stalks off back to the car.

For a moment I feel lost. I've become used to following Ven's orders. What should they do? They can't stay here. I look around. We're only a mile or so from the district.

'Split into groups,' I say to Patrick. 'You're too conspicuous all together. Stick close to the trees for cover and head for your original targets in the Media sector. You've still got time.'

Patrick nods. 'We'll get back on track, I promise.'

'Blake!' Ven shouts. 'We've got other problems to deal with!' He's already back in the car, holding open the passenger door for me.

'Good luck,' I say to Ilex and Patrick. I run over to the car and jump in.

Ven puts his foot to the floor and we speed away.

When we hit the district's shopping sector Ven says, 'Do you think Nard would definitely be able to make an actual bomb? He's not on the Defence team.'

I'm surprised by this question. 'I think Nard knows a fair bit about explosives. And guns. And weapons in general. Nard is pretty much into anything that can kill someone.'

'How do you know?'

'Apparently he talks about it a lot. Haven't you heard him?'

'I can't listen to the babbling of every member of the

313

Resistance. I've got a filter. When people like Nard speak, it just sounds like buzzing to me.'

'Don't you remember him going on about Plan Scarlett – which I heard involves blowing the Leadership up with a ton of explosives. You said it was a no-go.'

'I vaguely remember that.'

'I'm surprised that someone of your intelligence would forget a thing like that.'

He takes his eyes off the road to give me a heavy-lidded stare. 'Blake, I have to apply my brilliance to any number of plans that are actually occurring. I don't waste time on the ones I've rejected.'

Now isn't the time to get into an argument with Ven so I content myself with saying, 'Maybe sometimes you should give a little more thought to the ones you've rejected.'

'Where are we going?' I ask, realising that I have no idea where we're headed now.

'We're going to get into position ready for The Leader's speech, just like we planned.'

I blink. 'Is there any point if Nard's bomb is going to blow him up anyway? Shouldn't we be getting away? Or looking for the little girl?'

'We don't know for sure what Nard is up to. Maybe he's taken his explosives and his uniform elsewhere. No one has reported a missing team member yet. If there is an exploding child wandering around in the square, then we'll have to trust that Tanisha and Kurt have picked her up, because we are going to carry on exactly as arranged. We've worked too hard to abandon the plan now.'

He is seriously determined. So am I. I don't even consider trying to talk him out of it. There may be a bomb in the vicinity, but this is probably the best opportunity I'll ever get to kill The Leader.

We park several streets away and then walk over to the main square. We're well behind schedule and I struggle to keep up with Ven's urgent striding. As we approach, the air vibrates with the throb of loud music. The celebrations have already started. Balloons and long strings of bunting are swaying in the breeze.

The main square is surrounded by government buildings. All entrances have been gated for the occasion and admission is strictly by ticket only. As we get closer to the gate my heart speeds up. I'm afraid that the guards will know who we are. I focus my eyes on a man spreading a picnic blanket out on the grass for his family and let Ven hand over the tickets.

The guard on the gate says nothing.

I follow Ven through the swarms of people and stalls selling sweets and flags, until we reach a tall grey building on the other side of the square. Just as we expected, the main entrance is hidden by a large section of boarding which shows a display of 'Letters to my Leader' written by young children.

'Wait for it,' Ven says.

We hover for a moment and I wonder what it would be like to forget about all of this and just sit down on the grass and let someone else worry about making everything right.

The music cuts out and a voice says, '*Please welcome back your host . . .*'

There's a storm of clapping and the music swells. Ven slips behind the boarding and I follow.

Ven reaches for the door press-pad and taps in the code that I found for him by hacking into the building's security records. Once inside, we creep up two flights of stairs. Ven locates a caretaker's cupboard and produces an old-fashioned metal key. Inside, I'm relieved to see the bags that were sent ahead. At least some parts of our plot seem to have gone to plan. I pick up my bag and we move to a large open-plan office that looks out over the square.

'Keep low,' Ven says.

We drop to our knees and crawl to the windows.

I take out my rifle and calibrate the laser sight as quickly as I can. Slowly, I raise my head high enough to look out of the window. I've got a great view of the stage.

The presenter is bouncing about telling the audience what a wonderful day it is and what a great man The Leader is. The crowd are quite happy to cheer at the appropriate moments. It's just a day out for most of them. They're oblivious to the fact there might be a child sat next to them with enough explosives strapped to her to blow them all to smithereens.

My heart squeezes. Where is Kay? If a bomb did go off, would she be safe from the blast? Considering the quantities of explosives Ven was talking about, I'd be dead for sure. But I try not to think about that.

'The Leader will be on soon,' Ven says in a low voice.

There's a thump somewhere below and behind us. 'What was that?' I ask.

'What?'

317

'I heard something. There's someone in here.'

'I can't hear anything.'

The sound comes again. Ven's eyes meet mine and I know he's heard it too.

There's someone coming up the stairs.

318

I only have time to swing my rifle round so it's pointing at the door before it opens.

I squeeze my trigger finger and . . . stop.

Standing in the doorway wearing a Girls Guards' uniform is Kay.

'King hell, Kay! I almost shot you.'

'Blake!' she says, coming into the room.

'Oh, it all makes sense now,' Ven drawls. 'We should have realised before that your pixie friend was the perfect size for the uniform.'

'You've got to get out,' Kay says. 'Nard sent me—'

'We know Nard sent you,' I say. But my brain is fumbling to work out why.

'What the hell are you doing here?' Ven asks. 'Didn't he tell you to stay in the square?'

Kay frowns. 'No, Nard told me to get you out. He heard a thing on the guard communicators. They're searching all the buildings around the square, but we can't get you on the communicator here because guards listen to all com-municators around here. We needed to get into the square to tell you to get out, but no one can get in without a ticket, but Nard had a ticket for a Girl Guard—'

Ven grabs his gun and stands up to go. 'At least we don't have to worry about a bomb any more.'

'Wait,' I say.

'Blake, *they're coming*,' Kay says.

'Nard's not trying to blow anyone up, he's saving our behinds,' Ven says.

'No, wait! Think about it. When did Nard hear the guards talking, Kay? Did you hear it?'

'No. It was a little bit back.'

'And when do you think he kidnapped the girl?' I say to Ven.

Ven can see where I'm going.

'Nard didn't get hold of that uniform on the off-chance that he'd need to send Kay to warn us about the guards. He's planned this. He's . . .' I screw up my face. I don't know what he's doing. I don't even know if we should still be worrying about a bomb. 'Kay, did he give you anything to carry?'

'No. What's going on?'

I look at Kay's slight figure. There's no way Nard could strap explosives to her without her knowledge.

Ven's got his eyes closed in concentration. 'Let's think. He's sent us Kay. Why would he do that? What's special about Kay?'

Kay has paled. 'He said you're in danger, and he said it's bad that no one knows where you are, and I ...' She glances at Ven because of course she's not supposed to know where we are. I wasn't supposed to tell her, but Nard was banking on me not being able to keep my mouth shut. '... I said I know where Blake is, so Nard said I have to come to you because I'm the only one who knows where you are.'

Below us, the door crashes open.

Ven sucks in his breath. 'I don't think you're the only one who knows where we are any more.'

'That bastard Nard has betrayed us!' Ven says, grabbing his backpack. 'Come on, there's a walkway to the next building on the fifteenth floor.'

Footsteps are thundering up the stairs. It has to be guards. I snatch a revolver from my bag and press it into Kay's hands. We rush after Ven, who is taking the stairs two at a time. I hear a hissed command below us. I can't believe we were worrying about a bomb and all this time Nard just wanted to use Kay to show the guards where to catch us in the act. Does he really hate me that much? Enough to ruin our chances of taking down The Leader?

We keep running. Looking over the bars, I see a flash of red beneath us. It's guards all right. Ven and Kay are already ahead of me. I work my aching legs faster. We reach the next landing. My gun is heavy in my hands. What is Ven's plan? What can we do, even if we make it into the next building? I'm too breathless to ask him. The footsteps are louder and closer. I think about angles of sight. Once they reach the floor below us, will they be able to get a clear shot?

'Keep,' I gasp, 'to ... the wall.'

Ven and Kay obediently move towards the wall as they run on. I'm falling behind again.

I look up. We're still a long way from the fifteenth floor. I stumble on and risk a look back. The guards are definitely gaining on us. Outside, I can hear children singing.

'Ven,' I say, 'we ... won't ... make it.' We've reached a landing and I stop. It's better that we hide, so we've got the advantage when the shooting starts. Ven and Kay stop too. Ven looks back, and then up. He freezes. It's his first moment of indecision I've seen since we met. I move behind a pillar and try to pull Kay with me, but she steps in front of Ven, her back to his front, and flings his arm around her neck. The guards round the corner. They see a tiny blonde Girl Guard apparently taken hostage by a member of the Resistance.

'Help me!' Kay screams. 'They've got me!'

The bunch of guards look at each other in confusion. I put a bullet through the forehead of the nearest one. Ven and Kay send a spray of fire across the front row before they've even realised what's happening. They tumble backwards, knocking over those behind.

'This way,' I say, flinging open the door behind me and running into another open-plan office space. Outside, music is pumping. I dive behind a desk then twist on to my knees and raise my gun. A guard pushes through the door and I shoot him right in the chest. He falls. Another guard – Ven hits him first. Then a jumble of them push through the door together and we're all shooting at the same time. Red-clad bodies hit the floor again and again. We're killing them. Efwurding hell, I'm shooting guards and I'm killing them. Out of the jerking mass of red, one of the guards breaks free and runs towards me. I fumble and my gun slips as he lifts his and aims. He's only a few metres from me and as I duck I know that his bullet is heading straight for me. It whizzes past my cheek. The guard stops like he has hit an invisible wall and then crumples.

Kay has shot him in the neck.

I turn my gun back to the door, but there is no need. No more guards come.

Outside, the rousing music thumps and jingles on. Has no one heard all the shooting?

My heart is banging against my ribs. 'Kay? Are you all right?'

Kay stands up from behind a knocked-over table and gives me a shaky smile.

'Yes, thank you, Blake,' Ven says, from his corner of the office. 'So kind of you to enquire. I am entirely unhurt. Don't tax your limited emotional intelligence by worrying about me further.'

My hands are shaking. I put down my gun and press my palms to my face. I can't believe what just happened.

'I dropped my bag,' Ven says. 'Give me some ammo, Blake. Kay, check they're all gone.'

I toss my bag over to Ven. Kay moves to the door, stepping over the bodies. There must be a twenty of them. She pulls the door open a crack.

'I th— *Ah!*'

The guard lying nearest to Kay has grabbed her by the ankle. She swings her gun around, but he knocks it flying out of her hand. Kay twists and shakes, but the guard scrambles on to his knees and grips her arm.

'Get off!' Kay shouts.

I run towards them. The guard lets go of Kay for a second to pull a revolver from his waistband. Kay sees him. She spins round, flicking out a leg to kick the gun from his hand, but he pulls back and she misses. The guard snatches at the back of her jacket and, as she continues to turn, it rips right across the back. Something falls out of the lining and on to the ground.

'STOP!' yells Ven.

Everyone freezes.

Ven is still in his corner, holding my bag.

The guard clutches his gun centimetres from Kay's stomach.

I am near enough to reach out and touch him.

And we're all staring at the flashing red light on the bomb that has just tumbled out of Kay's jacket.

Oh God, Nard *did* want to blow everybody up. He just wanted to make damn sure that Ven, Kay and I were right at the heart of the blast.

Nobody moves.

'As I'm sure you are aware,' Ven says to the guard, 'that is a bomb – and I think it's safe to say that it's set to go off as soon as The Leader comes on stage.'

Outside the crowd are applauding someone.

'Which must be soon. You'd better stop waving that gun about, because this young man,' he points to me, 'is the only one in here who can disable it – and he's not going to like it if you hurt his girlfriend.'

Efwurd. Ven wants me to disable the bomb.

The guard stares at him. His eyes flick from Ven to me and back to Ven. 'Then I won't hurt her,' he says, 'for now.' He doesn't move the gun.

'Blake . . .' Ven says.

I'm regretting ever having mentioned my theoretical

understanding of bombs. 'I think it would be better if you did it,' I say.

He shakes his head. 'Unfortunately, Blake, I know so efwurding much about almost everything that there just wasn't room for a few things. This is one of them. You're up.'

King hell, it's all on me. I crouch down and take a look at the device. Out of the corner of my eye I see the guard turn and look at the door.

'I wouldn't bother if I were you,' Ven says to him. 'Doesn't matter how fast you run now, if this goes off you'll be dead. Or we'll shoot you as soon as your back's turned anyway.'

I'm afraid to even touch the bomb, but I reason that Kay brought it all the way here without it exploding.

When I get it open, I'm relieved to be able to identify most of the components. The design is fairly simple. If I can just disconnect the timing device then we should be okay.

'I need a knife.'

'I don't have any knife,' Kay says.

'Nor me,' Ven says.

The guard clears his throat. 'I've got one.'

'Then you'd better give it to me.' I put out a hand.

'You get it,' he says. 'Top pocket.'

He doesn't want to put down his gun. I reach inside his breast pocket and pull out a flick knife. Now, I just have to cut the connection to the timer. I pull up the wire and position the knife. I touch the blade to the wire.

Wait.

I need to be sure I'm doing the right thing.

Outside, the opening chords of the Leadership anthem blare out.

'Blake ...' Ven says. We both know that the music means The Leader must be seconds from appearing on stage.

Sweat gathers under my arms. I imagine Nard's smirking face. He wouldn't have made it this easy. There's bound to be a trap. I take another look. I think I'm right. It looks like he's wired it up so that cutting off the timer will trip the explosive. So first I need to break that connection. But there are two possible wires ... Which one is it? What do I do? Sweet efwurd, we're all going to die.

I tilt the device towards me so that the guard can't see. I don't know which wire to cut. There's no way of knowing. Either one could be a secondary trigger. The anthem rises to a crescendo. If I don't decide soon, we'll all be dead anyway.

Red. I'm going red. My hand moves in front of me and ... I cut the yellow wire.

I wince.

Nothing happens.

Quickly, I cut the connection to the timer, too.

The flashing stops. I've done it. I've disabled it. But I don't look up and I keep fiddling with the wires. The moment I stop, the guard is going to shoot Kay. Without moving my head, I use my peripheral vision. The guard's gun has drooped. Kay's knees bend very slightly. If she's moving, maybe she's got a plan.

I sigh loudly to keep the guard's attention on me. I keep prodding at the device.

From outside we clearly hear the announcer say, '*Ladies and gentlemen, please give a very enthusiastic welcome to the cause of our celebrations . . . It's The Leader!*'

'What colour does that wire look to you?' I ask the guard. 'Is that blue or green?'

Kay sinks lower.

The guard leans for a better look. 'Blue. It's blue. *Come on*,' he says in a thick voice. 'They're introducing The Lead—'

He doesn't finish because Kay snatches up one of the guards' guns from the floor and shoots him in the head.

Blood splatters across my face.

The crowd are going crazy.

'*Blake*—'

'It's done, Ven. It was done two minutes ago. I just couldn't let the guard know that.'

I turn to Kay. She's staring at the messy remains of the guard.

'Well done,' I say. 'Are you okay?'

'I'm okay.' She drags her eyes away from the guard. 'Well done for you. Doing that bomb.'

'Yes, you're both efwurding heroes,' Ven says. 'Of course it might have been simpler if any one of us had been ready with our guns when he came back from the dead.'

329

It's true. We're a disgrace. I wipe the blood from my face with my sleeve and exhale slowly. The last ten minutes are a terrible blur.

The smooth tones of The Leader penetrate my fug.

'... *celebration of our nation and of our achievement.*'

'It's him,' Kay says.

'Get to the window,' Ven snaps.

We rush back across the office.

I pick up my gun and run to the left-hand window, but my view of The Leader is obscured by a lighting tower. This isn't how it was supposed to be; this is not the floor that we planned to shoot from. I dash to the next window. It's the same problem.

Then it happens. The Leadership logo displayed on the big screen at the back of the stage changes to an image of The Leader's angry, jerking body at the Academy. The Leader's voice coming over the speakers is replaced with Ven's, saying, '*Our Leader is a man who encourages the use of starvation and electric shocks to control our children.*'

'It's starting,' Kay says.

'Efwurd, there's no clear shot in here! Next door,' Ven says.

We run out of the room and down the corridor. I'm aware of the complete silence of the audience while Ven's voice runs on.

'*Our Leader sends teenagers to work in factories with conditions like these ...*'

330

As we run across the room towards the windows I see the screen change to footage of the factory, featuring the twisted and melted face of one woman and the missing limbs of another. There's an audible gasp from the crowd.

I can see The Leader now. He seems bewildered by what's happening; he continues to speak into the microphone, even though all the crowd can hear is Ven's speech.

I reach to open the window. Where's the catch? Where's the efwurding catch?

A man scuttles on to the stage and starts fiddling with the microphone, but he can do nothing to bring back The Leader's voice. The Leader has now turned around and is watching the brutal images on the screen.

These windows are computer controlled. There is no catch.

'*We can tell the Leadership that we will not tolerate child abuse and enforced slavery. We can tell them that we demand to be heard.*'

Ven is effing and blinding at the next window along.

One of The Leader's assistants runs on stage and rips down the fabric screen. The image of an emaciated Academy child disappears.

'Break it!' Kay says, and she slams the butt of her gun into the glass. It holds.

Ven's voice continues. *We must all rise up and take back our country. Factory workers – down your tools. Learning Community students – refuse to be indoctrinated. Academy Specials – break out of your prison. We must say no to a government that hurts our children and attempts to control our minds. Fight for your freedom . . .'*

I grab a chair and slam the legs into the window. It cracks.

As I pull back, I catch a glimpse of the motionless crowd. How are they going to respond to Ven's call to arms? They don't seem angry. They just look stunned.

I hurl the chair forward again.

The glass shatters.

Kay and Ven are still hammering at their window with their guns.

Ven's commentary is lost to a high-pitched squeal of feedback. Someone somewhere has succeeded in stopping the broadcast. As I lift my gun, the insider at the media centre flashes into my head and I wonder if he is already dead.

I take my aim.

The squeal cuts out.

I fire.

In the same instant that I move my finger, a man from the crowd rugby-tackles The Leader and he hits the floor. My bullet tears through the screen behind them.

To my right, Ven's window finally shatters. Two guards rush on stage to pull the rugby-tackler off and more follow them to create a wall between The Leader and the audience.

I reposition my gun, but I can't get a clear shot at The Leader.

One of the guards jerks backwards, followed by the presenter. I look round in surprise. Ven is taking shot after shot; he's not bothered by who he hits in order to get to The Leader. I see a flash of black suit as The Leader is hauled off stage by the guards.

'Bastard's getting away,' Ven says. 'Jesus! We'll never catch him now.'

In the distance I hear an explosion.

Some of the crowd seem frozen, unable to take in what's going on, but others are surging towards the exits. People are being trampled underfoot. Why are they running away? Didn't they hear what the recording said? There's a small knot of people crowding around the stage, shouting. They look angry, but everyone else just looks terrified.

There's another explosion, this time much closer. I hope this means the teams sent to cause havoc at the power plants and the water suppliers have succeeded. I take my binoculars from my pocket and scan the crowd. A guard at one of the gates is bellowing at the people as they try to leave. A kid, shoved forward by the movement of those behind him, bangs into another guard and without hesitating the guard hits him round the head with a pistol. The boy's father grabs the guard by the collar and the mother punches him. The people around them shout and gesticulate too. I scan across the square. All over, the guards are treating families as if they're all proven revolutionaries and at least some of the crowd are reacting angrily.

The crowd are shaken up and appalled by the horrible images from the screen. The worst thing the guards can do is to treat them roughly, because they can't help responding in the way their adrenaline-filled bodies tell them to – fighting back.

'Why aren't they doing anything?' Ven asks.

'They are. Some of them are,' Kay says.

Shouts reach us through the broken windows.

'How can you treat children like that?'

'My brother's in a factory!'

'What the hell is wrong with you?'

But they're in the minority. I realise that most of the public are simply terrified. I don't think we've generated nearly enough anger. It's all gone horribly wrong.

Nevertheless, a pocket of the crowd *has* descended on a Leadership car. It seems unlikely that The Leader could be in there, but it serves as a representation of the whole government.

A man with thick sinewy arms starts banging on the window. 'Get The Leader out here now!'

People surround the car and start rocking it.

A man flings himself across the bonnet of the car. For a moment I think that he's trying to shield whoever is inside, but then I see the red splatter on the white shirt of the woman next to him and I realise that he's been shot. The woman's mouth opens in a scream that I can't hear above the shouting and shrieking around the square. The others circling the car realise what's happened and start to back away. Some people are still trying to get to the car and the result is a horrible crush of bodies. I see arms grabbing at anything, trying to stay upright, and I see several people lose their footing and get trampled underfoot.

And that's when the guards open fire.

This is not what is supposed to happen.

I swing my binoculars, but I can find no sign of The Leader.

'He's gone,' I say. 'What are we going to do now? How will we find him?'

335

'Less talking, more shooting,' Ven says. He's picking off guards one by one.

'We have to go,' Kay says. 'They're going to come for the shooters. They will be looking all places.'

Ven reloads and lifts his gun to the window again.

'Kay's right, come on,' I say.

'I'm going to finish what I started.'

'If you stay, you'll get caught. You're more use to the revolution alive than dead,' I say.

'It doesn't really matter. I'm staying.'

There's a roaring in the sky and people's flags and paper cups are sent blowing across the grass. A helicopter has appeared overhead.

A bullet hits the window between myself and Ven and shatters it.

'Blake!' Kay drags me backwards by the elbow towards the door. 'Ven, *now*,' she shouts.

'There are officials all over the grass,' he says, without pausing in his shooting. 'I'm not missing this opportunity.'

Kay pulls me across the office.

'Ven, come on! *Please*,' I say.

'I SAID NO!'

Kay pushes me out of the door.

'We shouldn't just leave him,' I say, but I let Kay drag me along anyway.

We get one floor down before we hear footsteps on the stairs.

'Hide,' Kay says. We duck through a door. Kay slips

down the corridor and through another door, but I turn around and crouch low so that I can watch the guards coming up the stairs, through the glass window in the door. They stream past. There are six of them.

Before I know what I'm doing I've pushed the door open and I'm following them back up the stairs. *Shoot them, shoot them*, my brain is saying, but there will only be time to shoot one or two before the others turn around and shoot back.

I'm almost on their heels when one of them throws open the door of the office Ven is in. Someone must have seen him taking shots. They know exactly where to find him.

I see straight away that Ven is in the middle of reloading again.

'Hands in the air!' one of them yells.

Ven doesn't move.

'Hands up or I'll kill you!'

Ven looks up. He clocks me. Slowly he shakes his head. He's telling me to go. They still haven't noticed me right behind them. I could creep away now.

The guard takes the head shake as defiance and lifts his gun.

Ven stares right into him. Doesn't he even care?

'Don't shoot!' I shout.

All six guards swing around to face me. The one with the raised gun frowns at my sudden appearance. 'You going to give me a good reason why not?'

I speak without thinking, saying the first thing my desperate brain comes up with. 'I'm The Leader's son.'

'Of course you are. That's why you're taking potshots at your daddy.'

I draw myself up. 'However things may stand between myself and my father, I think you'd better check things out with him first before shooting me or my friend.'

He thinks about it. I've seriously annoyed him. He's clearly unconvinced, but he doesn't want to get himself into trouble.

'Put your gun on the ground.'

I do as he says.

'Cuff him,' he says to another guard who does so, pinning my arms tight behind me.

'Let's get back to the enforcement centre.' He sneers at me. 'Just remember; as soon as someone tells me I can shoot you, it's done.' He turns back to Ven. 'And you—'

But Ven has disappeared.

'What the efwurd?' The guard starts kicking over desks and chairs, but Ven is nowhere to be seen.

'He's gone out the window,' one of the guards says.

'Well, get down there and find him!' He strides back to me.

I don't get to hear what happens next because he presses a stun baton to my neck.

When I come round I'm lying in a dimly lit cell, still in handcuffs. My head is pounding. I feel sore all over. Oh God, Kay. What happened to Kay? Did they find her down the corridor or did she get away? What about Ven? He must have been a right mess after jumping out that window.

I start to shake. Why can't the people I care about just be safe? I bury my face in my hands and press my lips together. It's all gone wrong. How did I ever think that I was going to manage to kill The Leader? And why did we think we could get people to fight for us after years of brainwashing from the Leadership? I should have known it would end up like this.

And now I'm completely at the mercy of the man who wants to kill me. I'm surprised they didn't just eliminate me when I was at the Learning Community. Did they think that if I was trained up as a good little future Leadership member that I would never learn about all this? Maybe I wouldn't have. It takes me a moment to remember the trigger point for this whole horrible situation. It was when I hacked into The Register to find out about my father. It's my curiosity that's brought me here. My questioning has led me to a place where I have fewer answers than ever. Should I regret that? Somehow, in spite of everything, I don't. I've found Kay. And even though I don't have the whole truth, I've learnt how important it is to keep searching for it.

The cell is three walls of solid brick and thick bars covering where the cell looks on to the corridor. The only thing in here is me.

A few minutes later, the door at the end of the corridor swings open and a guard walks towards my cell. He unlocks the door and manhandles me down the passage way and through several corridors. Neither of us says a word. He drags me into an office and pushes me into a chair in front of a desk. He steps away, but his hefty presence remains behind me. On the other side of the desk a man with grey hair and pale skin watches me without the slightest movement. I recognise him.

'My name is Radcliffe,' he says.

'You miserable efwurding bastard,' I spit. 'You're the one who shot Ali. You killed a little girl just because she wouldn't tell you what you wanted to know. You're scum.'

The man's face remains blank but his eyes hold disdain. As if what I've said is somehow distasteful.

He waits for me to settle down.

'Who are you working for?' he asks in a calm voice.

'I'm not working for anyone. You should give some thought to your own choice of boss.'

He leans forward in his chair and fixes me with a stare. 'The Leader wants you dead. I am the only thing between you and him. You should remember that when I ask you a question. Now, who,' he says in a voice so low that I can barely hear it, 'are you working with?'

'No one.'

'I'm waiting for an answer. We will remain here until I get one. If you have difficulty answering my question then I will have to persuade you.' He lifts a paper knife from his desk.

My hot anger chills to ice in my veins. If I don't give him what he wants then he is going to hurt me. In fact, whatever I do, he's going to hurt me. I want someone to come and save me, but I know that no one is going to.

I am alone and I am afraid.

I stare at the photos on the shelf behind him. I want this to be over.

'You talk or you suffer. The choice is yours. Who are you working with?'

I know what I am supposed to do. I've seen films where the heroes keep quiet under torture. I shake my head.

Radcliffe raises his eyes to the guard behind me. Before I even have time to turn and look the guard has grabbed me by the hair. He slams my face into the table.

'You're working with a group of unwashed idiots who call themselves the Resistance,' Radcliffe says. 'Tell me about them.'

'You obviously already know about them,' I say. My voice is high-pitched with fear.

'Start talking or he'll break your fingers. Although, I wouldn't worry too much about a mangled hand because unless you start cooperating I am going to kill you.'

The truth is that he's going to kill me anyway. No matter what I do. The guard grips my hand tightly.

'No,' I say.

He bends one of my fingers back. The pain runs right up the tendons in my forearm. I think I'm going to be sick.

'Give me a name,' Radcliffe says.

'No,' I say again, but this time I'm really talking to the guard. My finger is stretched to the point of agony. He's going to break it.

'What were their plans today?' Radcliffe asks.

I can't even answer.

He looks at the guard again. He yanks harder on my finger. I try to pull away but he holds me in the chair with his other hand. He's going to do it. There's an audible snap as my finger bone breaks. Christ. A whimper escapes me. The guard grips a second finger.

'Don't!' I cry.

'Their plans,' Radcliffe repeats.

The guard is wrenching back my next finger. I can't bear it.

'They're going to get The Leader,' I blurt out. 'And they'll get you, too.'

Radcliffe laughs.

I try to hold on to the thought that one day he will be punished for this, but my mind is scrambled by pain. The guard tenses and I hear my second finger break.

'Tell me.'

Nothing comes out of my mouth but a sob.

'Tell me about their leader,' Radcliffe says.

I try to shake my head. My hand hurts so much that I can't think straight.

Radcliffe nods to the guard who presses something against the skin on my arm. *Dear God.* Pain ricochets through me. I'm jerking in my chair. He's giving me an electric shock. My skin is flaming.

It stops. I gasp for breath. Their device is much stronger than the one at the Academy. The guard leans towards me and I flinch away, but he grips my arm and applies the device again. Pain knifes through me. My legs kick.

'His name is Ven,' I say.

I struggle to make my mouth form words. The guard shocks me again. Agony stabs at every inch of me. It stops. I retch. I force myself to focus my eyes on Radcliffe. I want him to ask me a question so I can tell him something and make this to stop. I can't take this kind of pain. I'm not strong enough. I can't take any more. I don't care if he kills me, I just want this to end.

He shocks me again.

I scream.

The desk blurs before my eyes.

There's a sound behind me. I swing my head round clumsily. The door opens. Someone has come. I want it to be Kay and an army of Resistance fighters carrying a whole lot of guns. But it's not my rescuers.

It's The Leader.

I struggle out of my haze to stare at him. Words have left me, but I fix my eyes on him and pour all my hatred and anger into my gaze.

He shifts uncomfortably and looks to Radcliffe.

The Leader doesn't care. He is responsible for this torture. How could a father do this to his own son? His face shows not a trace of sympathy. Why does he hate me so much?

He looks from Radcliffe to me and back again. His face pulled up in disgust.

This is it; The Leader, my father, is going to tell his aide to kill me.

Finally he opens his mouth. 'Who the hell is this?'

He's serious. My father doesn't know that he is my father. He's not faking it. He hasn't got a clue who I am. Hope surges in me. I try to focus my pain addled brain; how can I turn this to my advantage?

'He's a trouble-maker. Resistance,' Radcliffe says, non-chalantly.

Which doesn't make any sense. Radcliffe knows exactly who I am. Why is he hiding it from The Leader? What the hell is going on here?

The Leader scowls. 'What's he doing in your goddamn office, man? You should have let Lewis question him like the rest of them.'

'I didn't know you were here,' Radcliffe says. He seems a little annoyed himself.

They lock eyes for a moment. The Leader turns away. 'Get rid of him,' he says. 'Now.' He reaches for the door.

Once he walks out, I'm a dead man.

'Wait!' I say. I don't know what makes me open my

mouth. Desperation claws up my throat and once again I blurt out the only hope of leverage I have. 'I'm your son.'

The Leader turns back to the aide. 'What the hell is this, Radcliffe?'

'He's just trying to save his skin,' Radcliffe says.

'I *am* your son. He knows it—'

'Take him away,' Radcliffe says to the guard.

'Hold on,' The Leader says, staring at me hard.

'He's lying,' I say. 'He knows I'm your son.'

The Leader gives his aide an appraising look. I get the impression that this is not the first time Radcliffe has lied.

'It's true,' I say, trying to take advantage of his apparent indecision.

The Leader sighs.

'We've had kids turn up here before claiming to be The Leader's child,' Radcliffe says to me.

I shake my head. 'I'm not *claiming* to be his son. I *am* his son.' It's not as if I'm proud of the fact.

'What makes you so sure?' The Leader asks.

'My mother told me.'

'What's your mother's name?'

'Sir—' Radcliffe gets to his feet, but The Leader holds up a hand to stop him speaking.

'Anne Jackson.'

The Leader's eyes widen.

Radcliffe steps in between us. 'You haven't proved anything.'

'I don't want to prove anything. Just let me go and I'll forget all about this.'

The Leader lowers himself into Radcliffe's vacated chair.

I'm so close to him ... If only I had a gun now.

'When were you born?' he asks.

I tell him my date of birth and his eyes swivel up to the right as he makes mental calculations. He gives a slight nod. Then he fires more questions at me: my mother's job at the time, the colour of her hair, where they met. I find myself answering because I realise that I do want to prove something: that my mother is not a liar. But why does he need convincing? I thought he knew. I was sure he knew; after all, he tried to have me killed. Didn't he? But as he sits there questioning and nodding his head and staring at me, to try to find a resemblance between us, I really believe that this is the first time he's heard of my existence.

Which leaves me with the question that this whole thing started with: who wants me dead?

The Leader has the guard take off my handcuffs. Then he takes me by the elbow and steers me out of the room.

'Send a medic to my office,' he says to Radcliffe.

Radcliffe is clearly not happy that I am being plucked away from him, but he says nothing and reaches for the phone.

The medic patches me up. He puts a splint on my fingers and stitches a cut near my eye. I swallow the painkillers he holds out for me. I can feel his eyes on me while he applies antiseptic to my various cuts and grazes; he's clearly wondering who I am and why The Leader is supervising his attentions, but he hands me an ice pack for my swollen face and leaves without saying a word.

'Did you try to kill me?' I ask The Leader, before the medic has even closed the door.

His face doesn't betray any surprise. 'I did not,' he says.

'Then who the hell did?' My fingers are still throbbing,

but my fear has dwindled. I need to know what on earth is going on. 'My mother told me that your lot were after me and—'

'Now I recognise you,' he says. 'You're that crazy liberal kid from the Academy. You started a whole parcel of trouble.'

'I was trying to protect the inmates of that awful place. How can you let them treat Academy Specials like that?'

'Your mother liked to talk as well, didn't she?'

How dare he? I consider attempting to strangle him with my one good hand. 'Don't start on my mother, if it weren't for you she'd still be here.'

'Still be here?'

'Yes, she's dead! She died—' My voice wobbles. 'She died trying to protect me from the sick stuff that goes on inside an Academy. Where *you* sent me.'

'Me?'

I can't get this all straight in my head. 'Well, I thought it was you, or at least someone acting on your orders.'

'Listen, young man, before that nonsense at the Academy, I'd never seen you before – much less sent you anywhere. And, surely you'd be better off at a Learning Community. You're clearly pretty smart.' He says that with some satisfaction, as if he's a proud parent.

'I *was* at a Learning Community, but then someone tried to kill me and deleted my records. Someone who knew that I was your son. If it wasn't you behind it, then who the efwurd was it?'

349

He blinks when I swear.

'What?' I say, my voice rising. 'You don't mind having the blood of children on your hands, but a bit of swearing makes you twitch?'

He leans forward. 'Keep your mouth closed. Or I'll give you back to Radcliffe.' He turns away and lowers his voice again. 'And I wouldn't give a dog I liked to Radcliffe.'

I bite my lip. Letting him send me to be beaten to death isn't going to get rid of him and his damn regime. I've got to keep my head. 'I just don't understand why you've done the sick things you've done.'

The Leader sits back in his chair and presses his palms together. His smooth serious politician's face reappears.

'I know you're angry,' he says. 'And maybe I can explain a few things to you later when I've more time. I want you to know that I'm not unhappy to see you. A man should have a son. Now let me see . . .'

He turns to his computer and starts tapping away. This is crazy. I should just attack him. I look around for something, anything, to hit him with.

'Your records are pretty interesting,' The Leader says.

'I don't have any records, remember – someone wiped them and I disappeared.'

He looks me up and down. 'Your records are pretty interesting,' he repeats.

Clearly he has access to my files, even if no one else seems to be able to find them any more.

350

'You're a smart young man. Maybe I could make use of the family angle.' He flashes me that white-toothed smile.

Something inside me snaps. 'How can you talk about family? What about all the kids that you've hurt? Those children are all someone's son or daughter.'

'Like I said to you at the Academy, if young people can't buckle down and contribute to their country then we have to take action.'

'Action? Like giving them electric shocks?'

I spot a glass paperweight on his huge wooden desk. It's almost touching his right hand.

'We run the Academies to get the highest rate of success. You might not be keen on all our methods but—'

'You burnt that Academy down. That was your guards, wasn't it? How many kids died in that fire?'

'I didn't want those kids to die. Heck, I didn't want anyone to die.'

My eyes dart back to the paperweight. I'm pretty sure that one quick blow to the head with solid glass could kill someone. 'Are you going to spin me some propaganda about how you have to make sacrifices for the greater good?'

He lets his smile fall. 'Do you know what I've learnt? I guess it's what they teach all leaders. They tell you that you have to think of the population, not the individuals. That you can't look after every person, but you can look after your country. Well I've damn well done that. You've

351

no idea how I've protected this country, the sacrifices I've made.'

I shift forward in my chair. What is this nonsense? Does he really believe this? 'If you wanted to save people, why didn't you close down Academies? Why don't you treat factory workers like human beings?'

'It's not that simple.' He lets out a gusty sigh.

I'm still too far from the paperweight. I grip the bottom of my chair.

'We can't afford to pamper stroppy teenagers and lazy workers.'

I inch my chair a little further forward.

'They've got to learn – and it's my responsibility to make sure they do. By any means necessary. That's the way things are.'

My eyes snap back to him. 'What the hell are you talking about? You're in charge, aren't you? If you wanted to change things, you could.'

He stands up.

Now, I've got to do it now – but by the time I'm on my feet he's in front of me.

'Things aren't perfect,' he says, and I'm not sure if he's talking to me or himself. 'You have to make the best of what you're given.' He pushes me gently back into my chair, as if he thinks I stood up out of courtesy. 'I did what needed to be done.'

Oh my God, he really believes that he can somehow justify all the things he's done. I see now that it's not those who know they are doing wrong that we have to fear. It's the people who are unshakable in the belief that their actions are right, who will maim and murder – and much worse – in the name of their cause.

He takes my silence for acceptance. 'I have always done my best for this country.'

As soon as he looks away, I'm going to stand up and lean over the desk all in one rapid movement to grab the paperweight and embed it in his skull before he can stop me.

'If we're going to get along, you've got to toe the party line. You should remember that.'

'I don't want—'

He turns and takes a step towards the door. 'I need to speak to my secretary. Wait here for me.'

I fling myself across the desk and snatch up the paperweight. I push back off the desk, spin round and raise my arm.

He's disappeared out the door. It slams shut behind him. 'I don't want to get along with you!' I shout after him. 'I want to . . . *URR!*' I throw the paperweight down in frustration. How am I supposed to hold this man to account if he won't even recognise what he's done? Why didn't I go for him when I had the chance?

I don't know what I'm doing. I don't know if I should be trying to get out and find Kay, or if I can still do what I came to. There's no time to think. I try the door. The idiot has left it unlocked. I pick up the paperweight. I could still catch him.

I steal down the empty corridor and round a corner. Which way did he go?

I slip around another corner and bang straight into Kay.

I throw my arms around her. I can't believe it.

'Kay!' I stand there grinning like an idiot and she smiles back. I'm just so thankful that she's all right.

'What are you doing here?' I ask.

'I followed you.'

'Why?'

'To save you, stupid.'

My breath catches. She came to rescue me.

'They put you in the van. There was a – what's that wheel-thing we went on in the Wilderness?'

'A bike?'

She nods. 'I took a bike and followed that van and it went just a small bit to here. They got you inside. There were guards at the door, but after a time the guards saw people were shouting and fighting and they went to stop them, so I just walked in.'

'Really? Seems pretty slack for a Leadership building.'

355

'All things are—' She waggles her hands about. 'Things are broken and burning, and some places are all full of guards and some places just people smashing things and stealing things. And here I think lots of people are hiding in their houses.'

'Do you mean it's working? Are people actually rebelling against the Leadership?'

She frowns. 'I don't know. It most seems like a mess.'

That's a start. If the uprising has thrown things into chaos, that's a good start. Maybe this can still work.

'We have to find The Leader and then we have to get out of here,' I say.

Kay reaches for my hand, but I flinch backwards. She notices my bandage. 'What did they do to you?'

I shake my head; we haven't got time for this.

'Blake, we really need to go now.'

I know that she's right. I know that we're in danger. I don't want Radcliffe to find me, and I really don't want him anywhere near Kay, but still I can't bring myself to just give up on taking out The Leader.

'I can't just let him go.'

'Blake, listen to me, The Leader is already in big trouble. I don't think he's The Leader any more.'

'What?'

'When I came in I heard them talking, the men in the—' She pushes one clenched hand up under her chin and pulls the other one down her front, miming a tie. 'They said he's got to be out. They want a new Leader.'

356

'But—'

'I don't know how it is, Blake, but I know they said "Let's dispose of him". Dispose is killing, isn't it?'

'I . . . I suppose so.' My mind is reeling. Why would they want to kill their own Leader? Are they actually listening to the rioters? But what's this about a new Leader? We don't want another dictator.

'You don't have to get him,' she says. 'He's going to get got. Come on, Blake, please!'

I'm confused; there's so much to think about and no time to do it. Kay reaches for my other hand, but I'm still gripping the paperweight so she takes my elbow instead. I let her pull me down the corridor, but I'm still watching for The Leader. Just because some of his people have turned against him, it doesn't mean that his demise is guaranteed.

We slip down the thick-carpeted corridor. The place is deserted. Through open doors I see offices with huge oak desks and paintings on the walls.

'This is the way,' Kay says and takes a right turn.

At the end of the corridor is a security door. Kay stops.

'It was open before,' she says.

I take a look at the lock. It opens on fingerprint recognition. 'I can't do anything with this without tools.'

Kay takes the paperweight out of my hand and slams it hard against the pad.

'That's not going t—'

'Hey, you two!'

357

There's a man in a suit coming towards us. He raises a gun.

Kay pulls back her arm and hurls the paperweight at him. *Crack*. It hits him smack between the eyes and he keels over backwards.

'Quick,' Kay says and we rush down another corridor.

Striding in our direction is The Leader.

I stop dead. So does Kay.

'There you are,' he says to me. 'And who is this?'

My paperweight is gone. I've got nothing. He's here right in front of me and once again I'm powerless. 'Have you got a gun?' I ask Kay.

'Of course she hasn't, we don't allow weapons in Leadership buildings. Although, everything is up in the air today. We've had some trouble. I don't know where my team have got to. But you shouldn't be in here without a security pass, young lady.'

Kay looks up at him; her face is strange mixture of anger and fear.

Footsteps sound around the corner; we turn to see a red-faced man running towards us.

'Sir! Oh, thank God you're all right.'

'I'm fine. What's all this fuss about, Murray?'

'Sir, we have a situation. The public are, er, *restless* and—' he casts a glance at Kay and I but obviously decides we're the least of his concerns '—I'm afraid certain elements are proving disloyal.'

'What the heck do you mean?'

'There are calls for your immediate resignation. The public are angry and Radcliffe and his lot are trying to pin this all on you.'

'Radcliffe! I'll give him a piece of my mind.' He turns back down the corridor.

'No! Sir, we really need to get you to a safe place.'

'As soon as I've spoken t—'

'Sir, there's been a break-in at your house.'

'Good God, is my wife all right?'

'I'll take you to her. Sir, you've got to come.'

The Leader frowns. 'Yes. This is all getting out of hand. You kids had better come along with us.'

So we follow The Leader's man through the security door towards the main entrance. I haven't lost him yet. Behind his back I form my hand into a gun shape and give Kay a questioning look. I'm hoping she's still got my revolver.

Kay shakes her head. It's like a nightmare where I'm forced to watch events unfolding, but I'm completely powerless to act.

Murray is rapidly explaining which members of the Leadership have turned and how they're trying to manoeuvre things when I hear voices behind us.

'Quickly, sir,' Murray says, taking his arm.

'No need for panic,' The Leader says. But I can see that Murray is terrified. Are there really Leadership people who want to hurt The Leader? It just goes to show how corrupt and fickle the whole government is.

'It's him,' someone behind us says.

'Sir, I need to speak to you.' It's Radcliffe. I throw a look over my shoulder. Radcliffe and another man are advancing down the corridor, flanked by a pair of guards.

'Sir! It's important,' Radcliffe calls, but Murray grips The Leader's elbow and launches into a run. Kay and I follow suit.

'Surely this is unnecessary,' The Leader says.

'We're near the door,' Kay says to me.

We turn another corner.

A shot is fired.

'Good God!' The Leader says. 'What is he playing at?'

Ahead I see the main entrance. We sprint for it. I can hear Radcliffe and the guards running down the corridor. There are no guards on this side of the exit and I can't see any through the glass either. If Kay and I can just get through the door, I'll let Radcliffe deal with The Leader.

'It's not safe for you to leave the building!' Radcliffe shouts.

He shoots again. The wall ahead of us cracks.

Kay and I burst through the door. She drags me away to the left and we turn back on ourselves to hare down a narrow gap between the building we've just left and the one next-door. When we burst out at the other end, we find the remains of a street party. There are a crowd of people tearing through knocked-over stalls and emptying the snack vans. Kay and I run right into the middle of the throng.

'This way,' she says.

We duck behind a merry-go-round and down another alleyway. There's someone following us. I turn. It's The Leader. How has he made it out alive?

'Leave him,' Kay says.

We run on.

But I'm already out of breath. After my session with Radcliffe, my whole body aches and now an agonising pain rips through my side. I stop. Kay stutters to a halt.

'What is it?'

I double over, unable to speak.

The Leader catches us up. 'It's not safe for you here,' he says.

'We can cut through the park to the Westside offices. I'm sure that they'll be able to provide me with a car and a driver.'

I widen my eyes at Kay. He doesn't realise that I want him dead and he doesn't understand that he can no longer rely on the unconditional obedience of those around him.

The slap of footsteps on pavement rings out. I turn to see a bunch of guards round the corner of the street.

'Quick!' I grab Kay and push past The Leader. I run into the nearest building. It's a recreation centre and as soon as we get into reception I can see that there's been trouble here. The front desk has been thrown over and the digital posters have been torn from the walls. There's the sound of shouting and banging coming from further down the corridor. I decide quickly that it's best to lead the guards to where there are other people, and head in the direction of the noise.

We end up on a sports court where a handful of guards are trying to control several hundred people. Some of them are hitting back at the guards, who are trying to cut a path by stunning anyone who comes close enough. Others are ripping apart the court. There are shrieks and shouts and the slap and crack of punches being thrown. I follow Kay as she dashes across the court and up the steps between the tiered seats for the spectators.

A hush falls on the groups of people. I assume that this is because we've brought a whole load of guards with us, but when I look back over my shoulder I see that's not the only thing we've brought with us. The Leader has stumbled into the hall. He spots us and follows us up the stairs, seemingly unaware that everyone around him is frozen by his presence. I watch the expression of one woman switch from stunned to furious and I realise that there is definitely some bad feeling towards The Leader in here. And that it might look as if we are in some way connected to him.

'Don't stop,' I say to Kay. We push on up the steps with The Leader trailing behind. The room erupts.

'It's him! It's The Leader!'

'Get him!'

'He's the one who did all this!'

When she reaches the top of the steps, Kay runs along behind the seats to a door. She throws it open and we hurry through it. The Leader stumbles behind us before I can slam it shut.

I look around for something to block the door. 'Help me,' I say, clutching at a snack dispenser unit. Together, Kay and I slide it in front of the door. The Leader just looks on.

'If we could locate a member of staff then I could ask them to contact one of my assistants,' he says.

I stare at him. He just doesn't get that some of his people have turned against him.

'Come on,' Kay says to me and launches into a run again. The Leader moves with us. 'Leave us alone!' Kay shouts. 'It's you they're after.'

We run up the stairs, through another door, and find ourselves on a viewing balcony above the swimming pool.

'Keep down,' I say. Kay and I duck down but The Leader remains on his feet, with his back to us, still casting about for a helpful member of staff.

In the distance I hear shouting and smashing, but I don't think anyone is following us. I look at Kay; she pats the front of her Girl Guards' jacket, as if reassuring herself something is still there.

She's got an efwurding gun.

'Give it to me,' I whisper.

'Blake, are you sure th—'

'Give it to me.'

She hesitates, then slowly hands me the pistol. In one rapid movement I spring up and knock The Leader to the floor. He twists round to see me standing above him, the gun pointed at his head. He's bewildered. I almost pull the trigger but, looking down at his face, I hesitate.

All this time, he was a monster to me; someone so wicked that they were personally responsible for the abuse of thousands of children, the appalling living conditions of workers across the country and the oppression of a nation; a creature so devoid of love and kindness that he abandoned me. But when I look at him now, terror in his eyes, his weak chin trembling, he's not a monster. He's just a man. An ignorant, vain man who has been used. I am stronger and smarter than him. He is not the beginning of the evil in this country and killing him will not mean the end. There are thousands of people who are responsible for the terrible things that have happened, including all the people who turned a blind eye to what they knew or suspected was wrong. People like me.

The fate of this country is not just about my father. And it is not just about me.

I lower the gun.

His eyes are darting about all over the place. He's waiting for one of his aides to rescue him.

'You should be punished,' I say. 'But it should be done fairly. I'm not the kind of person who thinks he has the right to decide who should live and who should die, or even who should succeed and who should suffer.' I stare at him. 'I'm not like that. I'm not like you.'

364

'They came this way!' someone shouts from the direction of the stairs.

I spin round. Kay's eyes are wide with horror. She points at another door at the other end of the balcony. 'This way.'

I glance back at The Leader. He's getting to his feet. 'I'll speak to them,' he says.

I stare at him. 'They'll kill you.' It's not a warning. I want him to know. 'They hate you and they'll kill you.'

He carries on as if I hadn't spoken. 'You have to understand that they're afraid. The public need guidance at a time like this.'

I stride towards Kay. We both know that they'll rip him to pieces.

'You'd better tell my office where I am,' he says, turning back towards the thumping footsteps and yelling on the stairs.

He really is losing it.

'We're going,' Kay says, grabbing my hand.

I take one last look back at this strange man who is supposed to be related to me.

Even though he's only just narrowly escaped me blowing his brains out, he's put back on his politician's smooth, calm face. He holds up a hand. 'I'll speak to them.' He turns in the direction of the stairs and squares his shoulders. 'They're my people.'

He pushes open the door.

There's a moment's hush like the sucking in of breath.

'Citizens!' my father shouts.

The rest of his grand words are lost in the animal cries of a hundred angry people.

And a single gunshot.

52

Kay pushes me through the other door.

I don't let myself think about what just happened. What's important is that we get out of here. These people think we were with The Leader. We need to get away. The painkillers have really kicked in and my whole lower arm has now gone numb. I can think clearly and I'm strangely calm.

We sneak down another set of stairs and into a changing room. I pull a lifeguard's hooded top off a peg as we walk past.

'Put this on,' I say. 'It will hide your uniform.'

Kay helps me shrug off my own jacket and turn it inside out before draping it over my shoulders. Now, at least at first glance, we'll look different to the people they were chasing. We slink out of the changing rooms and back towards the front of the centre. Shouts are still coming from the rear of the building.

We walk past a bunch of teenagers ripping a screen from

the wall. Just as we're about to reach the exit, a man walks in and grabs me by the arm.

I see Kay readying to fight, but the man only says, 'Is it true? Is The Leader here?'

'I ...'

'Yes,' Kay says. 'That way.' She gestures behind us.

The man hurries off in the direction she pointed.

Once we're out of the building we begin to run. Eventually, we slow to a brisk walk.

'Why did he do that?' I ask. I can't make sense of The Leader's actions.

Kay knows exactly what I'm talking about. 'I don't know,' she says. 'Maybe he really thought he was going to make them not angry.'

'He didn't have an efwurding clue, he was on another planet.' There's a sort of buzzing inside me. I can't tell if it's anger or sadness or something else, but it feels bad and makes me want to shake myself to try to throw it off.

'They shot him, didn't they?' I say.

Kay nods.

The buzzing gets stronger. But this is what I wanted. I was going to kill him myself.

'Do you think he's dead?'

She nods again. 'I saw it through the door when we were running away. It hit him in the head.'

'Good,' I say. And I mean it.

But the buzzing doesn't stop.

It takes a long time to get back to the hospital. Fortunately, I still have metro passes in my shirt pocket from when I had to half carry Ven back from the factory, but the service has been disrupted. I hope it's because of the trouble the Resistance have caused, but of course there's no mention of that on the announcements about delays. We waste time sat on stationary trains. The painkillers start to wear off and my fingers burn and throb.

When we finally cross back over into the Wilderness, we find that the car that Ven drove this morning is still where we hid it. It's good that we have a car to travel back to the hospital in, especially now that it's getting dark, but the fact that Ven hasn't picked it up himself sends a chill through me. Even if he survived his jump out of the window, the guards must have got him.

When the hospital finally appears out of the darkness, it looks the same as it always did. I half expected to find it razed to the ground. We still don't know how much Robin's friend found out about the Resistance.

I park the car, but I hesitate before getting out. I check the revolver is still inside my jacket. There's no one guarding the back door.

'Ven!' I call. My voice echoes around the dark, dirty corridor. 'Paulo!'

No answer.

Kay looks at me with wide eyes. 'I'll go to the rec room,' she says.

I run down the corridor. It's horribly quiet. I fling open

the door of Tanisha's office. It's empty. I sprint into the
cafeteria and the kitchen. They're empty too. I run to the
stairs, where Kay is coming back up.

'I can't find any person,' Kay says. 'They're all gone.'

53

'Do you think they're all dead?' Kay asks. 'Or do you think the Leadership came and got them?'

I don't point out that those two possibilities probably amount to the same thing. I need to think.

'There must be something,' I say. 'Let's look upstairs.'

We run up to the first floor and start throwing open doors. There's no one to be found.

'Wait a minute,' I say and I retrace my steps and look into the room behind the last door I opened. It's the computer room. 'This door is normally locked. And ...'

'There's no computers!' Kay says.

'Kay, I don't think they were captured. I think they left.'

'What?'

'I think they've moved to another place. They took the computers with them.'

I expect Kay to smile, but instead she bites her lip. 'Maybe the Leadership took the computers to see all the things the Resistance do on the computers.'

My shoulders sag.

'What more things are gone?' Kay asks.

'There was food in the kitchen.'

'Wouldn't they be taking all that food, if they were leaving?'

'Not if they were in a hurry,' I say. 'In fact, we shouldn't be here. If they left, it was because they were worried that Robin had led the Leadership to this place, or even because of some other threat that we don't know about.'

We stare at each other hopelessly.

Kay's head jerks up. 'I know. I know what thing they would take and the Leadership would not take.' She strides up the next flight of stairs.

I follow more slowly. My hand is killing me again. Kay shoots into our ward. By the time I've reached the door she's triumphantly waving a pillow about. 'It's gone,' she says.

'What's gone?'

'Robin's bear. Only Robin would take the teddy. The Leadership would not take that.'

'What if she took him with her this morning?'

'No, I saw her saying goodbye to it. Robin has been back to here.'

Which I guess is enough to give us hope that the Resistance still exists.

'We have to find them,' Kay says.

I nod. 'You get whatever food and water you can find from the kitchen and I'll look in Ven's office to see if I can work out where they've gone.'

On the ground floor we split again.

I only hope that they've left some clue, because it could take us forever to find them in the Wilderness again.

I open the door to Ven's office and flinch.

We're not alone.

Crouched in the corner with chocolate smeared around his mouth is Nard.

'He was just keeping this stuff all for himself,' he says, waving a chocolate bar about.

I fly at him, grab his collar and haul him to his feet, then I punch him in the face with my good hand. He crashes backwards into a shelf of books. When he staggers upright, I punch him again.

'Why?' I shout in his face. 'Why would you do that? Why would you send Kay to die?'

He pushes me off him and shrugs his shirt sulkily back into place.

'Why should I care about your stupid girlfriend?'

'You liked her! You certainly spent enough time running around after her.'

'I thought that maybe we had something in common. I thought that maybe we understood each other, but it turned

374

out that she thinks she's better than me, just like everybody else. You all think you're better than me.'

Efwurd, Nard has got some serious issues. 'Maybe that's because we wouldn't try to kill someone just because they didn't want to kiss us.'

He screws up his face with disdain. 'I didn't set this whole thing up purely to kill Kay,' he says as if I'm the crazy one. 'I wanted to take out The Leader. Putting you three at the centre of it was just an added bonus.'

He is seriously twisted. 'We were already going to kill The Leader. And we were going to do it in a way that wouldn't blow up thousands of innocent people.'

Nard shrugs. 'What does Ven always say? Sacrifices have to be made.'

'Ven wouldn't make a sacrifice like that.'

'No,' Nard sneers. 'But he was prepared to sacrifice you, wasn't he, Daddy's boy?'

A line of ice runs through me. 'What the hell do you mean by that?'

'Oh, come on, do you really think that he took you along because you were an asset to the Assassination team?'

'I'm a good shot.'

Nard sneers. 'But not exactly a favourite with Ven. He knew who your father is and he took you along as an insurance policy.'

I don't want to give Nard the satisfaction of seeing me consider his words, but already my mind is whirling.

Could Ven have known? How does Nard know? The last time I spoke about my father was up on the roof with Kay, and then ... And then when I came down the stairs Ven told me I was on the team. He must have been listening. Nard is right. But Ven didn't use me. He saw me there behind the guards and he didn't give me away. He could have, but he didn't. I volunteered.

'Ven didn't betray me,' I say.

'How sweet. But I'll bet he shot a hell of a lot of people today.'

'With reason. He didn't try to kill anyone just because they pissed him off.'

Nard lets out a high-pitched laugh. 'Oh, please, I'm sick of you lot making out you're so principled and high-minded. All anybody is interested in is getting on. Grasping something better. Every single member of the Resistance would shoot anybody else in the back to save themselves.'

This is the way that Nard sees the Resistance. It's a wonder that he hasn't sold them out long ago.

'If that's how you feel, I don't know why you even wanted to kill the Leader.'

He pulls up his face to indicate my stupidity. 'Because he's a sick and twisted man,' he says.

My mind flips over in its effort to process this. My skin crawls. The fact that Nard thinks he is making perfect sense and that he judges The Leader's crimes, but not his own, is terrifying.

'You're wrong,' I say. 'There *are* people who will sacrifice themselves for others, Kay did it for me. I did it for Ven and I'm certain that Ven has done it more times than either of us are even aware of. The Resistance are good people who have strived their whole lives to help others.'

Nard rejects all the hard work and self-sacrifice of the Resistance with a dismissive shake of the head. Nothing I can say will change the way he thinks. What I need from him is information.

'What's happened here?' I ask in a more level tone. 'Where have they gone?'

'They left. They're afraid that Robin let a load of information out to that Jed guy. See? I'm not the only efwurd up.'

He's deluding himself again by putting Robin's foolishness in the same bracket as his own treachery.

'Where have they gone?'

Nard smiles. He knows.

'I don't know why I'm bothering to ask,' I say. 'It's not like you were anyone significant. They didn't trust you with the really important stuff, did they?'

'But I knew it all anyway,' Nard spits. 'They were like a bunch of kids with their secrets and their special groups. Did Ven really think we were going to keep out of his office just because he said so? I knew everything that there was to know around here. I knew about your father, I knew Ven's little secret, and I know that they've gone to the university.' He tightens his face in a 'so there' smirk.

He really is horrible, but at least now I know where they are. I remember Paulo mentioning that most of the university in the next district had remained intact. I'll bet that's the one.

'Go on then,' Nard says. 'Run along to your little friend, Ven. You're all a bunch of bastards.' He pulls a knife out of his boot.

'We're not the bastards!' My voice rises. 'Can you not see the terrible things that you've done? What is wrong with you?'

He takes a step towards me, pointing the knife at my chest.

My hand finds the gun in my jacket. The splints on my fingers make it awkward to hold the gun, but I manage to grip it and aim it at Nard.

'You wouldn't shoot me.' But I can see from his face he's scared.

He's right, though. I can't shoot him. Just like I didn't shoot my father, even though I despise the pair of them. But I've got to keep the gun on him until I figure out what to do.

Nard has paled. 'It's all gone wrong. You don't understand what it's like. People always expect the worst from me. All I ever hear is how aggressive I am. That stuff starts to stick. And then the time I try to reach out to someone, to tell a girl I like her, look what happens.'

'That's not a reason to plant a bomb on someone!'

'I know. I'm just a mess.' His shoulders slump and he covers his face with his hands.

I can't feel any sympathy for him. I don't want to. What can I do with him? Maybe Ven can talk some sense into him. 'Listen, Nard . . .' I say.

The second my guard is down, Nard throws off his fake despair and lunges for the gun. I step back at the last second and Nard falls against me, knocking me to the ground. I keep hold of the gun, but Nard is on top of me. He grabs my wrist with one hand and tries to wrench the gun from my grip with the other. It feels like he's breaking my fingers all over again.

'Did you think I was sorry?' he sneers in my face.

He's twisting the gun to point it at me.

I try to push him off me with my good hand, but he lands a lucky punch right on my jaw. My head cracks back against the floor. The gun slips from my grip.

And then it's pointing in my face.

'Don't do this,' I say. 'You don't have to be like this.'

'I never had any choice.'

He takes the safety-catch off the gun.

'Should have taken your chance,' he says. 'Shoot first or be shot.'

Behind Nard something moves. Kay leaps towards us. She lands on Nard, sending him slamming into me. I fight to push him off. He's yanked away from me. Where's the gun? I push myself up. Nard and Kay are rolling over on the floor.

'Let her go!' I dive towards them.

The gun goes off.

379

Oh God.

The two of them are in a heap. The gun is lying next to them. I snatch it up and aim it at the back of Nard's head. Kay is underneath him.

'Kay! Kay, are you all right?'

She pushes Nard off her and struggles to her feet. She's all right. Kay is all right.

But Nard's face is pulled tight in agony. He clutches his stomach and a moan leaks out of the corner of his mouth. His hands are red.

'We've got to ... We need ...' I start pulling off my shirt, thinking I can use it to staunch the blood, but it's already too late.

'Blake,' Kay says gently.

I stop tearing at my buttons.

Nard's eyes are unseeing.

'No,' I say.

'Come on,' Kay says, putting an arm around me. 'Come away from here.'

Out in the corridor, Kay stoops to retrieve the packets of food that she dropped in the corridor when she heard me and Nard fighting, and mechanically I bend to help her.

We go back to the car.

I rest my head against the steering wheel. I think of Robin. She will be very upset when she learns Nard is dead.

'King hell,' I say. 'That wasn't our fault. The gun just went off in the struggle.'

380

Kay puts a hand over mine. 'It wasn't our fault,' she agrees. 'But ... I fired the gun.'

I don't have any words left.

'Nard doesn't understand,' Kay continues. 'He doesn't get it. We're not murderers, me and you. We don't choose it. But we won't let people like Nard hurt the people we love. We're not murderers. But we are fighters.'

I try to hold on to Kay's words. She's right, what happened just then was self-defence. But even after what happened with The Leader, even though I've realised that it's not my place to decide if someone lives or dies, even though I knew I wasn't going to shoot Nard, there was a small part of me that wanted to. Not to protect myself or Kay, but just because I hated him. And I'm afraid that no matter how many decisions I take about what's the right way to behave, I'm always going to have to keep that vicious angry part of me under control. There's always going to be a new struggle to do the right thing.

When we escaped from the Academy, everything seemed so clear to me. We were the good guys and the Leadership were the enemy. But I'm realising that no one I know can simply be slotted into a 'good' or 'bad' category. I thought Janna was a traitor, but she helped us out. I believed I was the one trying to put things right, but I could so easily have killed two unarmed people today. I thought my father was pure evil, but he really seemed to believe he was doing the right thing. And

Nard – aggressive, predatory Nard – took the time to talk to a little girl everyone else ignored.

Maybe most people are capable of both great kindness and terrible things.

I know now that I am.

55

It's starting to get light when we arrive at the university on top of a hill. The first person we find is Toren.

'Blake! Kay!' He laughs in amazement. 'You made it! We heard you'd been taken and—'

'How did you hear?' I ask. 'Did Ven come back?'

Toren's smile disappears. He nods slowly. 'His leg was broken. Tanisha got him back. But—'

'Where is he?' I ask.

'He's in sick bay.'

'Where's that?'

'Upstairs, at the end of the corridor.'

'I've got to see him.' I head for the stairs.

'Blake, I need to tell you something!' Toren calls after me.

But whatever it is can wait. I need to see Ven. I need to tell him what happened with The Leader.

I take a right at the top of the stairs. At the end of the corridor I hear coughing. I peer through the last door. Sick bay has obviously been hastily assembled and the large room is full of an assortment of beds, cushions and sofas. There are a lot of wounded Resistance members sleeping here. And these are the ones that managed to make it back.

In the bed closest to me is Alrye, the boy who tried to interrogate Kay and me when we first arrived. His eyes are wide open.

'Where's Ven?' I whisper.

'In the back room.' He continues to stare at a spot on the wall.

I make my way between beds and makeshift beds and through a door at the back. It's a large room. The dawn light is pouring through a huge window. As I approach the bed, my footsteps slow. Something is not right. This limp body cannot be the twitching ball of energy that is Ven. He didn't look well before the uprising, now he looks terrible.

His eyes snap open. 'Blake,' he says in a rasping voice, fixing me with his gaze, 'it surprises me that a young man of your limited skills was able to escape the Leadership. I'm going to assume that some sort of friendly animal helped you dig a tunnel out.'

I open my mouth to speak.

'No, don't tell me I'm wrong. I'm enjoying picturing you with a badger.'

'Ven . . .' is all I can manage to say.

'Yes?'

'What happened?'

He rolls his eyes. 'If you look at my weakened state, the

384

shallow breathing, the internal bleeding and a few other details that I'll save for when I really need to induce nausea in you, then it all points to the fact I'm ill. I'm ill, Blake.'

I remember his sunken eyes and weight loss running up to the Big Day. I assumed it was stress and lack of time to sleep and eat, but clearly this is something much worse.

'Is it . . . Is it the Sickness?'

'Yes, Blake.'

I don't know what to say. Even though I knew that the Resistance die young, I didn't expect it to happen to the people I know. And certainly not to Ven.

'Now that we've got your eloquent and heartfelt warm wishes out of the way, tell me about what happened to you.'

'Kay found me. We escaped. But that isn't the important thing; it's The Leader, he didn't even know that I was his son.'

Ven raises his eyebrows.

'I know you know about that,' I say, seeing no point in pretending otherwise. 'The fact is The Leader didn't seem to know a whole lot of stuff. That Radcliffe man, it looks like he's got a lot of power, but he's turned against The Leader; he tried to shoot him.'

Ven's mouth twitches. 'It's nice that someone is picking up where we left off.'

'But you don't understand; Kay heard them saying that he wasn't going to be Leader any more and one of his assistants told him that there were Leadership members who were going to pin the blame for the uprising on him.' I remember with a jolt that it won't matter to him what they do any more. 'And he's dead,' I say.

My father's dead.

Ven jerks upright. 'Why didn't you say so? What happened?'

I hesitate; I don't want to share the moment in the recreation centre where I nearly pulled the trigger, so I just say, 'A crowd of people turned on him. They shot him.'

Ven's thin fingers clench into a fist. He closes his eyes to take in the fruition of all his hopes.

'Thank you, Blake. You've made me feel much better.'

'But ... I don't think it's over. I don't think that everything pivoted on The Leader in the way that we thought it did.'

'Well, it's an efwurding good start.'

He leans back and shuts his eyes, and for a moment I think he's gone back to sleep, but eventually he pushes back his blanket and I'm shocked to see how thin he is without his massive jersey. I can't believe how rapidly he's deteriorated. I can only assume that he was holding it all together for the uprising and that all that effort has completely drained him.

'So Blake, I'll admit that you've stayed alive longer than I ever expected. I'm almost moved to congratulate you on your cockroach-like tendencies.'

I give a half-smile. 'Thanks.'

'Let's move on from the pleasantries before I vomit on your shoes. I need to talk to you.'

I shift uncomfortably. 'Go on.'

'My body is slowly falling apart. I've been taking a cocktail of drugs for quite a while now. They can keep me alive for some time, but pretty soon I'll be useless physically.'

It seems so wrong to think of Ven bedbound. I don't know what to say. 'I'm ... I'm sorry.'

'I'm not the confiding type, Blake, but they say that you should try new things before it's too late, so I think I'll try some confiding in you.' He runs a hand through his hair. 'I had planned to die on the day after you arrived at the hospital. I should have died on that day. Then you turned up with your footage and I remembered that The Resistance weren't the only ones that wanted to get rid of the Leadership; that some people out there cared too. I realised that maybe now was the right time to rise up and that I could still be there to help.'

Things fall into place. 'That's why you were so insistent that we get on with it.'

He sticks out his chin. 'I thought it was as good a time as any to strike, I really did. I didn't do it just to make myself look good.'

I laugh out loud. 'I'm pretty sure you've never done anything to make yourself look good, Ven. Even the way you say good morning makes you look like an arsehole.'

To my surprise, Ven laughs too. Then he winces.

387

'Are you all right?'

'I'm dying, Blake.'

I can't help screwing up my face and saying, 'It's so unfair!'

'There's no denying that a mind and a body such as mine should rightly have been granted immortality. But I've had more than I ever expected. I was given an extra week. You can't imagine what it's like to live when you should be dead. To breathe and run and fight and laugh when you should be in the ground. Not many people get that.' He twists his mouth into a crooked smile. 'Bet you don't.'

My throat tightens. There's so much of Ven. It seems impossible that all that brilliance and anger and wit could be bound by a failing body.

Ven gives me an exasperated look. 'As long as you promise to stand at the back so as not to detract from the aesthetic appeal, you can join the procession of beautiful young people who weep for me when I'm gone, but don't start sobbing now.' He fixes me with his dark brown eyes. 'I need you to do something for me.'

Something about his sudden shift in tone sends a sliver of ice down my throat. Eventually I say, 'What is it?'

'I need a gun.'

I look away. What do you say when a man who has just explained that his suicide is overdue asks you for a gun?

I suck in my breath. 'If you want a gun, surely you can go to the weapons store and get one. Not that you should have a gun. I mean, can't the medics—'

'I need a gun. Paulo's got the keys for the weapons store. He's not going to let me in. He's afraid of being left in charge. I need you to get me a gun.'

'I don't think I can do that.'

'Oh, come on, Blake, even for someone as useless as you, it's a fairly small task.'

'It's not funny, Ven, I don't want to be responsible for your death.'

'I take responsibility for my own actions.'

'And what are the rest of the Resistance going to say when they find out that I've given their brilliant leader a gun?'

'They might be upset at first, but in the end they'll understand. This is the way that it works here. You know that.'

'I might know it, but I don't understand it.' I lean closer to him. 'Your mind is fully functioning. You're still an asset to this group. They need you. We need you.'

'I'm a burden. I need drugs, I need painkillers, and I need the medics' time. They could be using those things on the kids who were wounded. The kids who we need to grow up and carry on the Resistance.'

I look out of the window. I know I'm not going to persuade him that this is the wrong thing to do.

'Blake, soon I won't be able to go to the bathroom by myself,' he says.

I unfocus my eyes so that the crumbling building in the distance blurs.

'I'll be dead within the year, anyway. Let me do it my way.'

I want to tell him to ask someone else. I feel like a Learning Community boy trying to get out of his cafeteria duty.

As if he reads my mind, Ven says, 'I could ask Kay. She'd do it.'

He's right. She would do it. Kay is proud and she understands what it means to follow the expectations set by the community you grew up in. But if she does it then she'll have to carry it with her for the rest of her life. I don't want that for her. And anyway I've realised that it's not as easy as I thought it was to decide what's right and wrong. Or who is good and who is bad. One thing is for sure, you can't make those decisions for other people. And being a friend means that sometimes you have to support your friends with their choices even if they're not the ones that you would have made.

'Don't say anything to Kay. I'll do it.'

Ven nods. 'Toren said he's going to fetch me a wheelchair from the campus medical centre tomorrow. Could you come and get me in the afternoon?'

I want to say no. I want to stop this from happening, but I nod my head.

'Did you notice what I did?' he asks.

'What do you mean?'

'I asked you for help.'

'Oh.'

390

'Our last captain seemed to have some ludicrous concerns that I was an arrogant control freak. She always said that to be a really great captain I had to learn to ask for help. Well, there you go; I did it. Which probably brings me to the rank of best captain ever.' He leans forward and whispers, 'I've peaked. It's best that I die now.' Then he laughs long and hard. And it occurs to me that maybe the best way to deal with the hardest things in life is to find something to laugh at.

The following afternoon I find Ven in the room assigned to the babies, with Toren. Ven uses a crutch to manoeuvre into his wheelchair and announces that he and I are going for a walk. As I turn the chair he reaches out and touches Toren lightly on the shoulder; I have to look away.

Once we're outside I push him in his wheelchair, still holding his crutch, away from the university and into the barren countryside.

'There's a quarry not far from here,' Ven says.

We carry on in silence along a road bordered by stunted hedges. I keep my eyes peeled for wild dogs or violent Wilderness types. No one is going to spoil this for Ven.

As we approach the gates of the quarry, I feel dizzy. I ignore it and keep on moving. I swing the gates open and put my back into pushing the wheelchair up the incline until Ven says, 'Stop. You can leave me here.' He gets slowly to his feet, using his makeshift crutch, and holds out his hand.

I take the revolver from my jacket and give it to him.

'Since I'm trying out new behaviours, here's another one for you . . .' His lips twitch. 'Thank you.'

I nod. My throat is dry. I want to tell him something comforting, but my mind is racing around in circles. I can't think straight. I'm in such a heightened state of awareness that it's almost too intense to keep breathing. He holds out a hand again and this time I shake it.

'I'll take this opportunity to have the last word, Blake.' He smiles at me – the first real warm smile he's ever given me. 'Just remember, I'm always right,' he says, and he shuffles away from me using his crutch.

I push the chair back down the slope and out of the gates, and I stand very still.

Ven fires the gun I handed him.

Walking back to the university is hard. All my attempts to make sense of what is happening crumble away. Why are we fighting when our bravest efforts only lead to death? Ven was so smart, but even he couldn't find a way to fix things – and now he's dead. What's the point?

It takes a lot of effort not to just lie down in the dusty road. Instead, I keep putting one foot in front of the other until I find Paulo.

'Get Toren and Tanisha,' I say, 'and Kay.'

He doesn't ask why.

When they're all gathered around me, I steel myself to break the ominous silence.

'Where's Ven?' Toren asks.

'Ven's dead. He shot himself.'

The sunny lightness in Toren disappears as if a switch had been flicked. His kind open face buckles like he's been punched.

Kay takes hold of my hand.

'But he can't have,' Tanisha says.

'Why did he do that?' Kay asks.

'He had the Sickness.'

Tanisha nods. 'But he was okay. The medics were managing it. I mean, he didn't have to . . . He could have . . .'

Toren is rigid, but his eyes are wild with denial. 'He can't be. He wouldn't.'

'This is our way,' Paulo says. 'This is the way it is.'

'Don't you care?' Tanisha snaps.

'Of course I care!'

I've never heard Paulo shout before.

'Of course I efwurding care. How are we going to go on without him? I just, I just—' He gulps. 'He wanted to do it this way, you know he did.'

Tanisha presses her hands to her face. 'Why now? We really need him now.'

'We need him all the time,' Toren says in a voice horribly unlike his own.

'He didn't want to use up supplies,' I say, 'or to take up the medics' time. He didn't want to be a burden.'

Tanisha swings round to face me. 'How could you let him? Why didn't you stop him?'

'That's not fair, Tanisha,' Kay says. 'Ven does what he wants to do, you know that. This isn't Blake's choosing. Blake has done a hard thing.' She squeezes my hand and I know she understands. Thank God, I couldn't have borne it if she hadn't.

'Kay's right. This is the way he wanted it,' Paulo

repeats. His face is white and set. 'I, for one, am glad that he got to lead us in the uprising and that he got to do this on his own terms.'

I can only hope that one day this might comfort them. For now, I can see that no words can soothe the terrible loss.

'I want him back,' Toren says.

And he begins to sob.

Every gasp hits me like the sound of gunshot.

The weight of grief that immediately descends over the Resistance makes me realise just how much Ven meant to everyone. He wasn't just their boss. I can see now that even though his words were harsh, everything he did was to try to make things better for these people.

Kay finds me a bed and sits beside me until I fall into an uneasy sleep, but when I wake alone, I get up and pace the corridors until I bump into Tanisha, who takes me to the new computer room where Paulo and Kay are already working.

'We have to keep going,' Paulo says. 'Ven would say we can't sit around crying like babies.'

I don't say anything. Kay gestures to me, so I go over and sit next to her. She brushes my hair out of my face. Kay means so much to me, and I'm grateful to still be alive and to be with her, and yet the knowledge that so many people weren't as lucky as me, that Ven wasn't, burns like a brand pressed to my skull.

'We've got the computers set up,' Paulo says. 'Can you help us assess the reaction to the uprising?'

'Why bother?' I ask. 'Everything on the Network will have been filtered by the Leadership anyway. They'll just make us sound like bloodthirsty terrorists.'

'We still need to know what they're saying about us.'

I don't really want to have to wade through accounts describing me as a crazed gunman, but I don't want to sit around thinking about Ven either.

'All right,' I say.

I go to the Info's main news site to get their take on events first. I flip through the headlines. There's nothing there. I try a search. The only article about The Leader's birthday is an account of a ball hosted by the deputy Leader. King hell, this can't be right.

'There's nothing here!' I say. 'They're pretending it didn't happen.'

'I can't find anything either,' Tanisha says.

The blood has drained from Paulo's face. 'But . . . there must be something. We did so much . . . What about the explosions? The power station?'

'The power company's site says that disruptions to power are due to "necessary maintenance",' Tanisha says.

'And apparently the gas explosions were caused by sparks from a malfunctioning machine. They're trying to pretend that it never happened,' I say.

'But people know it,' Kay says. 'We saw people. They were fighting the guards. It was happening.'

'Maybe it wasn't as many people as we thought,' Tanisha says.

Paulo slaps his hands down on the table. 'No! Everyone saw our film. *Everyone*.'

I shake my head. 'This is what the Leadership does. It hushes things up. People know what they're not allowed to talk about.'

We stare at each other.

'I wish Ven was here,' Paulo says.

'It's better that he went thinking that we'd achieved something,' Tanisha says.

'We have done something!' Kay says, 'People will be asking questions about the Leadership now.'

There's a tap on the door and Toren pokes his head into the room.

'You okay?' Tanisha asks.

Toren comes in. 'I just needed to tell you,' he says to me, 'Ven said . . .' He bites his lip. 'I didn't realise what he was going to do! I thought it was just a conversation . . .'

'What is it?' I ask.

'Ven said that if anything ever happened to him . . . that you're in charge.'

Tanisha gasps.

I look at Paulo. There's nothing but relief in his eyes. He nods. 'Yes. Yes, it's got to be you.'

'No,' I say. 'No way.'

'He said you'd say that,' Toren says. 'He told me to tell you to remember that he's always right.'

That was the very last thing he said to me. Typical Ven. Sneaky bastard.

'I don't know,' I say. 'This isn't what I imagined happening next.' I look at Kay. She had her doubts about the Resistance before. Is she going to want to stick around now?

She nods her head decisively. 'You should do it,' she says.

An unbearable heaviness settles on me. 'What's the point?' I say. 'The revolt was a disaster. Resistance members were killed; members of the public were killed. And what for?' I throw a hand out in the direction of the computer. 'The Leadership have buried the whole thing. You can see why people are too afraid to stand up and fight. Look what happens when they do: they get knocked down.'

Nobody speaks.

'Hey!' Kay says pointing at Tanisha's computer screen. 'Go back! Go back to that thing.'

'What?' Tanisha asks. She clicks back to the previous screen and we all look at Kay.

'There!' Kay says.

I turn to watch the news report playing on the screen.

'What? What are you talking about? It's just the reporter glossing over what really happened, the same as before,' Paulo says.

'No, it's not,' I say. I push Paulo aside and tap the screen. 'His tie.'

Kay nods vigorously.

'Let me enlarge it . . . See?'

They lean in around me to get a closer look.

'Sweet efwurd,' Tanisha exhales. 'Has he got a Resistance symbol worked into the pattern of his tie?'

He has.

Paulo tilts his head on one side. 'I'm not so sure. Maybe it's just part of the design.'

'It's a deliberate part of the design,' I say. 'He's got that there on purpose. He's making a statement.'

'It's a bit ... subtle, isn't it?' Paulo is still frowning.

'He's a reporter! He can't wear a T-shirt saying "I'm a Resistance supporter", can he?'

'We're going to need more help than one subtle reporter,' Paulo says.

'Maybe it's not just him, maybe there's more,' Toren says. 'Let's look.'

'Where?' Kay asks.

'News sites. Community sites. Anything you can think of,' I say.

Paulo frowns. 'All those things are monitored by the Leadership.'

I turn back to my computer. 'That's why you'll have to look carefully.'

The longer we look the more we find. On a gardening site there's an artistic shot of a tree in flower, but on the wall behind there's a small splash of red graffiti, which is definitely the symbol. Then on a Learning Community site we find a scan of a child's report of The Leader's birthday which is all about the picnic she ate, but when you look closely at the number four in the date, at the top of page, it's another symbol.

'There's another one here,' Toren says.

'This is one,' Kay says.

'And here.' Tanisha points.

We search on and on, and all night Resistance symbols pop up like spots of light in the darkness.

We're not alone.

The people want to take back this country.

'Will you be captain now?' Toren asks.

Could I be captain of the Resistance? I'm not a natural leader. I'm not at all like Ven. Although, as it turns out, I didn't really know what Ven was like.

'Please?' Tanisha asks.

'I don't know if I'm the right person.'

'Ven seemed pretty sure that you were,' Paulo says.

This is all getting a bit much. 'Can I just have a moment?' I ask.

'Sure,' Paulo says, but his face falls as I turn towards the door.

Out in the corridor I feel Kay's cool hand on my arm.

'Are you all right?' she asks.

'I don't know why Ven wanted me. I couldn't command people the way he did.'

'You're smart. You're a good planner. You can think of what to do when the thing you wanted to do goes wrong. And you care about people.'

I press the heels of my hands into my eye sockets.

Kay puts an arm around me. 'You led the Specials at the Academy.'

'As I recall, you had to give the rousing speech because they didn't understand a word of mine.'

'You did a good speech for the Resistance. You made everyone want to do their best for all the people they had lost.'

I didn't even know she'd heard it. 'The point is, look how things ended up at the Academy. I didn't do a great job.'

'You made the Specials believe that things could be different. That was the most important thing.'

I shrug. 'No one at the Learning Community every thought of me as a leader. I was, you know, the brainer one who looks after all the maths and science. I wasn't good at being in charge.'

'Stop there. It's not about the things that you *did*; it's about *now*.' Kay's right. I'm not the person I thought I was. Since I left the Learning Community I've done things that I never would have imagined I could.

'Ven and all the others think you can do this.'

Maybe it is possible. 'What do you think?'

403

She smiles wide. 'Oh, I think you can do anything you want, anything at all.'

It's amazing what one person's belief in you can do, if it's the right person. I want to deserve her faith in me. I don't know if we will ever free this country from the Leadership, but I do know that you can't change anything unless you dare to believe that change is possible.

I push open the door behind us. 'Okay,' I say. 'I'll do it. I'll be captain.'

Their tense faces break into smiles.

And I stop thinking about who I have been and start thinking about who I can be.

About the Author

C.J. Harper grew up in a rather small house with a rather large family in Oxfordshire. As the fourth of five sisters it was often hard to get a word in edgeways, so she started writing down her best ideas. It's probably not a coincidence that her first "book" featured an orphan living in a deserted castle.

Growing up she attended six different schools, but that honestly had very little to do with an early interest in explosives.

C.J. has been a bookseller, a teacher and the person who puts those little stickers on apples. She is married and has a daughter named after Philip Pullman's Lyra. THE WILDERNESS is the second book in her series that began with THE DISAPPEARED.

HAVE YOU READ WHERE BLAKE'S JOURNEY BEGAN?

DELETED FROM THE SYSTEM. TAKEN FROM EVERYTHING YOU KNOW. HOW WOULD YOU SURVIVE?

THE DISAPPEARED

C. J. HARPER

"A BRILLIANT READ"
KISS

"PACKS IN THE PLOT"
SFX

"A REAL PAGE-TURNER"
THE BOOKBAG

F HAR

WARWICK
LIBRARY
SCHOOL